MYSTERIES
of SILVER PEAK

Dear Reader,

When I was a teen, I believed one true love existed for each of us in the world. But, I wondered, if my true love and I lived on opposite sides of the globe, how would we find each other? Fortunately, he happened to live only minutes away, and I met him while working at an afterschool job at a fast-food restaurant. We've been married thirty-eight years, and he is my true love.

But does lightning strike only once? What about people like the fictional Sadie and Edwin in this book who are widowed and still have plenty of love to give? In the years since my romantic teen notions, I've seen family and friends find love again—to have lightning strike twice in their lifetimes.

And why not? When it comes to love, God isn't stingy. As you read *When Lightning Strikes*, I hope you enjoy this peek into the way God blesses Sadie and Edwin with their reunion romance and brings them even closer as a result of the romantic mystery that began several decades ago.

Love and grace,
Carolyn Greene
writing as Carole Jefferson

Mysteries of Silver Peak

MYSTERIES
of SILVER PEAK

When Lightning Strikes

CAROLE JEFFERSON

Guideposts

New York

Published by Guideposts Books & Inspirational Media
110 William Street
New York, New York 10038
Guideposts.org

Acknowledgments

Every attempt has been made to credit the sources of copyrighted material used in this book. If any such acknowledgment has been inadvertently omitted or miscredited, receipt of such information would be appreciated.

Scripture quotations are taken from *The Holy Bible, New International Version.* Copyright © 1973, 1978, 1984, 2011 by Biblica, Inc. Used by permission of Zondervan. All rights reserved worldwide. www.zondervan.com

Cover and interior design by Müllerhaus
Cover art by Greg Copeland represented by Deborah Wolfe, Ltd.
Typeset by Aptara, Inc.

Printed and bound in the United States of America
10 9 8 7 6 5 4 3 2 1

Prologue

"IT'S TIME TO MOVE ON, SADIE."

Hearing her own thoughts uttered out loud caused fingers of dread to clutch at her heart.

"No," she said, shaking her head. "Edwin and I agreed that we would date others when we went off to college, then pick up again...at some point. One thing I am is loyal to the end."

Sadie's friend Frida turned in her chair to face her and leaned her elbows on her knees. "Maybe now is the end."

Sadie didn't want to hear it, but she had to ask. "What are you saying?"

Her classmate released a slow, measured sigh, the sound reminiscent of the time her mother had broken the news that a favorite church member—a sweet lady who had slipped her and the other children butter toffees out of her massive purse each Sunday—had passed away.

"Edwin has found someone else," Frida said.

It wasn't a question, but a statement. And, just as it had done when she was a child hearing of Miss Irene's passing, the breath left Sadie's lungs. But this time it was worse. Far, far worse, because Miss Irene had lived a long, full life. She and Edwin had barely begun their relationship together.

She knew Frida wouldn't have told her this without being certain of the facts, but she had to ask anyway.

"You're sure?"

Frida nodded her head solemnly, and Sadie wanted to discount what she was saying. But everything added up. First, there had been the dwindling contact from him. Then Edwin's ominous words that she'd tried to scrub from her memory: *One choice taken requires the release of another.*

Edwin had found someone else. During Edwin's unexpected visit two Saturdays ago, T.R.'s presence had obviously put a crimp in their having an open discussion, but even if T.R. hadn't been there, Sadie was sure her own nervous sense of dread would have made it difficult for Edwin to say what was on his heart that day.

She had always believed they'd resume their relationship at some point, and now her heart broke with the knowledge that their high school plans to marry someday and start a family together would not come to fruition.

"If Edwin has found someone else," Sadie said, "it was through no wrongdoing of his own. We had an agreement."

"Lots of couples agree to date others when they go off to separate colleges," Frida agreed. Then, apparently seeking to comfort her, she added, "High school romances rarely last. People grow and change and move on in different directions."

"I know." She drew in a deep, wavering breath and said the words that were so hard to admit. "I don't want him to feel beholden to me if he's found happiness with someone else."

The long hand of the clock on the wall ticked straight up, and the professor fumbled into the room, balancing slide carousels in one arm and a stack of books in the other.

Frida slanted a sympathetic look in Sadie's direction and turned to face forward in her chair.

Trying desperately not to cry, Sadie attempted to focus on the lecture. But no matter how straight she sat in her chair, and no matter how firmly she tried to paste a neutral expression on her face, inside she felt like she was crumpling into a soggy, wadded-up mess.

She took a notebook and pen out of her book bag and stared at a slide image of rock art at the Mesa Verde ruins. Ordinarily, the story behind the ancient cliff dwellers' drawings would have held her transfixed, but today her thoughts kept returning to Edwin.

Her overdeveloped sense of loyalty made it hard for her to let go. That must have made it even more difficult for Edwin who, knowing her as he did, must have wanted to spare her feelings. Ultimately, that loyalty and her sincere concern for him convinced her to do the hard thing—the thing he could not do when he was here last—and bring closure to their relationship.

The notebook lay open on her desk, and not even one word of art history notes had been scribbled on the paper. She placed today's date at the top of the page, then wrote what was on her heart, starting with her joy over having shared so many growing-up experiences and memories with Edwin. She continued the two-page letter by wishing him a contented and happy future. Finally, she ended on a note of hope.

Edwin, I thank God for bringing us into each other's lives. And though our paths may take us in different directions, I'll always consider you a lifelong friend.

Fondest regards,
Sadie

1

SADIE REINED SCOUT PAST THE TEMPTING NEW SPROUTS OF RUSH grass that had pushed their way up alongside the mountain trail near her Silver Peak home. The five-year-old chestnut gelding clearly wanted to linger as they approached the small fishing hole that held so many memories for Sadie. On any other day, she would have enjoyed pausing on this crisp April afternoon to savor the time with her daughter and grandchildren. But nature had other plans.

The weather that, until a moment ago, had been uncharacteristically warm for this scenic part of Colorado, suddenly gusted its chilly breath at the foursome. Fallen leaves scurried along the well-worn path before them, as if trying to escape the impending rainstorm that now darkened the sky. Such occurrences were common around here, and usually short-lived, but familiarity didn't leave room for complacency.

Fourteen-year-old Sara's horse danced sideways, and nerves showed on the girl's pretty face. Hank, Sadie's golden retriever, wisely gave distance to the excited equine. Sara was a good rider, but Sadie was also aware of the potential dangers presented by a frightened horse.

"Relax," Sadie reminded her as the bay filly sidestepped into her own horse. "You're sending your own nervous energy to Daisy."

Like any doting grandparent, she wanted to protect her loved ones from life's inevitable rough spots. But sometimes, such as right now, she just had to guide them through it, ask for God's protection, and let them ride it out.

As if the sky wasn't already dark enough, a heavy gray gloom settled over the area. The storm should be over in a matter of minutes, but it would be foolish to remain out in the elements until it passed.

"Let's go to Dad's old hideaway," Alice called from the back of the line.

"Good idea," Sadie called back over the gusting wind.

A rabbit skittered near the path, and Sara's horse tucked its hind legs as if it might rear up. Theo, thinking quickly, brought his horse alongside Sara's, grabbed the bridle, and quickly looped a thin rope through the ring near the bit. With the hastily fashioned lead in place, Daisy settled slightly, and Theo guided his younger sister's horse off the path and toward the rustic shelter that had been built there many years ago.

"You didn't have to do that," Sara protested with more than a hint of indignation. "I know how to ride a horse."

"You also know how to fall off," the seventeen-year-old said matter-of-factly.

The group had just about reached the shelter when the clouds ruptured. They all hastily dismounted and, although hitching posts sat on either side of the opening, they brought the animals with them into the bucolic sanctuary.

With its high roof, dirt floor, and open sides, the hideaway looked like a cross between a barn and a picnic shelter. What Sadie was most grateful for at the moment was its roof, which allowed none of the downpour inside. But the pounding of the rain on the tin disconcerted the already antsy Daisy.

"Let's give the horses some treats," Sadie suggested after they secured them to a post near the rear of the shelter.

Hank's ears pricked up at the word *treat*, and Sadie set out the food she'd brought for him while Alice rummaged through her saddlebag for a plastic bag of cut-up carrots and apples.

All but the skittish Daisy greedily took the treats, so Sadie dug into her own stash of goodies and set aside a drink bottle filled with an odd-colored smoothie. She handed Sara one of the homemade oat bars that she'd made that morning. "Here, try giving her this."

The granola chunks, slightly sweetened with raisins, shredded coconut, and a touch of brown sugar, would have been irresistible under normal circumstances, but Daisy's brown eyes widened at the distant rumble, and she jerked her head away.

"Waste not, want not," Sadie said and passed the bag of untouched granola to the humans in the group. Then, attempting to lighten the mood as the rumbles grew louder, she filled them in on news of a chocolate fest proposed by the Campfire Circle Ministry at their church.

"Why chocolate? I thought they usually did a 5K run to help needy families." Alice reached for another chunk of granola and took a seat on the sturdy picnic bench that commanded a large corner of the shelter.

At forty-one, Sadie's only daughter was not only taller and slimmer than she was—traits inherited from Sadie's now-deceased husband—but Alice had also claimed her father's auburn hair and green eyes.

"It's just a onetime thing to raise money for a local group that aids widows, single mothers, and other women who need a temporary helping hand," Sadie said. "Widows' Mite needs a larger place to store donated items that they pass along to the women. A number of churches in the area are participating, so our group thought it would be nice to do it too, and go for the chocolate theme."

"Women and chocolate. Ha-ha! That's a good one." Theo plunked himself down on the bench and dug through the bag his mother had brought. "Speaking of chocolate, did you bring any with you?"

"Sorry," Alice said, sounding not a bit regretful since the snack bag already contained more healthful options.

Sadie opened her smoothie. "Want to try this? It's a recipe I thought I'd try. I think it tastes interesting. A little sweet and a little savory."

Theo sampled it and screwed up his face as he decided whether it passed the taste test, then passed the bottle to his sister. "It's okay. What's in it?" he asked Sadie.

She hesitated. When the recipe arrived in an e-mail newsletter from a health magazine, she'd thought the ingredients seemed an odd but intriguing combination, and it had actually turned out better than expected. Still, it was probably not something she'd make again.

"Bananas, chia seed, coconut milk, peanut butter, honey, and of course chocolate powder." She wasn't sure whether they were interested in hearing the rest.

Sara lifted the bottle and examined the strange brown color with peculiar bits suspended in the liquid. "And...?"

Answering as if her granddaughter had asked what the brown morsels were in chocolate chip cookies, she breezily replied, "Bacon."

"Eww." Sara's nose crinkled, and she passed the smoothie, untasted, to her mother, who sipped it and nodded her approval.

"Seriously?" Sara gave her mother an incredulous look. "I bet Grandpa wouldn't have liked it."

"He would have tried it, even if only for your grandmother's sake," Alice said.

As often happened, whenever the subject of their grandfather came up, Theo and Sara reminisced about the things he'd said or done before he passed away a couple of years ago. Today, they laughed together as they remembered the time T.R. had tried to teach Theo to cast. The worm-covered fishing hook had snagged his favorite Denver Broncos cap and sent it flying into the water.

"He sure loved to fish," Sadie said. His first preference had been to enjoy the sport with her or other members of the family. But he'd also spent lots of time here with Milo's father, Philip Henderson. And, of course, Sadie's best friend's husband, Roscoe Putnam.

Sadie smiled in remembrance. They'd had a lot of good years together, and she still missed him. The rain, which had eased up for the past few minutes, now resumed with fervor.

As if sensing Sadie's nostalgia, or perhaps because she missed him too, Alice rose from the bench and put an arm around her shoulders.

Comforted, Sadie squeezed her daughter in return. It seemed that the only people who truly understood a loss were those who'd known the person themselves. And, although they no longer actively mourned him every day, she knew that T.R.'s presence and influence would remain with them for the rest of their lives.

"Mia says people only have one true love in the world," Sara announced. "She said lightning only strikes once. Does that mean you can never be in love with Edwin?"

"Sara!"

"It's okay," Sadie assured her daughter. Considering her words carefully, she directed her attention to Sara with a smile. "Let's just say that God isn't stingy about letting good people come into our lives."

Or letting them return to our lives, she added silently.

"Were you ever in love with Edwin?"

She had no idea what had sparked this line of questioning, but since Edwin had become an integral part of her life, it was important to her that all of them mesh well together.

"We had what I would call a young love in high school." For some reason, the term *puppy love* had always annoyed her, probably because their relationship had gone much deeper than a mere springtime romance. "But college took us in different directions, and it never developed into a more mature love that comes with time and experience."

"I like him. I think you should marry him."

Alice walked over to the front of the shelter and peered out into the tumultuous weather. "It's a little soon for them to be thinking about that. It hasn't been that long since Edwin moved back here to Silver Peak."

The words were spoken without emotion, but as always Sadie sought to tread carefully so that it never seemed to her daughter that she was trying to replace her father with someone else. Or, worse, that she'd carried a torch for her first love while married to T.R.

"Let's just say that we've picked up where we left off." She paused and studied her granddaughter. "Why are you asking so many questions? Is there a boy you like?"

Sara grinned, showing the row of metal on her teeth, and directed her hazel eyes at her brother. "No, but Theo's got his eye on someone." She pointed a finger at him and chanted, "Ella, Ella, Theo's your fella!"

To his credit, Theo didn't rise to the bait. He just shrugged and gave them a shy smile. "For once, Sara's right about something." He glanced up from where he'd been scratching Hank's belly, which caused the dog's hind leg to quiver. "Unfortunately, someone else beat me to asking her to the prom."

"I'm sorry to hear that." Sadie joined her daughter at the front of the shelter and peered out into the slowing rain. "It should be over pretty soon."

Almost as soon as she'd said it, an eerie, prickling sensation seemed to lift the very hairs on her arms. A streak zagged through the sky, emblazoning it like a neon brand on a gray-hided heifer, and a fraction of a second later, a megadecibel *clap* followed.

The horses shifted anxiously at their stations, but it was Sara's horse, Daisy, that yanked loose from her tie-up and bolted from the shelter.

Sara started after the animal, but Sadie stopped her with a hand to her arm. "The storm isn't over yet."

"But . . . !"

"Daisy knows how to get home," Alice reminded her. "It's not far. She'll find her way."

Sure enough, the little horse was making a beeline down the path, stirrups flapping against her sides as she ran toward neighbor Milo Henderson's ranch, a little over a half mile away, where all of the horses were boarded.

"You can ride the rest of the way back with me," Sadie said. "Scout is strong enough to carry us both."

She had just turned to pack up her belongings when that weird, hair-prickling sensation happened again. But this time it was much stronger and felt like it might lift the hair right off of her scalp.

A flash filled the sky, pointing to a Ponderosa pine tree a couple hundred yards away. At the same instant, a sharp *crack* sounded even louder than before and shook the earth beneath them. The open-air shelter suddenly seemed inadequate in the face of the power before them, and Sadie instinctively took a step back.

Fortunately, the remaining horses handled the light show and noise better than Daisy had.

In the next instant, a loud creaking and groaning ensued from the nearby tree that had been struck, followed by a loud rustling *whoosh* and a *whump* as a large branch fell to the ground and made impact across the trail leading home.

Like the close-bonded family that they were, Sadie, her daughter, and grandchildren had naturally gravitated to each other and clung together while the sights and sounds they'd just experienced registered in their brains and burrowed into the place that would hold it as a memory for many years.

"Well, I guess Mia was wrong," Sara said, gently breaking the awe-filled quiet that had followed the spectacular display.

Still reeling from the heavenly theatrics, Sadie wasn't following where her granddaughter was going with that out-of-the-blue statement.

"Wrong about what, dear?"

The girl looked up at her and smiled. "Lightning *can* strike twice."

———

From start to finish, the storm had only taken about twenty minutes. Most of the clouds had blown away, and the sky was almost clear again.

They walked the remaining three horses to where the branch blocked the trail. One option to get around it would be to double back and loop around near the lake. But they'd still have to contend with it the next time they came this way.

"Never fear, Theo is here."

Her grandson handed his horse's reins to Alice and struggled to drag the heavy branch out of the way. Sadie and Sara pitched in, but even with the three of them working at it, they still had a way to go before the path was completely clear.

Despite the cool midforties temperature, Sadie was sweating from the exertion. She loosened her jacket and wiped the moisture from her temple.

"Too bad the horses aren't trained to pull," Sara said with a grunt. "But they'd probably get scared, hearing it drag behind them."

Theo chuckled. "Yeah, like that mule deer buck I saw eating leaves from a sapling. While he was yanking on the leaves in front of him, the branch dipped down and touched him on the backside. He wigged out, jumped straight up in the air, and took off like a rocket." Theo adjusted his grip and helped muscle the broken branch the rest of the way into the woods. "The other deer in the herd looked at him like he'd lost his mind."

They all stepped back and paused to catch their breaths. Sadie took a close look at her grandson and was reminded once again how much he reminded her of his namesake.

So handsome. And close to the age T.R. had been when she'd met him. Someday Theo would make some fortunate woman a good husband. Sweet and thoughtful like T.R., Theo was also handy with whatever he decided to build or repair. Unbidden, the question nudged her, asking if Ella could be the one and they just didn't know it yet.

Her thoughts took her back to what her college friend Frida had told her many years ago...that high school romances rarely last. At the time, it had been an attempt at consolation, but now the remembered platitude had shown itself to be merely that.

She pushed her hair back off her forehead. If God intended for two people to be together, she was confident He would come up with a way to make their relationship last, no matter when they first came together.

Or reunited.

Theo, still puffing since he had done most of the pulling, seated himself on the thick branch they'd just moved. "Is this far enough?"

Sadie joined him, and watched as Sara went back to her mother to ask about inviting her friend Mia for a sleepover that night. She turned back to Theo, whose gaze had drifted to a nearby tree.

"Looks like a squirrel must have hidden something in that knothole over there."

Curious, Sadie rose from her spot on the downed tree branch and followed him to the tree to inspect it.

She rose up on her toes to look inside, but the view was obstructed by bark growth and her lack of height. Even so, it was clear something was in there.

At six feet one, Theo had no trouble getting a glimpse of the item inside. "There's definitely something in here."

He tried to push his hand into the hole, but his large knuckles would not fit into the overgrown opening.

"In school, we read about a man in Vermont who found a bunch of war medals and commemorative coins in a tree. Maybe this could be some sort of hidden treasure too." He poked his long fingers into the hole as if to wiggle it out.

"Don't do that. It looks like metal in there. You could get a nasty cut."

Or a bite, depending on what else might be hiding in there.

"Let's use a hoof pick to pry the bark off so we can get a better look before we go poking around in there," she suggested.

Theo went to get the tool from a saddlebag, and Sara followed him back to the tree.

"Mom says if we find a treasure that's worth anything, she gets a twenty-five percent cut."

Theo took another peek and called out his findings. "Whatever it is, it's mostly rusted, but there does seem to be some orange and black paint on it."

"I wonder who put it in there." Sara jumped up to confirm her brother's findings, her strawberry-blonde hair bouncing in time to her leaps, but her efforts were futile.

Sadie considered the possibilities. This area of her property was so far out of the way that not a lot of people ever came here. Her neighbor Milo and his family were always welcome, but the growth over the opening suggested the contents had been there for a long time. Perhaps even before her middle-aged friend was born.

"For all we know, it could be a bit of trash put in there by a crow or blue jay," she said. "And from the looks of that bark, it's been here for a very long time."

"Maybe a thousand years," Sara suggested, clearly excited by the possibilities.

Theo gave her a "get real" stare.

"Okay, a hundred."

Too short to gain leverage, Sadie stood back while Theo chipped away the bark.

"Be careful," Sara called. Sadie smiled at the concern the girl showed for her brother, until she added with a taunting tone, "Could be an owl in there. Or a rat." Sara paused as if to consider what might be worse. "Or giant insects with man-eating mandibles."

Sadie didn't even try to hide her grin of amusement. She'd been an only child, as had Alice, so the sibling dynamics that went on between these two were a never-ending source of entertainment.

Theo, slightly rattled by the possibilities of what else might be lurking in the tree, hesitantly reached in, pulled out a small tin box, and passed it to Sadie.

She cautiously accepted the find and gave it a quick going-over. On what appeared to be the front of the box, the word *Sweetheart* showed through the rust spots.

Now, how on earth could this box come to be in a tree's knot-hole in the middle of the woods? She stepped back from the tree while Theo poked around for more hidden items.

This tree was on the uphill side of the trail from the lake ... right across from T.R.'s favorite fishing spot. She considered the people who might have come this way and whether they had left it here for someone else, or to retrieve it later.

Sara clutched her arm, and now Theo joined them. "Open it, open it!" she squealed.

She paused. Curious, but at the same time hesitant, she placed her hand over the rusted lid. "I'm sure your mother would like to see what we've found."

The teens raced ahead, and after all were gathered, Sadie tried to push the tin lid off with her thumbs.

"It's rusted together," she said. "I can't open it without bending the lid."

As an antiques dealer, she always took care to avoid damaging the objects that came through her store, no matter how seemingly worthless they might be. Even if there was little monetary value, certain pieces might contain immeasurable sentimental value.

Like his mother and sister, Theo watched and waited to see what she would do next.

Once again, his eyes reminded her of T.R.'s. She remembered the times her small hands had difficulty opening jars, and T.R. had been there to help her.

"Here." She smiled and handed the tin to Theo. "Maybe those football muscles of yours can get some leverage on this."

She didn't have to caution him to try to preserve the tin and its contents. He'd spent enough time with her at the Antique Mine to know what to do.

Using the hoof pick that had helped chip away at the bark of the tree, he eased it around the rim to loosen the rust, then carefully coaxed the lid up with his thumbs. Rust scrapings fell to the ground, but the tin was otherwise undamaged. Once the lid had been loosened, he handed it back to Sadie for the unveiling.

They all leaned in.

"Hurry," Sara said and bounced on her toes. "I can't stand the suspense."

With some trepidation, Sadie slowly lifted the lid.

Inside, a water-stained card resided next to a black felt bag that had lost its luster over the years. Her curiosity over whom this item had belonged to loomed greater than her curiosity over what else might be in the box. She pulled out the card and glanced over it.

It was a romantic poem, painstakingly lettered and obviously a declaration of love, but there was neither an envelope nor an indication of the sender or intended recipient.

Three pairs of eyes leaned in, and for some strange reason Sadie suddenly felt like a voyeur in someone else's love life.

Alice pointed a finger at the object of her interest. "What's in the bag?"

Sadie carefully returned the card to its place in the tin and removed the felt bag. Alice held the tiny box while she took out the contents of the bag.

A ring. But not just any ring. This was a ring like none she'd ever seen before. This was a real beauty, worthy of a place on display. Perhaps even in a museum.

Intricate gold metalwork curved like vines toward a center stone of pink surrounded by green petals tipped with tiny diamonds. At least, they looked like diamonds. She squinted and took a closer look.

Alice drew in her breath, and Sara gave a low whistle.

Sadie had come across some finds in her days as an antique dealer, but nothing like this. The intricately designed and crafted piece bordered somewhere between ostentatious and worthy of a queen.

"That could be worth a penny or two," Theo said, obviously a master of understatement. "If you sell it at the shop, you could get a ton of money for it."

"That's a nice thought, but the first thing I need to do is try to find out who it rightfully belongs to."

Sara wistfully leaned her cheek against Sadie's jacketed arm. "Do you think it's from Grandpa?"

Sadie had already considered this possibility, and her heart had lurched at the thought. This was his favorite fishing spot, after all. He was the one who had spent more time here than anyone else. But all she knew for sure, judging by the growth over the tree's knothole, was that it had been here for a very long time. Perhaps decades. Perhaps much longer.

However, if the ring and poem had been placed here by T.R., it would be like receiving one final communication from him. Taking a chance, she tried the ring on and splayed her fingers.

A perfect fit.

However, one troublesome thought nagged for an answer. If this was from T.R. and he had meant it for her, why had he stashed it in the tree?

2

Sadie smoothed her dress and stood in front of the mirror. She followed an impulse to twirl, and the action reminded her of the time she had prepared for her own high school prom more than forty years ago. But this time, she was a chaperone, and her date had been invited to officiate over the crowning of the prom king and queen.

Tonight, as then, Edwin was her date, and she wanted to look her best for him.

She picked up a journal from her dresser and carried it to the back door, where she let the dog in, then moved to the front room, where she sat to wait for Edwin to arrive. Talking with her grandchildren today about her early days with T.R. and Edwin had resurrected memories—and feelings—of that pivotal time in her life.

Without having to search her memory for the date, she flipped the pages open to February of 1973.

The English Composition assignment had called for an account of a fork-in-the-road event in her life. A situation that had already changed—or would soon change—the trajectory of her future.

Her choices at that time had been few, but significant: The moment in kindergarten when she'd struck up a friendship with lanky, lovable, and laughter-filled Roz, who remained her best friend to this day. The defining moment that had convinced her that teaching history was the career choice for her. Or the event that, at that time, was still so raw that her heart felt like it was bleeding every time she thought of it. Which, unfortunately, had been often.

Never one to shy from a task merely because of its difficulty, Sadie had decided to write about her breakup with Edwin in the hope it would help her gain clarity about the unexpected and confusing turn of events.

Because she had often used the journal to sort through her thoughts and feelings, it seemed only natural to write the first draft of her homework in its pages. She decided to write the paper in the third-person point of view, as if observed by an outsider, partly because the professor had required it, but also because she felt that writing it objectively might help her sort through the situation. Sadie had changed the names when she'd copied it for class.

She glanced at her watch. Just a few minutes before Edwin was due to pick her up, so she began to read while she waited.

Saturday afternoon, February 10, 1973

The man maneuvered his way through the crowd at the Boulder Campus at the University of Colorado. Twenty-year-old Sadie Wright turned her head slightly to see if he was still following her.

He was.

She pretended not to notice him and continued weaving her way through the campus meeting hall, slipping through the throngs of people who, despite the overnight dumping of snow, had turned out in force for today's women-helping-women fund-raiser.

Sadie took note of his features...slim, almost six feet tall, dark auburn hair, and even from this distance his eyes appeared green. He was young, like herself. And quite handsome.

She sidled past the line of people queued up for chili, sugar-powdered elephant ears, or a ringtoss game with assorted prizes, and finally headed toward the art booth where her friend Frida drew cartoon caricatures of her customers.

But before Sadie reached her destination, the man who'd been following her finally caught up and clapped a strong hand on her shoulder to stop her escape.

Sadie gasped and whirled to face him. "Unhand me, you fiend!"

"Fiend?" T.R. Speers smiled down at her with those amazing green eyes and playfully chucked a work-roughened finger under her chin. "That's not what you called me when I repaired that antique music box you found at the thrift store last month. And why are you playing so hard to get?"

"You're right. I believe I called you the best friend a girl could ever ask for." She tilted her head up at him. "And I wasn't playing hard to get. I was just curious to see which you were trying to track down...me, or the carnival food."

In the two years she'd been attending UC's School of Education, she'd made lots of friends, and T.R. had quickly grown to be a fixture in her life. It was no exaggeration to say he was becoming her best friend.

She gestured toward the hot-dog stand. "Let me buy you lunch."

T.R. touched a hand to his plaid-clad chest. "Way to hurt a man's pride. How about *I* buy *you* lunch, instead?"

He reached for his pocket, but Sadie stopped him with a hand to his arm. "Get with the times, Speers. It's nineteen seventy-three. Equal rights, and all that. Besides, I owe you for fixing that music box."

Sadie stopped reading and rested the journal on her lap. After all these years, she owed T.R. for so much more than a repaired music box. He had been her best friend, life partner, confidant, constant companion, and sometimes challenger when the moment required it.

Taking care not to disturb the mascara on her lashes, she daubed at the moisture that had suddenly blurred her vision, then turned back to the journal.

T.R. seemed about to negotiate a different form of payment when Sadie's gaze fell on someone standing at Frida's art table.

The doorbell rang. On the off-chance she might not have heard the bell, Hank barked to alert her. But it was not a bark of warning. His wagging golden tail indicated the person on the other side of the door was someone he was happy to welcome.

Sadie put down the journal and retrieved her coat before opening the door to a dapper, silver-haired man in a dark suit.

"What a lucky man I am," Edwin announced after stepping back to admire the effort she had put into getting ready for him. "I get to escort the belle of the ball to the prom tonight."

3

AMID THE THUMPING OF THE PROM MUSIC THAT NIGHT, SADIE reached up and straightened Edwin's tie. The dark blue suit against his white shirt and the steely silver tie crisscrossed with blue served to play up his silver hair and vivid blue eyes. His powerful build had suited the judge position he'd held prior to returning to Silver Peak and winning the mayoral seat. And his appearance was just as impressive now, in his role as an awards presenter at Silver Peak High School.

Edwin had always been a big guy, and by virtue of his sheer size and confident personality, he made her feel safe and protected whenever she was with him.

"My, my, don't you look official and very mayor-ish," she said.

"Thank you. And you look like a dew-kissed rose in that pretty pink blossom of a dress." His smile let her know that, although his overly flowery description had been spoken in jest, he truly meant what he'd said.

"Are you all ready to perform your ceremonial duties?" she asked, knowing he would not be here if he wasn't.

At that moment, Virginia Radcliff zoomed past. Without slowing her step, she called out to Edwin, "Please don't go anywhere. I'll be right back to brief you on the presentation."

Sadie grinned up at him. "Crowning the prom king and queen. That's got to be more fun than sending people to jail."

He gave her a warm smile. "The best part is being here with you."

She had to admit it was fun being here with him too, even though her chaperone duties called for her to be cruising the crowd of students, on the lookout for signs of mischief, while Edwin performed his civic duties.

"Would you like something to drink?" she asked. "Soda? Water?"

Theo approached as Edwin made his request for water. "I'll walk with you to the drink table," he offered.

Her grandson looked so handsome in his rented tux. The bolo tie had been his idea, and Sadie had to admit the casual western accessory actually went well with the formal wear. Since his first choice of a date had already been snagged, Theo had ended up bringing a friend-date from his English class who otherwise would also have had to come alone. The girl was huddled with a group of giggling girlfriends on the other side of the room.

Sadie looked around the packed gym that now doubled as a dance floor. "Is Ella here?"

Turning ever so discreetly, Theo nodded to point out Ella, the pretty girl who'd been his first choice, and her date, Bodie.

Ella sported long dark hair that flowed over her slim shoulders. With large, expressive eyes, and a lean figure that was tastefully strapped into an elegant teal gown, she looked like an animated princess out of a children's movie.

Bodie, on the other hand, was noticeably shorter than his high-heeled date, and instead of a tux, he wore a navy sports jacket with tan slacks. And, whereas the girl stood confidently, her expression serene and relaxed, he seemed awkward by comparison, his posture hunched and his gaze randomly skirting the room.

"Ella's date seems rather young," she said, carefully avoiding mentioning her first thought…that he didn't seem to be Ella's type. "Does he attend this school?"

The music changed to a soft ballad. While she and Theo made their way past the couples swarming toward the dance floor, he explained that Bodie had skipped a couple of grades and was Ella's "super-smart" science lab partner.

"She got dumped by Garrick over there. He's our star football player," he said with a nod over his shoulder toward a muscular young man who looked more like an expected match for the attractive girl. The young man flashed a curious glance at Bodie but otherwise appeared uninterested in the couple.

Sadie could see why Ella had turned Theo's head. According to him, she seemed to have it all: good looks, straight As—except for earth science class, which was apparently the only one in which she struggled—and a sweet disposition.

By comparison, Theo explained that Bodie's social awkwardness prevented him from looking people in the eye.

"And he has this weird habit of listing things from memory. All the presidents, in order and backward. Things on the teacher's desk. The birthday presents he's received over the years. That kind of stuff." Her grandson's observation seemed borne out of curiosity and bemusement rather than judgment. "Bodie's so smart that everybody wants him in their class project groups, but nobody really wants to be friends with him."

Sadie lifted a shoulder as they neared the drink table. "Ella seems okay with him."

Theo tilted his head in mild disagreement. "Bodie asked her to the prom, but she made it clear that she's not interested in dating so soon after the breakup. She wanted to go as just friends."

Just by looking at Bodie's overeager expression, she could tell he didn't understand the nuance behind "just friends."

Theo confirmed her suspicion when he added, "Bodie thinks the friends agreement is only temporary, until she gets over her ex. He told me he's going to wait until she's ready, but I think he'll be waiting a long time." He shook his head. By way of explanation, he added, "He's got Hashberger's. He's a nice kid, but he's kinda clueless about a lot of things."

From his comments, it was clear that Theo liked Bodie and cared about him, even if he didn't fully understand him.

"You mean Asperger's?" Sadie idly wondered if it wouldn't have been kinder if the girl had turned him down right from the start.

"Yeah, that's it. It's kind of like autism, but milder, I think."

Talk of Bodie's condition triggered a childhood memory of Sadie's teenage neighbor with mild autism who had a fixation on the singer Hank Williams. Back then, people had called the girl "slow," but Brenda had memorized everything there was to know about her country music idol and passed along her love of the musician and his songs to Sadie, who'd only been about seven at the time. Sadie had sat with her on the front porch, an extension cord stretched through an open window to power the record player, and they sang along to the music. If not for Brenda's lingering influence, Sadie's dog, Hank, might have been named Johnny Cash instead.

Her memories of that time spent with Brenda were filled with happiness and affection, and she hoped Ella would be easy on Bodie's tender spirit.

Two girls, their hair piled high and hair-sprayed into elaborate styles, walked by and giggled. "Hi, Thee-oooh!"

Oh, the flirtations of youth! Sadie elbowed her grandson. "You should go make their day by asking them to dance with you."

Theo laughed. "My grandma is my wingman."

After he'd joined the girls, she turned back toward the drink table and noticed a shy, plain girl watching Bodie. The boy appeared oblivious to her interest. Instead, he left Ella at that moment and headed in Sadie's direction.

He and Sadie approached the refreshment table at the same time, but instead of doing the polite thing and letting her go first, by virtue of her age and chaperone status, he scooted in front of her.

She took her place in line behind Bodie and prepared for a wait.

The drink server, a boisterous girl in a bead-fringed, flapper-style dress, set down an open plastic water bottle with such vigor that droplets sprayed those closest to her.

"Dougie!" the server blasted. "Gimme a hand. This line is gettin' too long. Teacher is going to chew me out if it gets too backed up."

Sadie watched while the designated assistant stepped behind the table to help the girl dispense drinks.

From the back of the line, someone asked, "Sasha, why aren't you out there dancing, girl? You're better than all those knobby-kneed people."

"Baby, I gotta do 'community service,'" Sasha said with a sweep of her hand toward the coolers filled with bottles of water and soda. "Miz Fisher said I was cuttin' up too much in her earth science class. Can you imagine that?"

Then the girl proceeded to poke fun at all who passed by the table.

"Yo, look at that crazy glitter on that dress." She raised her voice and called to the wearer, "You think you're a fairy with all that fairy dust?"

Up ahead, a boy someone called Colin jostled Bodie out of the way. His attention interrupted by Ella, who had walked over and joined Bodie, Colin gave her the once-over.

Dougie reached into the cooler and withdrew a water and grape soda, still dripping with water from the ice in which they'd sat, and Colin passed them back to Ella and Bodie. In accepting the bottles, Bodie managed to sling water on all those around him, including Sadie.

"I'm sorry." Ella handed her a few napkins and proceeded to wipe down her own dress with the rest. "My mom says to daub. Don't rub."

While the girl busied herself, Garrick walked past like a campaigning politician, glad-handing everyone in his path.

"Thank you for voting me prom king," he loudly pronounced, even though the winner hadn't been crowned yet. "I will serve you peons to the best of my ability."

He clapped a couple of his "peons" on the back, then took a hard overhand whack at a balloon decoration. The unexpected *pop* caused a number of people, including Sadie, to jump at the sound. Pleased by their reactions, he popped a couple more balloons before one of the chaperones nearest him asked him to knock it off.

"More napkins?" Ella asked.

Sadie took another daub at the blot on her dress. "No thanks. It's just water. It'll be dry in no time."

Oblivious to what he had done to Sadie, Bodie handed Ella the unopened water, then unscrewed the plastic cap on his own bottle.

As soon as the cap came off, purple soda sprang like a multi-spouted fountain from numerous holes around the bottle. Taken by surprise, the bewildered teen turned in circles, spewing the dark liquid all over his tan pants and anyone else foolish enough to stand too close.

En masse, all those around him took a giant step away from the disaster in progress.

Finally, paralyzed with indecision, Bodie merely stood and watched as the drink continued to pour down on him.

Sadie wanted to help Bodie, but the boy went back to turning in circles, putting everyone who came near him at risk of permanent grape stains.

"Stop laughing!" Ella yelled. "It's an accident!" Unfortunately, Ella's voice was only one of many in the din around the table.

The music switched to a slow tune, luring some of the mockers to the dance floor. Theo, however, had noticed something amiss and returned to see what was going on.

As he approached, he gingerly removed the half-empty drink bottle from Bodie's hand and tossed it into a nearby trash can.

"Bode-Man, you're all washed up," Theo said gently.

The lighthearted tone was clearly meant to ease the teen's embarrassment, and Bodie seemed glad to be rid of the bottle that had thoroughly doused his pants.

"Look, why don't you go in the bathroom and rinse that stuff out of your pants?" Theo suggested. "Then you can hold them under the hand dryer. It shouldn't take long. You'll be out here dancing in no time."

Bodie seemed to appreciate being given a plan to follow, and he abruptly turned—without even a word to Ella—and headed toward the restroom.

"Use cold water!" Ella called after him.

Sadie couldn't be prouder of her grandson for the way he had taken command of the awkward situation and eased his fellow classmate's distress.

"Do you think you should go with him?" she suggested. Bodie might be plenty book smart, but he looked as though he could use a bit of supervision at the moment.

"Nah, that would just embarrass him more. He'll be fine."

The matter settled, she nabbed a bottle of water for Edwin and stepped away from the drink table.

Colin, taking advantage of Bodie's absence, asked Ella to dance. The girl glanced toward the restroom and back at Colin.

"I should wait for Bodie."

"Come on. It's just a dance."

Slowly, almost reluctantly, Ella accepted his offer, pausing once to glance over her shoulder in the direction her date had gone.

The matter settled, Sadie returned to Edwin where he awaited her with a white banner draped across his chest: *Prom Official.*

"Careful when you open this," she warned. "It might spring a leak."

Fortunately, Bodie's disaster was not repeated. After Edwin had quenched his thirst, he asked if Sadie would dance with him after the crowning of the prom king and queen.

Sadie grinned in response and made an exaggerated show of looking around her.

"Are you expecting someone?" Edwin asked.

"No. Just checking to make sure Lena Farrell isn't around. I had noticed that she kept trying to dance with you at our senior prom in 'seventy-one. She was so persistent, I wouldn't be surprised if she'd followed you here tonight."

"It upset you," Edwin said, obviously touched.

He reached out and touched her short hair that no longer fell over her shoulder as it had that special night so long ago. During their time apart, it had changed from a medium brown to salt and pepper. She'd also gained a few wrinkles and an extra pound or two over the years, but judging by the expression in his eyes, he either didn't notice or didn't care.

"Of course it did," she said, turning her cheek toward his hand. "I had the nicest and best-looking guy at the prom, and Lena was trying to move in on him."

Edwin shook his head and cast her a teasing grin. "I had noticed you were distracted that night. I assumed you were checking out the other guys."

Sadie burst out laughing at the unexpected teasing and playfully swatted his arm. "I did not!"

This was what she remembered most about their time together. The laughter. That, and an inability to be bored in each other's company.

Edwin's expression turned serious. "You're right. The truth is, the guys were checking you out."

She quirked her mouth and gave him a disbelieving look.

"Why else do you think I took you outside?" he said. "To get you away from the ones who wanted to steal you away from me."

The memory of that night under the clear sky, dotted with stars and filled with hope, drew a smile to her lips.

"We made a wish on the..." The rest faded away.

"Moon," he finished.

Her smile relaxed and quietly left her face. That night, they had wished to always be together, and to always be as happy as they were at that moment.

A glance at Edwin told her that he remembered that night—that wish—as well.

He tucked a finger under her chin. "We're together now."

As she gazed up at him, she realized he had that look like he wanted to kiss her. Despite the throng of hormonal teenagers she was supposed to keep in line, she wished he would.

"Yes," she said, whether in reply to his statement or in encouragement, she wasn't sure which.

Unfortunately, like the circumspect judge-turned-mayor that he was, he refrained.

Sadie's gaze drifted to the corner of the room where Bodie had disappeared to a little while ago. A number of boys entered and exited the restroom, including Dougie, who walked out and stood near the entrance. He administered a swipe and a few taps to his cell phone and grinned.

Dougie didn't seem to be doing anything wrong, but something about his behavior told her he was up to something. Her years as a teacher had given her a sixth sense for such things.

"Excuse me," she told Edwin with a grin. "This time I really am checking out another guy."

As she approached, Sasha walked out of the adjacent girls' room, past Dougie, who was laughing now. The boys' room door opened as the girl passed, and when she turned to avoid the person who exited, she apparently got a peek inside and burst out laughing.

Concerned now, Sadie picked up her pace. Theo, alerted by the hilarity, came toward them.

By now, Sasha had taken off her beaded headpiece and was waving it in front of her face like a fan.

"Dude," Sasha said to Dougie after she'd caught her breath. "Who wears tighty-whities anymore? That little guy cracks me up!"

Dougie showed her something on his phone, and they both convulsed into howls of laughter.

Sidling up to the pair, Sadie leaned in. "*Ooh*, prom pictures! Let me see."

After a second's hesitation, Dougie handed it over.

"Uh, I got work to do," Sasha said, her eyes wide with feigned innocence, and hustled back over to the drink table.

The phone was open to Facebook, featuring a photo of Bodie taken from behind as he stood near the sink. His skinny white legs showed, along with a small glimpse of white cloth under the tails of his Sunday dress shirt. He held the tan slacks under the hot-air hand dryer. The caption on the photo read, "Don't I look cute?"

It wasn't that the picture was that revealing. It was not. What bothered Sadie, and it had only taken a quick glance to know it, was that someone was intent on publicly humiliating the boy. Intent on bullying a sweet kid who probably wouldn't hurt a fly.

"What's this about?" she asked Dougie. She was so taken aback that she could hardly speak.

"I didn't do it! Bodie must have posted it," Dougie protested. "It was on his own home page. I only shared it. See?"

He clicked the screen that took them to Bodie's page, where the photo, posted only a minute or two ago, showed one share. Dougie's.

Regardless of semantics about whose page it had been posted to or how many shares it had rated, it was obvious that Bodie had neither taken the photo nor posted it to his own wall, as Dougie had suggested.

"I've seen a lot of funny things go on at this prom tonight," she said. "This is not one of them."

Theo showed up and looked over her shoulder before she could clear the screen.

"Did you do this?" he demanded of Dougie.

Theo's hands were balled into fists, and Sadie touched his arm to remind him to control his temper.

"Delete it," she urged Colin. "Before anyone else sees it."

"Too late," Theo said, taking the phone from her hand. "It's going viral. You should see all the shares."

From inside the boys' room, the electric dryer shut off, then started again.

The horse had left the barn and, unfortunately for Bodie, there was no way they could put it back in. But Sadie was determined that whoever did this would be set straight that any bullying—even via social media—was not acceptable.

Theo stood beside her, his face red with rage and indignation. She just hoped her grandson didn't get to them first.

4

BACK AT HOME THAT EVENING, HANK SEEMED TO SENSE THE
tension surging through Sadie and followed her from room to
room as she prepared for bed.

She put down her hairbrush and knelt to give her furry friend
a reassuring hug. Not surprisingly, the action calmed her as well
as the dog.

"Come on. Let's go get a treat for you and a cup of tea for me."
Perhaps the hot beverage would relax her enough that she could
drop off to sleep. And perhaps a little light reading would help too.

A few minutes later, she carried her tea and journal into the
bedroom and settled into bed. She picked up reading where she'd
left off when Edwin had arrived earlier tonight.

Could it be...? From the back, the dark, business-length
haircut and sturdy frame matched Edwin's and, in his
sophisticated clothes, the guy at Frida's art table looked
more "city" than most of the people around here. Yes, it was
definitely Edwin.

He hadn't told her he was coming back to Colorado
from Chicago. Then again, they hadn't talked or

corresponded in, like, forever. Well, it seemed that long.

T.R. moved closer and peered in the direction she was looking. "Something wrong?"

"Um, I don't know." She worried her bottom lip between her teeth. "It's Edwin, and I'm not sure why he's here."

"I thought you two broke up when you graduated and went off to separate colleges."

She turned away from Edwin and faced her friend while she gathered her thoughts about this unexpected turn of events. "I wouldn't exactly say we broke up. It was more like an agreement to date other people."

A temporary agreement, which had gone on far longer than she had anticipated. Although she'd accepted a few invitations from guys during that time, they'd been more like companion dates than romantic ones. In the back of her mind, she was always waiting to reconnect the relationship with Edwin. But, unfortunately, contact from him had gradually dwindled.

"Maybe he should have kept in better touch," T.R. mumbled.

Her best friend, Roz, had said as much, and Sadie wondered if the two had been talking. She shot T.R. a questioning glance, and he quickly adjusted his tone.

"Do you want me to leave?" He gestured toward the meeting hall. "Give you two space to air things out?"

"No!" she said with more emphasis than intended. It would be nice to have her friend's support while she figured out the reason behind Edwin's unexpected appearance here today. "I mean, I'm not even sure Edwin is here to see me. If you don't mind, it would be nice to have you stick around for a bit. Moral support."

T.R.'s expression softened with compassion, which made Sadie feel even more vulnerable than before. He was a good friend, and she appreciated his concern.

Edwin straightened from bending over Frida's art table, and his steely blue eyes connected with hers. He hesitated a moment, then said something to Frida, and headed Sadie's way. The crowd between them, as if sensing the determination in his stride, parted to make way for him.

T.R. eased closer to Sadie, like an early settler preparing to defend his homestead.

The grandfather clock in the hall chimed the passing of another hour. If she was to get up in time for church tomorrow and have plenty of energy to help Edwin declutter his aunt's closet in the afternoon, she'd better close the journal—and her eyes—for now.

Reluctantly, she laid the book on her night table. Amazingly, after all these years, she was still waiting to see how Edwin's and her story would ultimately turn out.

5

_____

"CAREFUL, DON'T HURT YOURSELF." SADIE LIFTED HER HANDS toward Edwin, where he was balancing precariously on a stepstool in front of his aunt's bedroom closet.

"Don't worry about me. Just stay out of the way in case there's a landslide."

Edwin had barely spoken the words when a pair of red ankle-strap heels broke loose on the top shelf and catapulted themselves down on his head. Before he could react, a small jewelry box followed, and a box of yellowed receipts rained down on him.

Pauline Marshall tottered into the room unassisted by walker or cane, an impressive feat considering her nearly one hundred years on this earth. Although she moved slowly, she remained in amazingly good shape.

"I've prepared some tea for us," Pauline said, oblivious to the near-calamity that had just occurred. "I hope you're okay with my Fiesta Ware tea set. I'm not like Edith, who uses different sets, depending on how important her guests are, don't you know. I use the same cups, whether it's someone important, like my grandson the mayor, or just regular folks like you," she said, apparently referencing Sadie as the latter.

Pauline smiled, and the bright red lipstick that lined her mouth showed two half circles on her upper lip, a replica of the rosebud lips of 1930s screen stars.

Rather than take offense at Pauline's inadvertent slam, Sadie smiled at the woman's obvious pride in her grandson and his accomplishments. Edwin drove to nearby Frisco to visit Pauline in her tiny assisted-living apartment every so often, as his schedule allowed. And Sadie occasionally joined him for visits with the quirky centenarian who never failed to entertain or sometimes even shock them.

"One lump, or two?" Pauline asked.

Edwin rubbed a hand over his head, gingerly probing it with his fingertips. "Probably three."

"You've made enough of a mess for the time being," Pauline chirped, taking in the receipts and old envelopes that lay scattered on the floor. "This would be a good time to take a break."

While Sadie and Edwin gathered the papers, Pauline returned to the living room to finish setting up the tea. A few minutes later, they were seated on the antique wingback sofa covered in faded gold velvet. Stoneware cups in bright teal, yellow, and adobe pink sat before them on the oval claw-and-ball coffee table.

Several bags of items from the closet sat near the front door for Sadie and Edwin to take with them when they left. Beside Pauline's chair, another bag awaited her final sorting. Each time they did this, Edwin had a harder time letting go of the pieces that pointed to a part of his aunt's life history.

Edwin sipped his tea, the cup looking very small in his large hands. "*Mmm,*" he said and pressed his lips together while squinting slightly. "Mighty sweet."

Pauline pursed her own lips, and the two half circles merged under her delicate nose. "Well, sweetie, you told me you wanted three lumps of sugar."

Edwin met eyes with Sadie but didn't bother to clarify. To do so would only launch his aunt into an unneeded safety lecture on proper stepladder use.

Sadie liked it here. Liked the way Pauline had decorated the place to suit her unique personality, and liked the senior-care facility that offered a clean and safe living environment for its residents. Best of all, Edwin and his family could rest easy, knowing their loved one had convenient access to prepared meals and social activities, all while maintaining as much independence as her mobility would allow.

"I'm so sorry to ask you two to handle all these things I've collected over the years. It's been hard to let them go, but at least every time I go through it, a little bit more goes out the door." Pauline thoughtfully sipped her tea. "Perhaps one of these days I'll be able to see the back of my closet."

They hastened to assure her that it was no problem at all to help her with the winnowing.

Sadie recalled Edwin saying that Pauline had come here to live after falling and breaking her wrist four years ago. Although Pauline had protested the change at first, the socially gregarious woman had quickly come to enjoy making new friends with whom she shared a love of crafting projects and going on planned excursions.

"How've you been getting along lately?" Sadie asked. "Have you gone on any interesting outings?"

"Oh yes, indeed." Pauline's voice pitched to a high lilt. "Last week, Muriel and I decided we wanted to go to that new yarn store, What's Needling U, but she said it was closed, and I didn't believe her. So we loaded up all our friends in the van, Howard snatched the keys off the reception desk, and I drove us down to Main Street to check it out for ourselves."

Sadie and Edwin both shot forward in their seats.

"You did what?" Edwin demanded, apparently knowing full well it was something his aunt was capable of doing. "You can't be out there driving, especially not in a stolen van. In the rain. And with a bunch of people who could have gotten hurt. Worse, *you* could have been hurt."

"*Pfft.*" Pauline waved away his concern with her slim hand. "Don't be ridiculous, dear. My license expired five years ago. Of course I didn't take the van for a joyride." She gave them a conspiratorial look. "But that doesn't mean I haven't thought about it."

Edwin stared at his aunt, disbelief and relief covering his handsome face. A few seconds later, after the shock wore off, he grinned at having been taken, once again, by his mischievous relative.

"You got me that time," he said and shook a finger at her.

"I'll save the van ride for after my centennial birthday party. Just in case anything goes wrong, and I get thrown in the slammer." She adjusted the clip-on earring attached to her ear. "I wouldn't want to miss my big birthday celebration."

Sparked by talk of the party, Pauline turned the conversation to her "much younger" eighty-nine-year-old friend, Edith, who would be hosting the event.

"I told her to feel free not to spare any expense. We aren't getting any younger, you know," Pauline said with a flash of a smile.

The woman picked through the bag beside her chair, pulled out a pair of bizarre-looking butterfly sunglasses, and put them on. Originally an old pair of cat's-eye glasses, they'd been altered with mesh-covered wire shaped into the form of wings on either side and bedazzled with colored rhinestones. Pink pipe cleaners, wrapped in shiny foil—possibly the cooking variety—arched over her forehead to serve as whimsical butterfly antennae.

"Oh, how cute," Sadie said. The image was both silly and adorable, both of which suited Pauline's unconventional personality. "Did one of your great-grandchildren make them?"

"No, dear," Pauline said, seeming affronted by the question. "I did, in craft class last summer."

She took them off and set them beside her on the marble-topped end table. "I'm going to keep these. They're too cute to get rid of."

Sadie suspected that would have been one item of Pauline's that Edwin wouldn't have had a hard time parting with.

"I always feel like a hoarder when I keep these things," Pauline chattered on.

Sadie laughed inwardly. Pauline had learned to keep her hoarder tendencies a well-kept secret. Not even a speck of dust dared to clutter a horizontal surface anywhere in sight. Instead, the things Pauline had saved over the years had ended up jammed tightly into every closet, pantry, and cabinet available.

"But then I remember all the knickknacks and whatnots you're always taking home with you, Sadie, and I don't feel so bad anymore." Pauline smiled, apparently clueless about the inadvertent insult she'd just delivered.

"Now, Aunt Pauley, you know that finding antiques is part of Sadie's job," Edwin said, coming to her defense. "And whatever she doesn't sell gets donated or used."

Well, most of it. Some of the treasures had made their way into her house, where she enjoyed looking at them, using them, or debating whether to keep or repurpose them.

"So tell me," Pauline said, unaware of the ripples she'd stirred up, "what have you added to your collection lately?"

Rather than take offense, Sadie cataloged a few of the more interesting pieces she'd found lately, but it was two gross of umbrellas, possibly from a wholesaler, that she'd received in a storage auction bid that caught the older lady's attention.

"Gross umbrellas? Why would anybody want gross umbrellas?"

"No, *a* gross. Twelve dozen. Times two. That's two hundred eighty-eight umbrellas in all different colors. I have no idea what to do with them."

For the next ten minutes, they had a blast imagining ways to use the unneeded umbrellas. Sadie and Edwin had come up with more predictable possibilities, such as donating them, but it was Pauline who came up with creative doozies, such as using them for frost protection over garden vegetables.

Sadie smiled at the mental image of almost three hundred umbrellas in assorted colors brightening a large backyard garden.

Considering how much they'd laughed since they came here after church, and how much they always laughed when they came by, she once again understood why Edwin offered no complaints about making trips to Frisco to visit his aunt. Unpredictable as she was, Pauline was definitely a lot of fun.

It was almost time to head back, but when Edwin checked his watch, Pauline declared how "worn out" she was, as if she'd been the one to lift the items from the top shelf of her closet.

"Let's just sit and visit for a while," she insisted.

Edwin raised one eyebrow at Sadie, and without words they agreed to extend the visit another fifteen minutes. But eventually, all good things had to come to an end.

After retrieving their coats, Edwin picked up a couple of the bags near the door, and Sadie retrieved a stray apron that had fallen to the floor. The front of it sagged, leading her to believe Edwin must have used the pocket for extra packing space.

"No, dear, not that." Pauline lifted the item from her hand. "That's my gospel pocket. Can't be caught without it."

The term was new to her, and Sadie was about to ask, but Edwin was already kissing Pauline's cheek and promising to be back soon. Although he wanted to get back to Silver Peak before dark, he never let it seem to Pauline that he was in any hurry to leave her.

Sadie loved how Edwin was so attentive to his aunt. If she was fortunate enough to make it to a hundred years of age, she hoped her loved ones would do the same for her.

———

They carried the bags onto the broad porch of the Victorian home that had once belonged to Edwin's parents, then wiped their boots dry of the springtime sprinkle.

Inside, they went through the items Pauline had sent home with them and sorted them into piles to sell, keep, donate, or toss. Antique or not, any salable items would be offered on consignment at the Antique Mine and the proceeds given to Pauline to feed her yarn addiction.

"Your aunt is precious," Sadie said. "She never fails to make me laugh."

"Or cringe."

She considered his comment. "That too. But you always know exactly where you stand with her."

Edwin pulled several stapled sheets of elementary school–lined paper out of the bag he sorted and placed it on the trash pile.

Thinking it was something from Edwin's earlier days, Sadie snatched it up and read out loud from the amateurish handwriting.

"I will respect other people's property. I will respect . . ." She turned the pages over and found each repeated sentence numbered from one to a hundred.

"Don't tell me," she said with an impish grin. "We've known each other forever, but I never thought of you as the little stinker who had to copy punishment sentences."

Edwin looked up from his work, and she handed the paper back to him.

"Be careful that you dispose of this carefully so the press doesn't get wind of it," she said, continuing the goading. "You never know how that kind of negative publicity could affect your next election."

With a finger to the name on the paper, he handed it back to her. The corner of his mouth lifted on one side.

"That's my cousin Joanie's doing," he said. "She went through a light-fingered phase for a while. The sentences must have done the trick, because she never stole anything else after that."

Sadie remembered Joanie. The girl had looked up to her older cousin and wanted to follow him everywhere. Edwin had been unenthusiastic about having the kid tag along, but Sadie had thought she was sweet and sometimes played dolls with her when she visited at Edwin's house.

"Maybe we should let Joanie make the decision of whether to throw this away," she suggested. "She might get a chuckle out of seeing it again."

Sadie had done all she could, sorting through the bags, and the rest would be for Edwin to decide. Only a few items remained, so rather than get in his way while he finished, she drifted to the bookshelf in the large drawing room and perused the titles while she waited. His reading tastes were even more eclectic than hers, so she welcomed the opportunity to see what latest tome had attracted his attention.

Hmm, a couple of mysteries. A biography of Abraham Lincoln. A home owner's guide to fix-it-yourself projects. And a slim volume by regional TV personality Mathis Root, which drew her to pull it from the shelf. She flipped the pages past an assortment of short stories and essays. The cowboy poet and humorist had been a fixture around the area for the past forty years or so and was often sought by the media for sound-bite quotes about anything involving Colorado or cowboys.

She carried the book back to where he had just finished up and showed him the cover.

"I didn't realize you were a fan," she said.

"Oh yes. There's a little of something for everyone in his writings. Humor, politics, romance, and the great outdoors. But mostly I like his stories about the day-to-day life of real cowboys, and the struggles they went through."

Edwin, even though he had spent most of his adult life in an urban setting, had always loved the great outdoors. But she shouldn't have been surprised. Edwin had always loved hiking and enjoying the mountains and waters of their scenic hometown, and he never turned down an opportunity to go adventuring. It was just that his lifelong judicial career and current political position often kept him indoors and at a desk.

"I've met Mathis," she told him. "He used to spend time with Milo's father and grandfather, and T.R. sometimes hung out with them."

Edwin seemed suitably impressed. "I wouldn't mind meeting him someday. Love the way he spins a yarn."

Speaking of T.R. made her think of the tin box and its contents that she'd found yesterday. They'd both been so busy she hadn't had the opportunity to tell him about her exciting find.

"Speaking of T.R., I found something really beautiful and sweet that he left for me." She still didn't know for sure that T.R. was the one who'd left it there, but he seemed to be the most likely person to have done so. That's certainly what her heart wanted to believe.

"That's nice," Edwin said, then halfheartedly pushed a pile of giveaways to the corner of the room and joined her near the fireplace.

She wasn't sure what kind of reaction she'd expected, but it wasn't this. It was possible he was distracted by the work needed to put Pauline's old mementos in the right hands, but a part of her wondered if he felt awkward, hearing about a gift left by her now-departed husband.

She had always accepted his wife's history with him as a good thing. Without his experiences with Rose, Edwin wouldn't be the person he was today. And Sadie believed that he felt the same about her and T.R.

"Theo found the gift in a knothole in a tree near that fishing spot of T.R.'s."

"I'm very happy for you," he said, his gaze ever so sincere as he pulled her into his big arms for a tender hug.

His embrace made her feel cared for and protected. Very much cherished. In some ways, it was like they'd never been apart for almost forty years. She knew him so well.

Well enough to know that he enjoyed hearing about all of her discoveries...of antique finds, of interesting developments with her grandchildren, and of new understandings about certain Bible passages. Yet this was the one time he didn't ask her to tell him more.

"I, um, just thought you'd like to know."

"Of course," he said.

Edwin had never shown signs of jealousy, but there was something about his response that made her wonder if this time was an exception. Out of respect for him, she decided it would be best not to show him the treasures she'd found. At least not now. Maybe later, when the time was right.

6

After Edwin dropped her off at the house and said good night, Sadie returned to where she'd left off in the journal. Talk of T.R.'s gift had her once again thinking of their beginnings. And Edwin's apparent disinterest in hearing about the discovery took her back to the first meeting of the two men.

At that moment, Edwin seemed to notice T.R., and a slight hesitation interrupted his purposeful approach.

As he neared them, Sadie silently debated how former steadies such as she and Edwin—separated by time, distance, and minimal communication—should greet each other. Uncertain and feeling somewhat awkward, she impulsively stuck out her hand.

Edwin closed his fingers around hers, pulled her to him, and lightly kissed her on the cheek. It could have been a let's-pick-up-where-we-left-off kiss or a citified mannerism he'd picked up in Chicago. She couldn't tell which.

"Sadie, it's good to see you."

She frowned. From his greeting, it sounded as though this might be a happenstance meeting rather than a planned encounter.

T.R. cleared his throat and extended his own hand, thereby forcing Edwin to let go of her and acknowledge him.

She peered up at her friend in response to his unexpected gesture.

T.R. just flashed a neutral smile at both of them.

"Um, Edwin, this is my friend T.R. Speers."

She hesitated, trying to remember whether she should have mentioned the newcomer's name first, or the name of the person she'd known the longest. Why did all of Emily Post's manners tips escape her when she needed them most? For some reason, her uncharacteristic concern over social protocol prompted a strange impulse to curtsy, and the thought of doing so almost sent a nervous giggle to her throat. She squelched the urge.

"T.R., this is..." How did she summarize the relationship of the person she'd known almost all her life? The person she'd gone steady with from their junior year in high school until departing for college? The person whose intentions she no longer understood. "This is Edwin Marshall."

"Yes, I've heard about you," T.R. said, still pumping the other man's hand.

"And I, you." The formal wording sounded snooty, even for Edwin, who seemed to be trying to comport himself like the lawyer he was studying to become.

Sadie took a deep breath. "T.R. and I were just about to have lunch. Edwin, would you like to join us?"

"*Aaarooooo!*" Hank howled, his fuzzy face lifted toward the ceiling.

His eyes darted to Sadie as if to see whether he had her attention.

"*Rooooo!*" he added, clearly determined to make it known he wanted something from her.

"You want a cookie?" She rose from her seat on the couch, and he pranced ahead of her to the kitchen, where she prepared the bedtime snack he'd asked for.

After he licked the bowl clean, she stooped and rumpled his soft ears. Satisfied, Hank trotted off to find his bed.

Still thinking about the journal entry and the circuitous path that had, almost miraculously, brought Edwin back into her life, Sadie thought it was probably time for her to do the same.

7

Spring came late to Silver Peak's high elevation, but it seemed determined to make itself known this early May morning. Sadie stepped out of Flap Jack's restaurant across Main Street from the Antique Mine, her hands loaded with a to-go bag of steaming pancakes and a side of berries to pile on top. The sun streamed down, promising temperatures hovering close to sixty, and for perhaps the first time since opening the shop, she wanted to dawdle before going in to work.

The sign in the window of the Antique Mine had been turned to *Open*, an indicator that her assistant, Julie, had already taken her place behind the cash register. With a twinge of guilty pleasure, Sadie succumbed to the lure of the metal bench in front of the Silver Peak Opera House.

Against the backdrop of the majestic Rocky Mountains, the charming little mining town that she called home was growing lush with green, and planter boxes in front of the businesses offered up an array of early-blooming colorful flowers for passersby to enjoy. And in front of the bank, a small rosebush budded with the promise of beautiful blossoms to come.

Across the street, perched on the back of an outdoor café chair in front of Arbuckle's Coffee, a male mockingbird called out to a different kind of beauty. The female, observing from the tree on the sidewalk in front of Arbuckle's and the Antique Mine, seemed unsure of his intentions.

Soon, the male seemed to realize that repeatedly calling out "*Chack!*" wasn't going to cut it with this one. He needed to step up his game. So he swooped to the sidewalk, stretched up high on his toes, and spread his wings to display the patches of white on his gray feathers. Like a birdie version of *Romeo and Juliet*, he continued the feathery show and called up to his love interest where she sat on her branch-balcony.

To further convince her of his sincerity, the mockingbird moved to the base of the tree where a small circular object glittered in the dirt. Picking it up in his beak, the bird gave it a toss as if trying to pitch it up to her.

Sadie leaned closer to see that the silvery object that had caught the female's interest was a metal washer, minus the bolt.

While the feathery Juliet was making up her mind about her suitor, another male entered the scene, a turn of events that the first bird did not appreciate. The two contenders faced off in the middle of the street while the female clung to the side of the tree and watched.

After a brief flutter of wings and bumping of downy chests, the challenger retreated in front of the Antique Mine.

The dispute apparently over for now, Sadie retrieved her breakfast, then crossed the street and entered her shop, where Julie greeted her with a smile and eyed the bag in her hand.

"*Mmm*, goodies from Flap Jack's."

Sadie handed a cup of coffee to her employee and kept the other for herself. "I would have gone next door, but Arbuckle's doesn't serve pancakes."

Back at her desk, she pulled out the old diary from her purse that she'd stuck in there this morning. After taking another look last night at the tin that had been found in the tree, she'd managed to make out a faded date on the front. It appeared to be a commemorative tin, celebrating some event, or perhaps an historic anniversary, in 1973.

Prior to discovering the date, she had intended to consult with an arborist to determine how long it would have taken for the bark to have grown over the hole as much as it had. But now, the tin itself had revealed that it couldn't have been placed there before 1973. But that didn't mean it couldn't have been placed there later.

She hurriedly ate the pancakes that had grown cold by now, but were still delicious, then put the takeout container back in the bag and stuck it in the trash can beside her desk.

A laugh sounded from the front of the shop.

"You should see these mockingbirds battling it out," Julie said. "It's like watching a soap opera."

Sadie wandered back up front and peered out the plate-glass windows at the feathery display that was still going on.

"The female seems a little confused about which one to choose," Sadie said.

By now, a couple of customers had joined them at the glass to see what was going on.

Julie laughed again. "If I were her, I'd have a difficult time choosing too. They're both so cute."

When a pedestrian walked past, the first suitor moved aside, and that's when the second one swooped down, snatched the metal washer, and flew off with it. The female glanced back and forth between the males, then flew after the second-comer.

"Awww," the customers said in unison.

The challenge over, Sadie was about to return to her desk, but was stopped by Julie's comment.

"Poor guy," Julie said of the first male. "He looks like he's not sure what to do now."

Indeed, he did. The bird lifted a foot behind his wing and scratched his head. Then a moment later, he flew across the street and perched on the rosebush.

The diary beckoned Sadie back to her desk. After having determined the date on the tin, the possibility had occurred to her that something written in the book might jar her memory. Perhaps something T.R. had said, or a mention of a visitor to the property.

After their marriage that had followed college graduation, she and T.R. had moved to the farmhouse, about a mile from the Silver Peak town limits, that had been in her family for many years. Until the Depression, it had been a large, prosperous ranch, but over time portions had been sold off until only a small plot remained. That was where she and T.R. had raised their children, and where she planned to stay for what she hoped would be many more years.

She randomly flipped the pages in the diary. Not every day had been journaled, because she'd had a busy time keeping up with classes, friends, and growing a new, closer relationship with T.R., but there were enough entries to jog her memory of events that occurred during that time.

The writings discussed her likes and worries about her new semester classes at UC-Boulder. Then there was the summer vacation with her family, and a signed agreement between her, Roz, and a new roommate at the beginning of the next school year, defining how they would divide the household chores.

Settling in, she turned back to the beginning of the journal and began to skim the entries. And then she came to that day in early February.

Edwin had shown up unexpectedly, as if there had been a reason other than a couple of hours of visiting behind his sudden appearance. He had acted odd that day. At first she'd thought it had something to do with T.R.'s presence, but the two had hit it off like old friends, so she doubted that was it.

She'd finally chalked up Edwin's reserved demeanor to his having found another girlfriend while they'd been apart. Not that she faulted him for that. They both knew when they left for separate colleges that it could happen.

Edwin must have had a hard time breaking the news to her, the task made even harder by the noise of the carnival, and later by T.R.'s and Roz's presence in the apartment.

It had been tough for him. And it certainly was a tough time for her, but her friends had gotten her through the sad parting.

She skipped forward to the following volumes recounting their marriage and the move into this house. Although Sadie had offered to help T.R. unpack his things, he had refused her assistance, and she had laughed that he must not have wanted her to see the holes in his socks.

For a while, she got lost in the memories of her life with T.R.... most of them good, some of them difficult, but all of them cherished and a blessing. One of those entries, all but forgotten until now, had been a conversation triggered by a news account of a politician's questionable actions. Although T.R. hadn't defended the man's choice, he had commented that everyone—himself included—had done at least one thing in their lives that they weren't proud of.

He hadn't elaborated at the time, and she hadn't pushed him to explain, but now, all these years later, she wondered what his less-than-proud moment had been.

Sadie stooped, her knees bent and back straight, braced her hands under the inlaid chest of drawers, and struggled to lift one end onto the flatbed dolly that rolled away each time she tried to load it. She had managed other large pieces of furniture like this before. Just scooch one end up, then wiggle the rest into place.

But today that wasn't going to happen.

She wandered from the back room to the front to see if Julie could give her a hand, but her assistant was helping someone decide about a telephone table with a built-in seat.

Rather than disturb Julie, she decided to go for some young male muscles instead. She had seen Josh Ralston in here earlier in the day. The twenty-six-year-old rented space from her to sell his Adirondack chairs and other woodwork items and usually offered to lend a hand with lifting whenever he came to the shop. Today she would take him up on his offer.

However, it appeared that he'd already left.

Sadie retraced her steps through the store, stopping momentarily to answer a customer's question about a vintage hat, and returned to the back.

The rear door swung open, and Theo stepped inside, his handsome smile lighting the room brighter than any crystal chandelier or Tiffany lamp could do.

"Hey, Grandma."

"Theo, you're just in time." She gave him a warm hug and stepped back to squeeze his biceps. "Might I hire you for a little lifting?"

Theo nodded enthusiastically, but when he caught sight of the chest with one end propped on the low dolly, he turned a reproving gaze back on her.

"You weren't trying to lift heavy furniture by yourself again?"

"Not after the first attempt." She was pleased for his concern, but she didn't consider herself a washed-up weakling just yet. Even so, she was glad he cared. "Aren't you supposed to be on the track about now?"

Theo pulled on a pair of work gloves and pushed aside the stacked boxes of umbrellas Sadie still hadn't figured out what to do with. Then he maneuvered most of the dresser onto the dolly by himself, pausing only to nod for Sadie to adjust the back end so it wouldn't jostle off when they rolled it into the shop.

"No practice today because Coach had to go home for his kid's birthday party. We're supposed to do some cross-training with weights at home."

She grinned. "Looks like you're getting a workout right now."

Her grandson flexed, and a small bulge popped up on his lanky arm.

"Bodie's upset about missing track today," he continued. "It's his favorite part of the week."

"I didn't know he was on the team."

Theo opened the door and backed the wheeled conveyance into the shop. Sadie followed and made sure the piece didn't wobble off its perch.

"He started out as equipment manager. But I suggested he train with us for the fun of it, and he turned out to be pretty good. So Coach put him on the team."After the dresser was unloaded in the spot she'd cleared for it along the side wall, she and Theo batted around a couple of ideas for the best way to display it. Ultimately, they decided to open the top drawer and fill it with colorful scarves, their tails flowing over the edge to catch the attention of shoppers. And Theo had suggested dangling one of the umbrellas from the corner of the mirror and hanging necklaces and decorative pieces from it.

While they worked, talk turned to the Facebook photo of Bodie.

"Most of the shares were taken down after the principal came down hard on the people who had put them on their pages," Theo said in answer to her question. "But who knows how many other copies are out there? It probably won't be long before some total stranger gets hold of the picture and makes a meme out of it with a goofy caption. Then it'll be making the rounds all over again."

That was the way of the Internet. Anything that appeared on it could stay there forever, popping up again and again when least expected.

"Then when Coach told us we wouldn't be running today, Bodie was putting his track shoes away and a homework assignment fell out of his backpack. He got all weirded out when he saw me look-ing at it, but he wouldn't tell me what was going on." Theo paused as if this information was somehow significant, so when she didn't respond, he added, "The homework was for earth science class."

Sadie waited for the rest. "And?"

"Bodie's not even in that class." Theo splayed his arms for effect. "He's taking an AP course that covers everything in that class, plus a lot more."

From her days as a high school history teacher, Sadie recalled that some of her higher-achieving students had taken advanced placement courses to get a head start on their college requirements.

"Then why would he have the assignment in his backpack?"

"That's my point. The only reason Bodie would have earth science homework is because he's doing it for someone in that class." Theo paused to let her consider what he'd just said. "Pair this with what happened on prom night—the spilled drink and the Facebook post—and I think he's being bullied."

She frowned. "Wait a minute. The Facebook post could defi-nitely be called bullying, but the drink on his pants was just an accident. Don't you think?"

Theo shook his head as if lamenting her naïveté. "Someone punched holes in the plastic bottle. Water displacement theory 101." Then he went on to explain, "For the water to go out, it needs an equal amount of air to enter the bottle to replace what leaked out. So the water stayed inside the bottle until the cap came off and allowed air in."

Yes, she recalled, that was the way it had happened. And if the bottle had leaked slightly before being uncapped, no one would have noticed due to all the ice water that had clung to it from sitting in the cooler. When Bodie had tried to recap the bottle, he had squeezed the sides, which pushed the purple drink out of the holes even faster. All along, she had thought it had been caused by a defect in the bottle.

Theo toyed with a string of beads to be hung from the mirror that sat atop the chest, and she knew him well enough to recognize the abashed expression on his face.

"You know I don't usually gossip about people…," he began.

It was one of the many things she appreciated about her grandson.

"…but I have a couple of ideas who might have rigged the drink, and maybe the Facebook picture too."

"Well, if you want to talk it out, anything that's said will stay between us," she said confidently.

"Thanks, Grandma. I knew you'd understand." He went back to draping decorative items over the chest of drawers. "Sasha is the first one who comes to mind."

"That's possible, but unless there's more than one person involved, it's probably not Sasha."

Theo turned away from his work to give her a questioning glance.

"Sasha walked by after the picture had been shared," Sadie explained. "And it appeared from the angle of the shot that the photo had been taken from inside the bathroom."

He nodded. "Whoever did it might have hacked Bodie's Facebook account to post it from his profile, but that's not likely because there wasn't enough time to bypass his password. More likely, they took the picture with his phone and posted it from there."

Sadie touched a finger to her chin, and they batted around ideas of possible culprits. Colin was the first to come to mind since he'd had access to the drink bottles at the serving table.

"And Colin danced with Ella," Theo interjected. "Maybe he was taking her attention away from Bodie so one of his henchmen could snap the picture and post it on Facebook."

Sadie felt a grin spreading across her face as he looked up at her. "Henchmen?"

Theo laughed. "I've been reading some of Mom's mystery novels."

The acorn didn't fall far from the tree.

"Then there's Dougie, who'd been at the table serving drinks," she suggested.

Theo shot that idea down, explaining that Dougie was being tutored by Bodie, so it wasn't likely that he would harm the person who was helping him to get into the dream college he always talked about.

Her grandson used the tail of his flannel shirt to dust the drop-leaf secretary sitting next to the chest they'd finished decorating.

"What about the girl who was watching Bodie all evening? The sandy-haired girl with the flower on her shoulder strap."

Theo shrugged. "I don't know about a flower, but you're probably talking about Hayley." He lowered his voice, as if someone might be eavesdropping. "She's only interested in Bodie because he's as awkward as she is."

Maybe it was someone less obvious.

"If Bodie is being forced to do someone else's homework, and I think he is," Theo said, "he's protecting their identity. I think he's afraid to rat the person out."

He paced the floor and pushed his fingers through the dark strands that fell over his forehead.

Although she appreciated that her grandson wanted to right a wrong, there was a chain of command that needed to be followed.

"Perhaps you should take these leads to the principal," she said.

"I already did, and he said he's working on it. But when other kids were picked on in the past, nothing was ever done about it. The school doesn't know how to find out who's doing the bullying or how to make them stop."

She nodded her understanding.

"If I hadn't seen the homework assignment fall out of Bodie's backpack, nobody would have known anything about it. He's determined not to tell what's going on. I think he's scared of what might happen to him if he does."

Sadie stepped back and took a final look at the chest they had just finished arranging for display. She sensed that her grandson had something else to say, and she waited for it.

"I still remember Bodie's face when he was standing there with grape drink all over his pants," Theo said. "Someone humiliated him just because he's a little different."

She anticipated what he was going to say next, and she was behind him one hundred percent.

"I'm going to find out who's bullying Bodie, and why."

She trailed a hand across the chest of drawers that gleamed under the new finish that she had recently applied to it. "Whenever I decide to restore a scratched or damaged piece of furniture, there's always the chance that I could end up causing more harm to the piece than if I'd just left it alone."

She snagged her grandson's hand, squeezed it, and firmly met his gaze with her own.

"Whatever you do, be careful not to accidentally make things worse for Bodie."

8

_____

On her afternoon break, Sadie pulled the journal out of her purse and continued reading where she'd left off. If she'd wanted to, she could have skimmed through the whole essay in a single sitting, but for some reason, she liked the aspect of taking it in small "tastings" that could be savored for a while afterward.

She leaned back in the chair and put her feet up on a mahogany footstool with a tattered, poorly stitched needlepoint cover that needed to be replaced. The rest of the piece was magnificent, but the shabby cover had put off potential buyers at the recent yard sale she'd visited. So she'd picked it up for a song, and after some careful repair work, she'd likely be able to sell it for a nice profit.

Edwin shot an assessing gaze at T.R., his stance reminiscent of an Old West gunfighter squaring off against an opponent. But after a brief second he accepted her offer to join them for lunch. The three of them hung around the commons area where the carnival was taking place, making small talk and trying to pretend that it wasn't so out of the ordinary for Edwin to show up after gradually slipping away over the past couple of years.

Sadie hoped she hadn't made matters worse by inviting the two most important men in her life to share a meal with her.

After the initial stiffness wore off, Edwin and T.R. found some common-ground subjects to talk about and even seemed to enjoy each other's company. But despite the friendly tone, there seemed to be an undercurrent in Edwin's demeanor.

They finished their meal, and while T.R. took the trash to throw it away, Edwin quietly said, "I was wondering if we could go back to your apartment. And talk."

"Sure. Roz will be there. I'm sure she'll be happy to see you."

Her friend since kindergarten, and now her roommate, Rosalind would be able to read the vibes going on between them and give them the privacy they needed to reconnect. And, well, perhaps to determine the future of their increasingly neglected relationship.

"Good. I look forward to seeing her again. Excuse me a minute. I'll be right back." Edwin made his way to the art table he'd visited earlier, paid Frida, then tucked the purchase in his coat pocket.

While Edwin was away, T.R. returned from disposing of the trash, and Sadie filled him in on the latest developments.

"We're going to my apartment to hang out for a while," she said.

"Cool." T.R. shrugged his coat onto his lean frame.

She appreciated his understanding and was thankful once again for the wonderful friends that filled her life.

Edwin returned and offered a vague expression that was something between a smile and concentration. "My car is outside," he said. "Want to ride with me?"

"That'd be great," T.R. replied. "We walked over earlier, thinking the snow would have melted by now. It'll be nice not to have to trudge back in the slush."

Edwin blinked twice.

"T.R. lives just around the corner from my place," she explained. To T.R., she added, "I'm sure Edwin won't mind dropping you off."

T.R. shrugged. "No need. I've got all afternoon to kill."

Sadie put the journal down again, and let her thoughts wander. To the events she'd recorded, so dispassionately it seemed, in her writing assignment. To T.R and her life with him. To Edwin, whose reappearance in her life had been such an unexpected blessing. To the hidey-hole near T.R.'s old fishing spot where they had discovered the tin holding the ornate ring in the lightning-split tree. Since the day of its discovery, the thought had nagged at her that there might have been something else wedged into that small opening. In the excitement of the moment, she hadn't thought to look further. The hole didn't look very big from the outside, but she had no idea how deep the hollow went on the inside. Or what else might be hidden in its inner recesses.

It was time for another visit.

9

AFTER CLOSING SHOP THAT DAY, SADIE RETURNED TO THE TREE near T.R.'s fishing hole. But this time she came armed with a small folding box stool, a flashlight, and a wire coat hanger.

Sara's talk of insects in the knothole and the discovery of the tin had distracted her and Theo from probing further. But now she intended to find out what else might be tucked away in this old secret place.

Hank's lack of interest in her search couldn't be more evident as he roamed the surrounding area. Sadie had set up the stool and put her foot on it when she heard the sound of splashing nearby. Uncertain what the dog was up to now, she walked back to the trail where she could see down to the stream-fed pond.

Hank stood belly-deep in the water, his ears aimed forward and his body quivering with excitement. A second later, he pounced. Water splashed in all directions, and he plunged his golden head beneath the surface of the water. A moment later he came up, his face and ears dripping, and looked at Sadie as if to ask where the fish had gone.

She laughed. The refractive properties of the water must have made it look as though the fish had been swimming in one place, when in reality its exact location had been distorted. She made a mental note to give Hank a bath before she let him have the run of the house tonight.

Turning her attention back to the tree, she stepped up on the stool, switched the flashlight on, and prepared to scramble away if her poking around managed to dislodge an insect nest or, worse, a resting snake. Maybe she should have asked Roz to come along for moral support.

At first glance, there appeared to be nothing else beyond the broken bark that she and Theo had pried apart to open up the hole. But a sweep of the flashlight showed something soft. And pinkish.

Sadie drew back. A nest perhaps? Maybe newborn squirrels?

She shook her head. No, the lack of nesting materials told her it probably wasn't an animal. But just to be sure, she used the rounded end of the clothes hanger to give it a little nudge.

Nothing happened.

Braver now, she fashioned the hook to snag the part nearest the opening and gently pulled. Whatever it was came out as she tugged, and it kept coming. It must have been five feet long. The possibility occurred to her that it might be a dead and thoroughly flattened snake, but this looked nothing like any snake she'd ever seen.

The thing crumpled in a heap as it fell to the ground. Sadie stepped off the box and looked closer. Soiled by time and weather, it required a second look for her to notice the faded image of a rainbow trout. Emboldened, she picked it up and noted that it felt like polyester.

A necktie. No clips, but the kind you tie yourself. And perhaps the ugliest of its kind that Sadie had ever seen. The artwork of the creature's expressionless face reminded her of fish on ice at the supermarket, but this one's mouth was open as if preparing to strike at a bait offering. But instead of the usual insides of a fish's mouth, the opening was filled with stylized lettering: *GATT.*

Puzzled, Sadie turned the fabric over to see if a manufacturer's label might give a clue, but there was none. Nor was there any writing or personalization of any kind.

She set the tie aside and went back to the tree. This time she retrieved a pair of men's socks that matched the tie, both in ugliness and in the plasticky fabric they were made from. But, in this case, the fish's gaping mouth would appear to be swallowing the wearer's ankle. Across the toe, once again, were the letters *GATT.*

"Ugh!" She set the socks on top of the necktie. Because of the location near T.R.'s fishing spot, it was only reasonable to assume he'd left the tin and its contents here. But this? There was no way he would have ever owned such a—what was the word for it?— *unique* garment. T.R. had been a down-to-earth kind of guy who wore jeans and flannel shirts when he wasn't taking care of business at his small law office, but he also liked to look good no matter how dressed-down he might have been. There was no way he would have worn these items, and she couldn't imagine why he would have had them in his possession... if, indeed, they'd ever belonged to him at all.

She went spelunking one more time in the tree, poking thoroughly with the wire hanger to make sure she hadn't overlooked anything else.

Confident that the opening harbored no more gifts, whether elaborate or ugly, she tucked the flashlight, hanger, socks, and tie in the box stool and whistled for Hank.

Another glance at the day's find reminded her that her trip back here had raised more questions than it had answered.

———

That night, Sadie kicked off her slippers and slid into bed. A wave of loneliness had hit her unexpectedly, and the gradually lessening—but always present—hurt in her heart made itself known. It wasn't like her to pine away, so she chalked her mood up to the strange items she had retrieved from the tree near T.R.'s fishing hole.

She'd initially been hopeful that the discovery of the ring and poem had been one final gift from T.R. But then the questions had settled in...questions that might never be answered. That is, not until she saw him again in heaven. And then there had been today's discovery of the awful tie and socks. She straightened the blanket over herself.

To chase away the melancholy mood, Sadie picked up the tin box to give it another look over. She wasn't sleeping anyway.

T.R. had often referred to the fishing hole as his thinking spot. If he'd been the one to place this tin—as well as the fishing-themed clothing items—in the tree, what had he been thinking?

Still convinced that he'd intended the tin and its contents as a gift for her, she was determined to find out why he had put them in a knothole, of all places.

She ran a finger over the red paint on the tin that had faded to a rusty pinkish orange, and she traced the partial word of fragmented letters that spelled "...*eland*," followed on the next line by the word *Sweetheart* and some other words that were too obscured to read. The front of the tin sported a stylized rendition of a cowboy and cowgirl kissing. On the back, a small faded photo image of a real cowboy in his thirties smiled back at her. Only part of the face showed through the rust, but something about the thick mustache and smiling, crinkled eyes looked familiar.

She looked closer, and an image of the man with T.R., Milo's father, Philip, and Milo's grandfather Buck flashed through her mind.

Of course! This cowboy had been the same one who used to get together with them when he was in town, referring to his companions as the Rocky Mountain Boys, a tip of the hat to an old Jack Benny show comedy sketch.

Mathis Root. Back around the time Sadie had graduated from high school, he had started his own TV show and was billed as "Colorado's Most Famous Cowboy." He'd been quite the up-and-coming celebrity at that time, filming his TV show in Loveland and airing the episodes throughout Colorado and beyond. His half-hour show eventually ended after a couple of decades of sharing his unique brand of humor, folklore, and life in the Colorado outdoors. Mathis would be in his seventies now, but he still made guest appearances on various TV shows and was the go-to cowboy expert whenever news reporters needed a pithy quote.

With this insight, Sadie took another look at the lettering on the front of the tin and was finally able to fill in the blanks: *Loveland, Colorado…America's Sweetheart City.*

Considering the 1973 date on the tin, she surmised that the city and Mathis Root's producers must have teamed up to promote both Loveland and its famous cowboy with this commemorative tin.

Sadie scooted back against her pillows, and Hank lifted his head to see if his assistance was needed. When she didn't say anything, he laid his chin back down on his front paws.

Truth be known, her heart wanted to believe that T.R. had placed the items there for her.

Next, she pulled out the poem and looked to it for hints that might lead her to the answers she sought.

The romantic tone and allusions to the Colorado mountains that they had called their home for so many years seemed like something T.R. might have said about her, even if the style was considerably more flowery than the way he generally spoke. The writer painted word pictures of their trails converging and love blooming in the spring thaw. It ended on promises of climbing to the peak together.

Sadie closed her eyes and pressed her shoulders against the pillows stacked behind her. Spring of 1973 was when her romance with T.R. began. She hadn't said much to him about her breakup with Edwin, only that it was over. T.R. hadn't asked many questions, for which she was grateful at the time, but he'd held her and comforted her when she'd needed it most. And from that time on, their love had grown exponentially.

Their trails had converged and begun to bloom that blissful spring, and they had climbed toward the peak together for forty years.

With a sigh that couldn't begin to convey her sense of both gratitude and loss, she opened her eyes and pulled the ring from the felt bag that had become shabby after all this time in the tree.

The ring—exquisite by another's taste, perhaps, but bordering on gaudy by her own—was large and heavy. Full of gold. The adornment displayed a pink stone as the centerpiece and was trimmed with clear stones. The name of the pink stone eluded her, but the whites were possibly diamonds. If so, the cost of this piece would have been formidable. Petals of green stones, presumably emeralds, added an interesting third dimension to the design.

The piece—larger and fancier than her taste—was not her preferred style of jewelry, but perhaps T.R. had acquired it for her before he'd come to know her preferences.

She rolled it over in her hand and noticed a set of initials engraved on the inside of the band: *A.M.H.* If this had been outside of T.R.'s price range, perhaps it had been handed down to him.

She got out of bed, and this time Hank didn't even bother to lift his head. She moved around to the nightstand on the other side of the bed and pulled open the bottom drawer to retrieve T.R.'s family Bible.

She sat on what she still considered to be his side of the bed and opened the Bible to the page showing his family tree. She checked his mother's branch first, since the original owner of the ring had apparently not been a Speers, judging by the lack of an "S" in the initials, but none of the last names began with an *H.* To be sure, she checked the first and middle names for a match in case the *H* in A.M.H. was a maiden name. No hits on those.

Then she tried the same on T.R.'s father's side. Once again, none of the names fit those initials.

If the ring had not been passed down through T.R.'s family, where had it come from?

———

Sadie watched while Fred Sunshine of Bless Our Souls Jewelry put the jeweler's loupe to his eye and inspected the ring. His wife, Debbie, looked on.

The eccentric pair, former hippies who'd turned gray, still proudly wore their long hairstyles and funky clothes of the seventies. Much of the jewelry they sold through their shop reflected the individualism and artistic expression that they valued, but they also carried a substantial number of contemporary, mainstream pieces to appeal to the varied tastes of their customers.

Sadie had come here, only a few doors down from her own shop, to ask for a professional opinion of the ring. At any other jewelry store, such an ornate piece might raise eyebrows and prompt a flurry of excited gossip about it, but she knew she could trust Fred and Debbie not to mention the find to anyone else. Even so, all she'd told them about its discovery was that this was something she had recently "come across." If they assumed she meant she'd bought it at an estate sale to sell in her shop, she wouldn't bother to correct them.

To ensure that word didn't get around and inspire dishonest opportunists to come forward to claim the ring, she had already asked Alice and the kids to keep mum about the find.

Fred set the glass down, and his wife picked it up to take a look. "These are emeralds and diamonds, as you expected, and the setting is gold. Not plated either, but fourteen-carat gold," he added, apparently impressed. "And the pink centerpiece is morganite. Very nice quality, at that."

Sadie remembered from her research on previous pieces of jewelry she'd sold through her shop that morganite was a type of beryl stone mined in Colorado. Also known as rose beryl, it was sometimes referred to as tourmaline.

"If I'm not mistaken, I would say this could be one of Chameli Youta's designs," Fred said. "What do you think, Deb?"

His wife set the eyepiece down and reluctantly returned the ring to Sadie. "If I were a betting person, I'd put my money on it."

Sadie lifted one eyebrow. The name sounded vaguely familiar, but she couldn't put a finger on where or under what circumstances she'd heard it.

In response to her curious expression, Debbie added, "Chameli Youta was a Colorado-born designer of both East Indian and Native American heritage. She liked to combine the two styles and was a sort of rock star in the jewelry industry, known worldwide for her unusual designs." She gave Sadie an affirming smile. "You're very fortunate to have found this."

Sadie agreed, but for reasons other than financial. "Isn't it odd to have morganite as the central piece? I would have expected, I don't know, a ruby or another gem."

"That was one of the designer's trademarks," Fred offered. "She liked to combine expensive with less expensive, well known with rare, and even bright with dull."

Sadie thanked them, grateful for a name to go on that would give her a starting place to research the piece.

"Don't you want to know the value?" Fred asked.

"Oh. Yes. Of course." She'd been so focused on its origin that its monetary value had totally slipped her mind.

"Well, it was expensive back in her heyday in, what?" he asked Debbie. "The fifties or sixties?"

"I'd say the fifties were when she really hit her stride. People couldn't get enough of her work, but except for a few of her more affordable designs, she refused to mass-produce them."

"Since her demise in the nineties," Fred said, "the value of her work has soared. If this belonged to a whole set, which is mostly what she created, you could buy a nice cabin in the woods with the proceeds."

Sadie's heart nearly shuddered to a stop. She had known from first glance that it would be expensive—too high for T.R.'s budget back then—but the price would be absolutely formidable now.

Sadie thanked them again and asked that they not speak of her acquisition to anyone else. "I'd rather no one know of it until I get it insured and decide what I want to do with it."

Debbie pantomimed zipping her lip, then offered to put her in touch with potential purchasers if and when she decided to sell the ring.

———

The information she'd learned was still swirling in Sadie's head when she returned to the Antique Mine, where her friend Roz awaited her.

"Uh-oh. What's going on now?" Roz asked. Despite the warm-for-Silver-Peak temperatures in the sixties, her best friend was decked out in layers that involved a long-sleeved turquoise shell, a multicolored orange and tan tunic over brown leggings and boots, a knitted vest that hung to midthigh, and a brilliant gold scarf wrapped intricately around her neck that, amazingly, brought together all the colors and textures of her ensemble.

Her friend had known her long enough to read her, even when she said nothing. Perhaps *especially* when she said nothing.

"Promise you'll keep a secret?" Sadie asked.

"That goes without saying."

Roz followed her to the back, where Sadie showed her the contents of the tin and filled her in on how she and Theo had found it, as well as on the information she'd learned at Bless Our Souls Jewelry that morning. She didn't bother mentioning the socks and tie because she wasn't sure if they were connected in any way other than merely being stashed in the same knothole.

"Well, honey, what are you waiting for?" Roz demanded. "Let's look up this Chameli Youta woman!"

A few minutes later, their heads almost touched as they bent together over the computer screen. They found the designer's bio and photos of some of her better-known work, which did indeed show a strong similarity to the ring now sitting on the desk before them. Unfortunately, there were no photos of this particular piece.

On a hunch, Sadie added the word *sketch* to her search request, and sure enough, a page popped up that showed early pencil sketches of Youta's designs. After a few minutes of scrolling, they came upon a set featuring a heavy bangle-style necklace from which the same floral pattern hung. The design was also repeated in large chandelier earrings.

Roz whistled. "I'd wear that in a minute."

Sadie grinned and turned back to the Web page. A handwritten scribble, presumably by the designer, indicated that this was the *Verge* collection.

Roz's cell phone rang, and she looked down at the screen. "It's Roscoe. He probably wants me to help him at the hardware store."

After her friend stepped away to take the call, Sadie entered another search, this time including the word *verge* as part of her criteria, and found an image of an old, grainy photo. The accompanying caption summarizing the newspaper article that the photo had been copied from described it as a one-of-a-kind set that had been commissioned by an unnamed client in Silver Peak.

With a sinking sense of foreboding, Sadie read the rest of the short caption: *The ring and earrings were believed to be stolen in the late 1960s and never recovered.*

She felt sick at the possibility that nagged at her. How had T.R. gotten hold of the ring if, indeed, he was the one to have left it in the tree? And what had happened to the earrings?

Roz returned and stood behind Sadie to peek over her shoulder. "Yep, I've gotta go. They've been slammed with customers all morning, and Roscoe wants me to fill in so others can take their lunch breaks."

Sadie clicked to a different screen before Roz could read the troubling report. She knew the information wouldn't go beyond Roz, who had always been there for her and would undoubtedly stand by her—and T.R.'s memory—if it was determined that he had indeed taken the jewelry. But she didn't want to inadvertently cast aspersions on T.R.'s good name, not even to her best friend.

After Roz said her good-byes and left the shop, Sadie was left with even more unanswered questions than she'd started with that morning.

But one thing was for certain. She had to find out how the ring came to be in the tree so that she could clear her husband's name, even if only to herself.

10

———

IT WAS PROBABLY JUST AS WELL THAT ROZ COULDN'T JOIN SADIE
for lunch. A solo lunch of coffee and a sandwich at Arbuckle's
would allow her a quiet opportunity to mull over what she'd
learned that morning about the history of the ring that she and
Theo had found.

Trouble was, the thoughts and possibilities—and especially
the questions—kept swirling through her head until she couldn't
keep the details straight.

Perhaps she needed to clear her mind. Think about something
else for a change. She took a sip of her coffee, then reached into
her purse for the journal she'd been reading lately, taking her back
again to 1973...

Sadie unlocked the apartment door and called out
to Roz that she'd brought guests. Although her friend
was one of the most down-to-earth people she knew—
with an eccentric, Bohemian style that fit her relaxed
personality—Roz wouldn't appreciate her inviting guests
into the house without first giving her an opportunity to
run a brush through her hair.

Roz came out of the bedroom where she'd been studying, her long hair perfectly smooth. She greeted everyone warmly and asked a few questions to catch up on what had been going on in Edwin's life.

Relieved for her friend's steadying presence, Sadie asked her to join them in the living room. She offered the invitation partly because Roz always livened up any gathering she joined. But the bigger reason was that Sadie feared that Edwin's recent long silence followed by this unexpected appearance meant he had come to tell her good-bye. T.R. seemed to have picked up on her fearful vibe, which probably explained why he had tagged along.

She knew she would have to talk to Edwin eventually and sort out what was going on between them—or not—and she would try to arrange an opportunity for a private chat in a little while. But for the moment, while she prepared herself for the heart-to-heart talk, she appreciated the buffer zone created by her friends. And Roz, bless her big heart, had always been there for her when she'd needed her most, such as times like this.

"Sorry, chickie-poo, but I've got a paper to write for English Comp," Roz said, swiftly and effectively breaking her loyalty streak. Then she added pointedly, "You know…the paper you haven't started yet?" She smiled. "Maybe next time, huh?" Roz went back to her bedroom and closed the door.

Pulled from her reverie by the lunch crowd surging into Arbuckle's, Sadie closed the journal and relinquished her table to a couple who were standing around awkwardly, waiting for a place to sit.

She exited through the interior door that connected to the Antique Mine. Reluctantly, she accepted the fact that Roz hadn't been able to help her back then by serving as intermediary, and she couldn't help her now by serving as a sounding board. Not when Sadie wanted to keep T.R.'s possible role in the theft of the ring a secret. At least for now.

At least until she'd had time to figure out what connection T.R. had to the valuable piece of jewelry.

11

SADIE CHECKED HER WATCH. EDITH RYKER HAD ALREADY KEPT her much longer than she'd anticipated to discuss the plans for Pauline's upcoming centennial birthday. Sadie would have to leave soon if she wanted to grab some dinner before the planning session for the chocolate fest began at church in a couple of hours.

"Well," she said, picking up the list from the elegant coffee table in the spacious living room. After a minimal amount of party planning interspersed with numerous stories about Pauline and their mutual friends, she was ready to wrap it up and head out the door. "It looks like we've taken care of all the preliminaries for now. I'll make a copy of this list and get it back to you in the next day or so."

After making the commitment to consult with Edith about his aunt's party details, Edwin had learned he would need to attend a board of supervisors' meeting this afternoon. Unable to be in two places at once, he had asked Sadie to fill in for him with Edith, and she had readily agreed. Edith, pleased to have a woman's perspective on all the tiny details she had thought of for the event, had readily welcomed her.

"Oh dear." Edith rose from the couch and placed her hands on her head. Apparently not finding what she was feeling for in her curls, which had been dyed a bit too dark for her fair complexion, she turned first one way and then the other, scanning the room as she did so. "I've gone and done it again."

"Done what?" Sadie found herself searching too, even though she wasn't sure what she was supposed to find.

"My glasses. I've left them somewhere and can't recall where they might be." The near-ninety-year-old's voice rose with concern and a touch of panic. "I need them to watch *Wheel of Fortune* tonight. If I don't have my glasses, I won't be able to see the letters and guess the words."

"I'll help you find them," Sadie said and began making a sweep of the room. "Do you remember where you were the last time you had them on?"

Edith stood there, staring off to a corner of the ceiling while she tried to access that part of her memory. "I do believe it was in the bedroom. I had gone up there to get the tablecloth that I want to use for the party. I keep the extraspecial pieces in my chifforobe."

As far as Sadie was concerned, everything in the house qualified as "extraspecial." From original artwork on the walls to antique furniture and thick Persian rugs, the place looked more like a museum than a home. No wonder Pauline had referred to Edith as Silver Peak royalty. Sadie had a silly urge to lift an auction paddle and start bidding on the items in this glorious house.

She followed the older woman upstairs to find the private quarters of the house just as opulent and carefully decorated as the more public areas.

Edith took her through the stately room, recounting everything she'd touched and her reasons for doing so, which only lengthened the search time.

Sadie checked her watch again. If she just dashed home to feed Hank, then grabbed a quick meal at Los Pollitos, she'd be able to make it to the chocolate fest meeting on time.

They searched all the horizontal surfaces in the room, then checked the master bathroom without success.

"What about the closet?" Sadie asked, naming the only place they hadn't investigated.

"Why, yes! I went in there to try on my new party dress and see how it looked with my gold shoes."

No wonder Edith had taken so long when she had supposedly come in here with the sole task of retrieving a tablecloth. "Do you mind if I take a peek inside the closet?"

"By all means."

Judging by Edith's enthusiasm, Sadie wondered if she was just happy for the opportunity to show off her pretty things. A pile of clothes, scarves, and hats on the bed later—and a story to accompany each—and Sadie's suspicion was confirmed.

"I'm sorry, Edith, but your glasses seem to have disappeared."

She stretched out her arms in a gesture of futility, and her hands didn't make contact with anything in the enormous closet. She had moved to the door and was about to flip the light switch off when she noticed what looked like a small cattle brand etched into the woodwork.

She leaned closer. A lowercase *h* had been tilted on its side and a curved line added to its bottom to make it look like a rocking chair.

"This looks like the Hendersons' brand for the Rocking H Ranch," she said, referring to her neighbors' place.

"Oh yes," Edith said, and touched the mark with her pink-shellacked fingernail. "Philip Henderson enlarged my closet many years ago. With all my things in there, my husband—God rest his soul—didn't have any room for his suits. So he hired Philip—may he rest in peace too—to do the construction work." She tapped the mark again and stepped back into the bedroom. "His heart was in ranching, but he did a few side jobs, and he signed all his work with his brand."

With the introduction of this new subject, Edith was quickly off and running with another story.

"That Henderson fellow was the nicest man. And funny too." Edith blocked Sadie's exit from the closet, making her a captive audience for this latest anecdote. "The very first sentence he said to me when he showed up here to do the work accidentally came out in a rhyme. So I answered the same way. The ending words in all of our sentences all rhymed with *clay*."

Edith chuckled at the memory.

"Next thing you know, it became like a game, with each of us trying not to break the rhyme. Even my husband got in on it. The funniest part was when Philip asked for something to drink, which did not fit with the sound of *clay*. He said, 'Might I have some water, of which to *partay*...k?' Get it? Partake?"

Sadie smiled at her obvious enjoyment of the recollection. "That was quite a stretch."

"He was quite the poet," Edith said, her voice softening.

Unable to resist following up with a rhyming cliché of her own, Sadie asked, "But did he know it?"

"Oh, indeed," Edith said, taking her comment seriously. "I hired him to write something for me. A very sweet, romantic anniversary poem for my husband. Pretty enough to put on a drugstore greeting card. And he even did some artwork too."

Sadie's eyebrow raised as she considered the possibility.

"Oh, indeed," Edith said in an apparent effort to convince her. "On the front of the card was a beautiful picture of Silver Peak with a man and a woman riding together along a trail. I'd never ridden a horse before, but the thought was sweet."

Trails converging. Could Philip Henderson have been the poet who left the tin in the tree? He had, after all, spent plenty of time at the fishing hole with T.R., so he had certainly known the surroundings well. She would have to look into this further.

Back in the bedroom, Sadie paused at the sight of all the clothes and things on the bed.

Edith crowed with delight at the sight. "Goodness, I'd almost forgotten about that."

Oh no. More planning? "Forgotten about what?"

"Little Joanie Marshall. She used to come over here with her aunt when she was just a little thing." Edith smiled and held her hand palm-down near her waist, obviously cherishing the memory. "I would pull out a pile of clothes, and she would dress up and clomp around in my shoes while the ladies and I played bridge."

Marshall? "Edwin's cousin?"

Edith thought about it. "Yes, I do believe so. Joanie would have been the daughter of Edwin's father's brother."

Going by her convoluted way of explaining their simple relationship, Sadie almost expected her to add "twice removed" or some such qualifier.

Edith laid a soft hand on her arm. "Edwin is such a nice man."

Sadie smiled. "Yes, I think so too."

She gathered up some of the folded clothes they'd taken off the closet shelves to search for Edith's glasses. "Would you like me to put these back?"

"Oh no, dear." Edith took them from her arms and laid them back on the bed. "I'm going to be like Joanie tonight and play dress-up to see which outfit I should wear for Pauline's birthday party."

One of the assortment of porcelain dolls lined up in front of the pillow shams toppled forward at the movement, and that was when Sadie saw the glasses cradled in its lap.

"Here they are." She handed the glasses to Edith, relieved that the task was accomplished, tonight's *Wheel of Fortune* plan was salvaged, and there were no other obstacles to her leaving in time for dinner and tonight's meeting at church.

"Why, bless you, dear! I'm so silly." Edith popped the wire-rimmed glasses onto her nose and blinked a few times. "My children tell me I have attention deficit disorder, but the truth is, I have an allergy, and my skin itches after any kind of metal has been touching against it for a while. So I sometimes take off what's bothering me without even thinking about it. Then I forget where I've laid them."

———

Sadie pitched in to help put chairs away in the church's fellowship hall and offered up a silent prayer of thanks that progress on the chocolate fest event this evening had gone more efficiently than the planning of Pauline's birthday party. She gathered up a few empty chocolate wrappers—samples that had been used to prime the pump of enthusiasm for this fund-raiser—and tossed them into the trash. If the organizers were going to bribe people to serve on a committee, that was the way to do it.

She was reaching for her coat when Sally Henderson, the chairwoman of the event, looped an arm through hers and steered her away from the others who were now making a beeline for the exit.

"I just wanted to tell you that Nana and Pop Henderson's sixtieth anniversary is coming up soon." Sally lifted the recently low-lighted hair from her neck and toyed with a strand. The effect made her look too young to be Milo's mother, which was probably what she was going for. "We're going to be throwing an anniversary party for them here at church."

Sadie hesitated. It sounded as though she was being recruited to help plan yet another event. "Sixty years. I'm so happy for them."

"It's going to be held here at the church, and everyone's invited." She softened her expression and gently got to the point. "I know that you and T.R. shared the same anniversary date as my in-laws, and it seemed only right to let you know." She choked. "It's hard…"

The woman paused and held back a tear. That was enough to tighten the lump that had lodged in Sadie's throat at mention of the anniversary party. A few times in the past, she, T.R., and Buck and Mil Henderson had been invited to Sally and Philip's place for a low-key celebration of their mutual anniversaries… usually after the men had spent the day fishing together. Even though there'd been some age difference between them, they had shared a number of common interests, and they had enjoyed sharing their anniversaries as well.

The dam broke, and the hot tears in Sadie's eyes overflowed down her cheeks. "Yes, it's hard."

In the next instant, the two women locked each other in a consoling embrace, each truly understanding what the other was feeling.

They both missed their husbands, though Sally had been a widow for a much longer period of time. The pain was not as raw or aching as it had been in the beginning, but it made itself known from time to time. It crept up on her in a way that made her feel that an unnamed something was strangely "off." Judging by Sally's heartfelt reaction, Sadie could see that the grief never completely went away. Hers hadn't, but she was learning to live with it.

Philip had only been in his thirties when the tractor he'd been repairing had slipped and pinned him under its massive weight. His dream had been to make the ranch a huge success...a dream he had unfortunately never lived to see. The insurance money had paid off the mortgage, allowing the ranch to provide a living for the wife and sons he left behind. But it wasn't until Sally moved closer to her hair salon in town and Milo took over the ranch that it began to see the kind of success that Philip had envisioned.

Afraid that they would draw attention from the chocolate fest–planning stragglers, she gave Sally a squeeze and stepped back. She wiped the moisture from her cheeks and offered up a weak smile.

"I remember how the Henderson men used to go fishing with T.R. at his favorite spot where our properties met. T.R. always came back with a string of fish and a batch of ridiculous stories to tell."

Sally nodded, her mind apparently recalling those times as if they'd only happened yesterday. "And then there was that time when we hit that rough patch in our marriage. Milo was a newborn, and I was having a rough time, not feeling like myself.

People didn't know what postpartum depression was back then. All I knew was that I was taking out all my frustrations on Philip."

Sadie remembered. T.R. had been Philip's confidant. Although he hadn't shared the details with her, she knew that the couple had been having a hard time.

"T.R. counseled him through it, and Philip seemed to be more patient and understanding after spending time with him." Sally laughed softly. "One time, when Milo woke up for his two o'clock feeding, I was so exhausted and stressed out that I plopped him down on Philip—who was still snoring, I might add!—and said, 'Here, *you* nurse him for a change.' Then I left the house and went for a walk."

Sadie chuckled at the memory. It hadn't been so funny back then, but at least Sally could find the humor in it decades later.

"Poor Philip. He was torn between trying to calm the baby, who was screaming his little lungs out, and wanting to go after me before a mountain lion got to me."

"I remember T.R. getting that call from Philip in the middle of the night. T.R. didn't hesitate to get up out of the warm bed and go look for you."

Sally grinned. "I was sitting on the front porch, listening to all the noise in the house and wondering if it made Philip feel as overwhelmed as it did me."

"According to T.R., it did."

Unbidden, the thought came to her that the ring and poem might have been placed in the tree by Philip, intending it as a kiss-and-make-up gift for Sally. Could he have stolen the ring and left it there, planning to wait until the attention from the theft died down before giving it to his wife?

"He couldn't afford to buy me fancy clothes or a new car," Sally said, continuing her reminiscing, "but we had everything we needed. Namely, each other."

Sadie shook off the thought, hoping Philip was no more likely to steal the ring than her own husband was.

12

THAT NIGHT IN BED, SADIE TURNED TO THE JOURNAL THAT HAD become her favored reading material lately. Though she and Edwin had gone their separate ways for so many years, she was finding that he fit very comfortably into her life now. The trip down memory lane, by way of the journal, was helping her to put their past and present together in a way that allowed her to see parts of God's grand design for their lives.

She pulled the cover up under her chin and continued where she'd left off, reading her youthful account.

Sadie stared at Roz's closed door for a moment before turning to join the two men who chatted amiably in the living room.

"Would either of you care for some coffee or tea? Maybe hot chocolate?"

"Coffee would be nice, but don't bother yourself. I'll get it." Edwin rose from the couch and turned to T.R. as if he himself were the host and T.R. were his guest. "How about you?"

"Sure."

Sadie hesitated a moment, then left T.R. behind and followed Edwin into the kitchen. Edwin promptly shut the cabinet door and made a show of knowing just how she liked her coffee.

Black. No fancy flavors. No frills.

Edwin remembered. He had always taken care to notice the little things, which was partly how he had endeared himself to her in the first place. Edwin had always been a kind and considerate person...someone who went the extra step to show that he cared. Knowing this about him made it hard to understand why he had not been more present in her life these past months. Why her long, chatty letters had been answered with only brief postcards or sometimes not at all.

"I take it you've been very busy at school," she said.

Edwin nodded, looking slightly abashed, even though it hadn't been her intent to chastise him. "It's been...things have taken a turn."

Her breath caught in her throat. "A turn?"

Sadie stopped herself and put the journal away. Even after all these years, it was hard to read on.

13

SADIE PEERED OVER HER POSTLUNCH COFFEE AT LOS POLLITOS and studied Edwin, who sat across from her. With his silver hair, imposing build, and dark blue suit that matched his discerning eyes, he could have looked out of place in the casual, come-as-you-are restaurant. But no matter where Edwin happened to be, he always managed to fit in.

And, like the final piece in a jigsaw puzzle, Edwin was fitting very comfortably into her life. There had been a time after T.R.'s passing when she couldn't imagine spending time with any other man. But things had taken a turn after Edwin had moved back to Silver Peak. Back into her life.

Perhaps a more fitting analogy to his place in her life would be as a pair of bookends. He'd been there in her early years as they grew and learned, and now he was here again, years later, supporting her in a way no one else ever could.

She set her coffee down and reached into her purse for her ever-present lip balm and applied it. The Colorado winter had wreaked havoc on her skin this year.

Edwin sat sipping from his cup, and she realized she enjoyed the silences with him as much as the conversations. She was less comfortable with tiptoeing around certain subjects as she had today with the matter of the tin and its contents.

Whenever she had come across any curiosities in the past—whether an oddity acquired for her store or a strange occurrence in her life—she had enjoyed analyzing them with him to try to uncover the answers she sought. But in order to spare him any potential discomfort, she'd taken the matter of the ring and poem off the table for discussion. Instead, she had filled him in on the bullying situation Theo was looking into at school. And, as always, Edwin had been observant, supportive, and helpful with his suggestions.

Apparently picking up on the affectionate feelings that she must have been broadcasting, Edwin gave her a slow smile and reached into his jacket pocket. He withdrew a slim book and handed it to her.

Ridin', Ropin', and Rhymin': A Cowboy's Perspective by Mathis Root. Sadie flipped the pages of the book she had perused at his house after returning from visiting Pauline. Essays, jokes, short stories, poems, and other writings. There seemed to be a little something for everyone and every occasion.

"I noticed your interest in it the other day," Edwin said.

She looked up from the book and smiled her thanks, pleased that he was so aware of things that caught her fancy.

On casual examination of the work, the pacing of the writing and certain word choices rang familiar, vaguely echoing the pattern of the poem that she'd found in the tin.

Rhymin'. Could he have…?

Considering the lettering on the tin and the poem's similarity to these writings by Mathis Root, she naturally wondered if he could have been the one to leave the items in the tree.

The pages flipped under her thumb to the section of poems. Though she didn't have time at the moment to closely examine them, many seemed at first glance to be about unrequited love. Had Mathis planned to give the ring and poem to the mystery woman he wrote about in this book? And if so, who might she be?

Most people thought of cowboys as living a life of bare necessities, with all their earthly possessions strapped to the backs of their saddles. But the author of this book was a celebrity in his home state of Colorado, and beyond. She supposed that at the height of his TV and personal appearances career, he might have been able to afford a ring of this caliber. So it didn't completely make sense that he would have been involved in its placement in the tree.

Then again, another theme in the book was that of the outlaw cowboy. Could he himself be an outlaw...one who took it upon himself to steal a valuable ring?

"Fascinating," she said, thinking of the possible connections.

Edwin smiled his pleasure over what appeared to be yet another common interest they shared. "Mathis Root is going to be at the rodeo in Loveland on Friday. Afterward, there will be a reception and he'll read some of his poetry. If you'd like, we could go together."

She closed the book and handed it back to him. "Thank you. That would be lovely."

Obviously, the best part would be spending time with the man she cared so much about. But the added bonus would be the possibility of seeing Mathis Root again and perhaps learning a little more about him...and whether he might have had something to do with the items hidden on her property.

Edwin pushed the book back across the table toward her. "Keep it for now. You might enjoy going through it before the rodeo and poetry reading."

Edwin settled their tab and escorted her to her car to put the book away for later. Outside, a passerby ran toward them, waving his arms and ducking his head before dashing inside the restaurant door they'd just opened.

Across the street, a young mother hustled a baby stroller down the sidewalk, repeating the arm actions of the man who'd just passed them. A gray feathered blur dipped and swooped behind the woman.

Thinking quickly, Edwin removed his jacket and held the coat over Sadie while she placed the book on the backseat of her car. "Hurry! I'll cover you back to the shop."

"No," she said, playfully pushing him toward the city hall building, where he was to return to work. "Save yourself. Run for your life!"

"You're sure?"

"Yes, go!"

She watched him jog up the street, the little bird dipping and diving around his head. She giggled. A few seconds later, the bicycle helmet she'd brought with her now covering her head, she made a dash to the Antique Mine. On the way, a couple of *ping*s resounded from the helmet.

As she neared the shop, her breath coming heavily from both exertion and excitement, the door swung open to welcome her into the safety of its interior.

Julie, by now breathless with laughter, had bent over double and stomped her foot with glee. "Oh my," she said, gasping to catch her breath. "That has to be the funniest thing I've seen in months."

While Julie wiped the moisture of mirth from her eyes, Sadie ducked inside, removed the helmet, and smoothed her hair back in place.

"You speak a word of this to anyone," she said, grabbing at the stitch in her side, "and I'll tell everyone about the time you accidentally locked yourself in the bathroom."

Undaunted by the empty threat, Julie only laughed harder.

Sadie joined in, knowing it was only a matter of time before they would both be retelling this story.

———

Still curious about the necktie and socks she'd recovered from the tree, Sadie settled at her computer and opened a Web browser to do some research on a 1930 scrip coin from a mining company in Powhatan Point, Ohio. She would have liked it better if the "company store" currency were from a local mining company, since tourists loved to take a bit of Colorado home with them, but some enthusiastic numismatist would enjoy discovering this particular piece.

She pushed the coin aside and laid the fish tie and socks on her desk.

Julie walked past and raised a curious eyebrow, but said nothing.

Typing *GATT* into the search engine brought up a Web site on the General Agreement of Tariffs and Trade, which additional reading revealed had later transitioned into the World Trade Organization. This most likely was not what she was looking for.

Next up was the Generic Attribute Profile, also abbreviated GATT, on a Bluetooth development site. Since the fish garments had most likely been in the tree for at least a couple of decades, judging by the amount of growth around the knothole, Sadie expected they had been around much longer than Bluetooth technology had existed.

Then there were listings of people whose last name was Gatt. And, finally, after taking a guess and typing in *1970s*, a small article appeared about a company called Great American, which had developed a fishing lure called a "Trout Tickler," hence the letters *GATT*. The logo letters matched the design on the socks and necktie.

"Yep, this is it," she said to herself and kept reading. According to the article, the device had been a good concept but was considered too complicated for the average recreational fisherman. Fishing diehards willing to put in the effort to learn it did well, but most people weren't interested because of both its complexity and the high cost. In the late 1970s, Great American Company merged with another, larger business, and the conglomerate shifted their focus from recreational fishing gear to commercial equipment. It was at that time that the GATT was dropped from production.

A search of YouTube archives brought up a cheesy TV commercial from the period. One of two fishermen in tackle vests was baiting a hook, and the other handed him a Trout Tickler. The second man did a goofy jig followed by a casting motion, all while singing the product's jingle: "Gotta getta GATT!"

So what did all of this have to do with the clothing items she had found on her property?

At the moment, she didn't have a clue, but the discovery warranted a trip to Andy's Hunt & Lure.

———

"Here's another album," Sadie said and sat on the sofa beside Theo. "He was about your age in this one."

They'd been at it for a little while this evening, going over family photos and reminiscing about the teen's grandfather. The time a snake invited itself into their tent during a campout. The repair projects around the house they'd worked on together. And the silly pranks they had pulled on various family members.

And the lopsided picture of her and T.R. kissing. Her husband had taken a selfie long before the word had been coined.

She smiled. "Your grandfather always said my kisses were the sweetest sugar." She sighed, then noticing Theo's discomfort, she changed the subject. "He was very protective. Not a fighter by nature or overly possessive, but he always had my back. He was that way for all of his family."

This was a bittersweet experience, reliving the fun times they'd had with T.R., and missing him.

If not for Theo's last-minute request to look through the family albums for his college application essay, she would have stopped by the hunting and fishing store on the way home to ask a few questions about the GATT tie she'd found.

Family first.

"Do you mind if I include some of these pictures in my essay?" Theo asked.

Naturally, Sadie had been flattered when her grandson had explained that he wanted to write about how T.R. had inspired him to be a person of integrity. Of course, she wanted to help him in any way that she could, but lending the photos came with the risk that they could be damaged or lost.

"I don't know," she said. "The negatives have been misplaced over the years, and there are no copies."

"Don't worry. They don't have to leave the room." Theo pulled out his cell phone and aimed the tiny lens at a close-up shot of T.R. relaxing on the bank next to the water, a fishing pole propped in his hand. "This way, I can just insert them into my paper and size them how I want."

Theo set two photos side by side—a recent one of himself and one of T.R. about the time she first met him—and snapped a shot. The two faces, their features so similar, could have been mistaken for brothers rather than grandfather and grandson.

The next few photos, which Theo admired before turning the album page, had been taken after the honeymoon. The first showed T.R. carrying her over the threshold of the house that she still lived in. And another of T.R. balancing boxes in his arms to move in. He'd been quite adamant about needing no help unpacking and putting his things away.

She watched while Theo quickly scanned the remaining photos. It heartened her to know how much Theo treasured the memories of his grandfather...that T.R.'s influence lingered on.

"How's the bullying situation?" she asked. "Have you made any headway into who might be responsible?"

Theo closed the albums and stacked them on the coffee table, then reached into his backpack. "These are the earth science homework instructions that I got from Bodie. I told him I needed to take a look at it, and he let me borrow it."

Although the boy may have assumed Theo wanted it for his own homework, Sadie was proud that her grandson had not lied about his intentions.

They scooted closer on the sofa and studied the photocopied homework together.

"Do you see what I see?" Theo asked.

Sadie leaned in and adjusted her reading glasses. The typed instructions indicated the subject matter that was to be written about, relating to geology, the length of the paper, and deadlines for turning in each phase of the report.

On the upper left corner, the person who had photocopied the paper had done so without fully closing the copier cover. His or her thumb pinched one corner to hold the sheet in place.

"This?" she asked, pointing to the fragment of fingernail that had been copied along with the paper. "It looks like a bruise."

"Yep," Theo said proudly, as if he were Sherlock Holmes praising Watson for his observation skills. "Left thumbnail. No polish. Nails bitten down."

Without thinking, Sadie stuck a fingernail between her own teeth.

"Could be male, judging by the lack of manicure," Theo continued, "but it could also be a female. It's hard to tell with such a small fragment to go on."

"Maybe you could check among your classmates to see who has a bruised thumb."

Theo shrugged. "This assignment was made a couple of weeks ago. The bruise is probably healed by now."

He rose from the sofa, and Sadie walked him to the door.

"Thanks for letting me look through the pictures, Grandma."

"Anytime." She kissed him and watched him cross to the door.

He grabbed the door frame like T.R. used to do when he left for work each morning.

"Uh, Theo?"

"Yeah?" The teen turned back toward her, his hand still gripping the wall. His grandfather's green eyes peered back at her from beneath the mop of dark brown hair that fell over his eyebrows.

She used to ask T.R. to stop leaving hand marks for her to clean off, but it had been an exercise in futility. Eventually, she had just stopped saying anything and watched him go.

"Just…drive safely, sweetie."

Theo grinned and gave her a mini–eye roll, then was gone, the sound of his aging Grand Am growing quieter in the distance.

Sadie sat back down, and Hank pushed against her knees for a backrub, which she obliged. "Kind of quiet around here without any other humans in the house, huh, boy?"

Hank tilted his golden head to give her better access to the tender spot behind his ear.

After the canine massage was over, Sadie picked up the copy of *Ridin', Ropin', and Rhymin'* that she'd left on the side table. With only two days until the rodeo, she would need to do quite a bit of reading to be reasonably knowledgeable for the upcoming encounter with Mathis Root.

She might not get much of an opportunity to speak with him, she acknowledged, but the better she knew his work, the better equipped she would be to initiate a brief conversation with him.

With time so limited and impatient fans clamoring to meet him, she would do her best to cut straight to the chase.

Normally, she would have started at the beginning and read all the way through the book. After all, the little bit she'd already read of the short stories and essays had been alternately entertaining, amusing, or heart-wrenchingly poignant. But for now she would keep to the poetry section.

She could be grasping at straws. Trying to make random pieces fit where they didn't belong. As someone who preferred to believe the best about people, she didn't like being suspicious of them or their motives. But as someone who needed to know the answers to this dilemma, she could not afford to overlook any possibilities.

After a while, her eyelids became heavy. She fought to keep them open. She was just about to close the book for the evening, when she came across a poem that looked somewhat familiar.

Trails converging. The budding of spring.

She sat upright, and Hank lifted his head.

"I'm afraid you can't help me with this," she told him.

He laid his chin on his paws.

She retrieved the poem from the tin in its safe hiding place and sat back down to compare the two poems.

Except for certain words that had been changed to make it specific to Silver Peak, they were identical.

As if of its own accord, her hand smoothed over the crisp calligraphy. She had known the wording was more flowery than T.R.'s style, but perhaps the message in this poem had spoken to him. Had said what he had in his heart but could not express in his own words. It would have made sense for him to change the wording that alluded to other regions of Colorado and personalize them for her.

We've all done things we aren't proud of, T.R. had once told her. Was this what he was referring to?

Had her husband been not only a thief, but passing himself off as a poet too?

14

GOING THROUGH THE PHOTOS WITH THEO HAD STIRRED UP SO
many memories. And questions. The only way to answer them
was to push through her resistance and find the truth... whatever
it might be. And no matter how painful it might be.

But it was too late at night to look into what role T.R.
might have had in the items he'd placed in the tree. She put the
scrapbook away and retrieved the journal.

This next part would be difficult to read. She considered
skipping past a few pages, but instead muscled up the willpower
to forge through and found herself drawn once more to the pivotal
events of 1973...

"No cream for me, Sadie," T.R. called from the living
room. "Just a little sugar."

"Okay," she answered, more than a little distracted by
what was unfolding right there between her and Edwin.
The small kitchen suddenly seemed more cramped than
usual.

Edwin's blue eyes met hers. "I've been remiss in talking
to you about what's going on. It's just that I'm torn between

what has always been, on one hand"—he tipped his hand like a balancing scale—"and what's new and untested, but seems like a better fit, on the other."

"I…" Hot tears burned at the corners of Sadie's eyes. "Are you saying…?"

Edwin reached to touch her arm, then stopped himself. "There's a lot for us to talk about," he said. "Perhaps now isn't the best time."

"But when?"

"I'm sure we'll be talking very soon."

It was clear his comment was meant to be reassuring, but his expression seemed uncertain. In all the time she'd known him, Edwin had always been confident and straightforward. It wasn't like him to be so vague.

T.R. eased into the tiny kitchen and nodded toward the green light on the percolator. "Coffee's done."

He turned his attention to Sadie, his gaze fixed on the flecks of moisture that had collected in her eyelashes. Then he directed a stern glance at Edwin.

"Is everything okay in here?"

Sadie put the journal down and pressed a weary hand to her eyes. No, everything wasn't okay. Not yet.

But it would be. Soon. She would keep pushing through to find the answers she sought about the stolen ring. And no matter what the results—good or bad—she had faith God would use the experience for a higher purpose.

15

"WHAT'S THE MATTER?" THE SILVER PEAK HIGH SCHOOL OFFICE assistant pushed a box of tissues toward Sadie. "Are you all right?"

Sadie smoothed her windblown hair and daubed the moisture from her eyes. Today's weather was moderate for May, but a stiff breeze had tousled her hair and brought tears to her eyes.

"I'm fine, thank you. It's just a bit brisk outside this morning."

She signed in on the visitor log and made her way through the teeming hallway to the locker number Theo had indicated.

Her grandson stood there, waiting for her, leaning against the locker as if he were modeling his Denver Broncos hoodie for a fashion ad.

She handed him the track shoes he'd left at home.

"Thanks, Grandma. You're the best." Theo bent to kiss her cheek, then tucked the shoes in his locker to be used later that day. "I've gotta go to Bodie's locker. You wouldn't believe the huge stack of books he carries around all day. So I offered to put some of them away for him."

She followed him to the next bank of lockers and waited while he spun the lock.

"How's the college essay coming?"

Theo shook his head and gave the padlock a yank to pull it open. "It's hard to sum up everything about Grandpa when the word limit is so short," he said over the noise in the bustling hallway. "I don't really know where to begin."

She nodded. Even after many decades of knowing T.R., she felt like she'd only begun to scratch the surface of who he was as a person.

"Pick one event that stands out to you. Then focus on just that."

Theo opened the narrow locker door and shoved the small pile of books on top of some loose papers on the top shelf. The bottom two-thirds of the locker had been divided with temporary plastic shelves, and the items on them were ordered into neat stacks according to the boy's classes.

"It looks like those books go down here," she suggested.

From what she knew about kids on the autism spectrum, a commonality among them was the desire for order. It might be better to place the books according to his method than cause him stress later when he found them on the wrong shelf.

"Hi, *Thee-oooh!*" Two girls who had flirted with her grandson at the prom sashayed by and batted their eyelashes at him.

Sadie grinned as Theo waved at the girls, then moved the books where they belonged. A couple of spiral notebooks and a loose paper fell to the floor.

Sadie helped him gather the notebooks so he could return them to the top shelf. She was about to hand him the paper, when she noticed Ella's signature on the sheet.

Her hesitation must have alerted Theo, and he followed her gaze to the signature at the bottom of the page.

"Ella? What does it say?" He stretched out his hand to take it from her, but she pulled it back.

"We shouldn't read this. It might be personal."

Her grandson nodded in agreement, but added, "Bodie is either not willing or not capable of standing up for himself. This could be one of those times when the benefit of our looking at it outweighs the negatives."

She wanted to do the right thing. Set a good example. But there was a lot of truth in his reasoning. Pauline had once mentioned something similar, saying that sometimes it was necessary to look at the bigger picture. After all, hadn't Rahab hidden the men of Israel and claimed she didn't know where they were? The woman of the Bible had later been proclaimed righteous for her actions.

"You read it first, and if it's anything I should know, you can tell me. Whatever's in there will stay between us," Theo promised.

"All right," she said at last, and turned to the paper.

Dear Bodie, the letter began. The *i* in his name had been dotted with a hand-drawn heart. The next bell would ring soon, so Sadie read quickly.

Her heart sank at the confirmation that Bodie was, indeed, being taken advantage of.

"What?" Theo prodded.

She looked up from the paper. If her grandson was to help his friend, he would need to know this. But it would hurt Theo to know that the girl he cared about was doing this to a naive boy.

"It basically says that Ella will be Bodie's girlfriend if he'll write her earth science term paper for her." Sadie tried to ignore the stricken expression on her grandson's face and continued on. If she showed sympathy, it would only make him feel worse. "In it are instructions on where to leave the homework and a caution never to speak of it to anyone, including herself."

Theo opened his mouth to say something, then closed it again.

Earth science class. The only class, according to Theo, in which Ella struggled.

The bell rang, signaling the impending start of the next class period.

"You'd better go now," she said, "before you're late for your next class. We can talk later."

"It's okay. I have lunch now. Let me buy your lunch as payment for bringing me the track shoes."

Sadie didn't have to consider the offer more than a second. Any opportunity to spend time with her grandchildren ranked an automatic "yes."

She followed him toward the cafeteria, and on the way he ducked into the calculus classroom to pick up a binder he'd left behind.

The sight of the empty classroom, with its neat rows of desks, marker-smudged whiteboards, and decorated bulletin board brought back fond memories of her years teaching history and business classes. Sometimes she missed teaching, especially the students, but the pleasures of owning her own business and finding and restoring antiques more than made up for the loss.

Having retrieved his binder, Theo walked to the cork bulletin board and slapped a calculus paper that was tacked to it.

"Another A+ for Dougie," the teen said. "Top score makes him Math Man for the week."

"Math Man?"

"Yeah, if a girl gets the title, she's Wo-Math Wo-Man." He shrugged. "The teacher is kinda goofy like that."

Sadie stepped closer and took a look. "You didn't do so badly, yourself, Mr. 'A' Man."

"Yeah, well, Dougie wants to get into the School of Mines, and he's obsessed with making perfect grades. So he keeps stealing the title from me."

Something about Bodie's and Dougie's papers seemed a little off. She peered at them, comparing the two, and discovered an unmistakable similarity.

"The handwriting is the same," she said, pointing to the papers in question. "Do you suppose Dougie could be behind the bullying? Maybe coercing Bodie into doing his homework for him to keep his grades high enough to get into Mines?"

"You think he's being chumped by Ella *and* Dougie?" He shook his head. "I don't think so. Dougie is a high achiever, but he's more direct about getting good grades. He pays Bodie to help him study."

But could that tutoring payment come with the fringe benefit of having Bodie do the work for him? Was Bodie being bullied into doing other people's homework... or being paid for it?

They left the classroom and headed toward the cafeteria.

At the open cafeteria doors, Theo groaned and pushed his hand through his hair. He stepped aside to allow her through before him. "I'm sorry, Grandma."

"For what?"

"I just remembered... today is mystery-meat day."

———

After they'd gone through the lunch line, Sadie crossed the crowded cafeteria with her tray while Theo scoped the room for a place to sit. She looked down at her tray. The meal didn't look so bad.

Theo led her to the table one row over that had just opened up, and he pulled out a chair for her before sitting down across from her. "Cool! We've got it all to ourselves."

Sadie sat down to her mystery meat, and the unwelcome thought crossed her mind that perhaps Theo didn't want her to sit with his classmates. At this age, Alice had gone through a phase of not wanting to be seen in public with her. Sadie had hoped Theo would be past that stage by now.

"That's the geek table over there," he said in explanation for having chosen this table over the one where Colin, Bodie, Bodie's admirer, and another girl sat. Then he closed his eyes for such a brief second that all he could have said in that time was "thank You, God," then dug into his meal.

"Geek table?"

He attempted to shrug off the comment. "I don't really know what to talk about with them. They're supersmart."

"You said Ella is smart."

"Yeah, but she talks about stuff other than school."

"What about Colin?" The boy seemed out of place with the others at his table.

Theo opened his roll and buttered it. "He got banished to the outcast table after getting in trouble too many times."

Something told her there was more than a lack of common interests that kept her grandson from sitting with Bodie.

Theo put down his knife. As if reading her mind, he said, "He's a nice kid, but he acts—I dunno—thunderstruck every time he's around me. It's hard to be around someone who looks at you like you're Moses on the mountain all the time."

Oh, so that was it. Theo hadn't wanted to say it in so many words, but Bodie apparently had a case of hero worship.

At the next row over, Bodie took out two squares of what looked like chocolate cake from his brown lunch bag. Judging by the way the sandy-haired girl was eyeing him, Sadie supposed one of them might be for her.

But, no. The boy handed one to Colin. When Bodie started to take a bite of the remaining one, Colin snatched that one from him, as well.

"Did you see that?" she asked Theo. "Colin just took the dessert right out of Bodie's hand."

Theo snorted his disgust. "The guy's a jerk ..."

He interrupted himself to wave someone down.

"Hey! Come sit with us. I want you to meet my grandmother."

Sadie smiled and greeted his friends. So maybe he'd outgrown that stage after all.

———

On her way back to the Antique Mine, Sadie stopped at Andy's Hunt & Lure. The business was relatively new, but it had quickly developed a reputation as the place for hunters and fishermen to go for quality gear at a reasonable price.

Inside, the humble decor didn't even try to compete with the big box stores and their fancy displays. The wide-plank wood floors in the old building sloped at a dizzying angle, and the dark beams on the ceiling, from which all kinds of merchandise hung, were used as extra display space.

A clerk who appeared to be barely out of his teens approached to offer assistance. Sadie doubted he was old enough to have heard of the gadget she sought information about, but she gave it a shot anyway. Maybe he could at least give her a lead to follow up on.

"I was wondering if you could tell me anything about a Trout Tickler. It was made by the Great American Company back in the seventies." She showed him the image on the pages she'd printed from the Web site.

The young man leaned in and studied the picture, then poked his hand into his unruly dark hair. "Never heard of it," he said, "but I bet my boss would love to see this. He's an engineering geek from the Rochester Institute of Technology. Andy goes nuts over stuff like this."

He left and returned a couple of minutes later with the store's owner, a blue-eyed man wearing blond dreadlocks, and surprisingly younger than Sadie had expected. Perhaps thirty at most. She didn't hold out much hope that he'd be any more knowledgeable than the first guy she'd spoken to.

She repeated the question and let him examine the pages she'd printed. But instead of answering her, Andy called over another employee and a couple of customers who'd been perusing some fish-cleaning gadgets.

Unfortunately, none of them seemed to know anything about the device or its origins either, so Sadie spontaneously danced the jig she'd seen on the commercial, gripped her hands together and swung them as if she were casting a lure, and sang, "Gotta getta

GATT!" She paused, waiting to see if it sparked any memories. "Ring any bells?"

They stared at her as if she'd lost her mind.

Maybe they were too young to remember the commercial, which by now had turned into an earworm for Sadie.

Andy flipped the page and started reading the accompanying information. "I've never heard of this, but it's pretty slick." He tugged at one of the fuzzy dreads on his head. "This is a good concept, but it could be made better using today's technology."

"You should make one," one of the customers suggested.

Andy frowned and nodded, then handed the paper back to Sadie. "I might do that."

Sadie still didn't understand how the old technology worked, but if he wanted to try to improve on the device, more power to him.

"So I suppose you don't know of any stores around here where these might have been sold?" she asked.

He shook his head. "Sorry."

"Yeah," she agreed. "Me too."

16

_____

WELL, THAT TRIP TO THE SPORTING GOODS STORE HAD BEEN A waste of time.

No, she took that back. Sadie opened the slice of cake that she'd packed for her snack and took a bite. Just as Thomas Edison had to go through thousands of experiments that _didn't_ work to eventually come up with the lightbulb that _did_, she had just worked through a possible lead that hadn't come through in the way she'd hoped.

That put her one step closer to the one that might provide the answers she sought.

She polished off the cake and considered what to do next. Business was slow at the moment. Julie was making busywork up front by rearranging a display of cobalt jars and antique medicine bottles. A sad-looking wall cabinet with chipped white paint over its beautiful, solid-oak frame needed to be sanded, but she wasn't ready to start that messy job just yet.

So she leaned back in her chair, retrieved the journal, and continued where she'd left off.

Edwin looked down at his shoes, then up at Sadie. "Yes, everything's fine," he told T.R. "I was just about to tell Sadie that I need to go. Got to squeeze in a visit with my parents before I head back to Chicago."

He smiled down at her, his expression more cautious than it should have been. "Would you mind walking with me to the door?"

The two men shook hands, and as she and Edwin exited, Sadie let the kitchen door close behind them. She waited in the foyer while Edwin shrugged on his coat and wrapped a gray-and-blue woolen scarf around his neck. The scarf she'd knitted for him...the colors carefully chosen to play up the blue in his eyes.

Edwin took her hand in his, stroked his fingers over hers, then drew a wavering breath as if to say something, but nothing came out.

Sadie offered a smile of encouragement. "With all the noise our ancient refrigerator makes, there's no chance T.R. can overhear us."

Edwin squeezed her hand. "College is a time of crossroads, Sadie. As a famous cowboy once said, 'the calf roped spares the calf that loped.' One choice taken requires the release of another."

He moved to the door, but Sadie drew him back. "Edwin, am I to understand that..."

"There's not enough time to talk about this now. Let's table it for a day or two, then follow up with a phone call. Okay?"

Edwin briefly rested a hand on her shoulder, then he disappeared down the snow-covered sidewalk to his car, leaving her to wrestle with topsy-turvy emotions that weren't sure whether to rejoice in his brief homecoming or mourn his departure.

The jangle of the bell above the shop door, followed by a hubbub of voices, alerted her to an influx of customers. She reluctantly set down her old journal, then joined Julie at the front of the store, greeting her customers with a smile. Further exploration of the 1973 events would have to wait.

17

THE CALF-ROPING COMPETITION NOW OVER, SADIE AND EDWIN turned their attention to the next rodeo event that was just beginning.

The little Palomino swung wide around one barrel, then raced toward the next, its eleven-year-old rider leaning over its neck, urging it on. Sadie leaned forward from her seat in the stands, urging the tiny competitor on. Beside her, Edwin put his fingers to his mouth and whistled his encouragement.

At the next barrel, the girl reined the horse to take the curve tighter than the last and shave a fraction of a second off of her time, but the pair overcompensated and bumped the barrel. The lightweight obstacle wobbled momentarily, then went down on its side. Though she completed the course, the girl's heartbroken expression tugged at Sadie's heartstrings.

Sadie slumped back on the hard bench and rubbed her hands together to warm them. "What a shame. She was doing so well until that last turn."

Edwin patted her hand reassuringly. "It'll make her a better competitor next time. The announcer said she's a tough little girl. She'll learn from it."

Sadie appreciated his pragmatic point of view. He'd once told her that in his position as a judge he'd seen people make lots of mistakes. Rather than look upon their failures as the sad state of humans today, he had prayed that the experiences would test those who had gone through them and challenge them to make better choices for the future.

Edwin looked so handsome in his blue jeans and chambray shirt. And she had gone all out for the event, wearing a pearl-snap shirt with a teal floral yoke, jeans, and a stunning pair of turquoise-trimmed boots that sported brown leather fringe on either side.

"You cold?" he asked.

"A little." She rubbed her hands together again. The arena where the indoor event was being held hadn't quite kept up with the evening's dropping outdoor temperatures, but it was still too warm for her coat.

Edwin unfolded the blanket from under them and wrapped it around both their shoulders.

Sadie smiled and leaned against him. She remembered sitting like this with him when they were still in high school. They had attended a school football game and huddled together for warmth. Then he had pulled out a heart-shaped ring and asked her to go steady with him.

"Aren't you forgetting something?" she prodded, wondering if he had taken a brief trip down memory lane along with her.

His grin told her he had not forgotten. Edwin took her hands in his and breathed on them to warm them, just as he had done after placing the sweetheart ring on her finger all those years ago. But this time her left hand was bare, and a silver wedding band—scuffed by years of wear—rested on her right ring finger. And this time he playfully choked after blowing on her cold fingers, pretending he'd run out of air.

She gave him a gentle punch on the arm, and they went back to watching the event that now featured a young cowboy competing in the roping event.

"When is Mathis supposed to perform?" she asked.

The celebrity, well into what would be retirement age for cowboys doing the circuit, no longer competed, but she'd heard that his skills were still honed enough to put on an entertaining show.

"About halfway through, and then again at the end." Edwin leaned back and studied her. "Are you a big fan of his now that you've read his work?"

She shrugged away the uncomfortable feelings the question raised. "I like his writing, but I'm not particularly a fan of his."

Edwin seemed surprised by her statement.

Now that she'd brought it up, she supposed she owed him an explanation.

"He used to come over to spend time with T.R. and the Hendersons. He had a big, boisterous personality, which was probably an asset when it came to his public appearances, but on a personal level it was a bit ... overdone. Especially when he acted as if I wouldn't know anything about fishing just because of my gender."

She paused and considered what she'd just said.

"That sort of attitude was fairly common back then, so I should probably cut him some slack."

Edwin narrowed his eyes at her as if he knew there had to be something more behind her less-than-wholehearted acceptance of the man.

"And, well, there was that time when I went for a ride and found him lurking on our property. He caught me by surprise and acted a little shifty." She had almost forgotten about the incident until just now.

"Maybe he was fishing," Edwin suggested.

Hmm. Fishing for what?

"Maybe, but I saw no sign of fishing gear. Besides, our fishing and trail-riding guests usually called first to let us know they were coming. They didn't just show up uninvited."

In fact, Mathis had seemed as surprised to see her as she was to encounter him so unexpectedly. She wasn't normally a suspicious person, but something had prompted her to believe that he might have had something to hide that day. From that point on, she'd always been a little leery of him.

Someone moved up the steps, heading for a row higher up.

"Well, look who's here!" Virginia Radcliffe backed up to greet them. "Are you enjoying the show?"

"Oh yes. How about you?"

Virginia had taken over Sadie's position as history teacher when she retired, and they'd been friends ever since. Theo was in one of her classes, and Virginia enjoyed relaying positive or funny stories about him. Her grandson certainly provided plenty of material for them to share.

They chatted for a brief moment, and Virginia said, "I hear you received a belated gift from T.R. recently. That is so sweet."

Sadie started at the knowledge that news of her find was getting around. Theo must have mentioned it. She wondered how much he'd revealed, but she didn't want to say anything and encourage any questions from Virginia.

"It was," she said and left it at that.

She hoped the information would not find its way back to the *Chatterbox* before she was able to search out the history of the items they'd found. The blog-slash-online newspaper was run by someone who seemed to have his or her finger on the pulse of everything that happened in Silver Peak. For that reason, it was a must-read for anyone in the community who had access to the Internet. And even those who did not own computers or smartphones usually found out through the grapevine what had been reported in the *Chatterbox*.

Edwin rose from his seat and stepped out into the aisle. "Would either of you like something to drink?"

They declined, and he left to go to the concession stand.

"Oh, Sadie, I'm sorry," Virginia said. "It was insensitive of me to say that in front of him."

"It's no problem," Sadie assured her. "He's not the jealous type."

Even so, she was taking care not to inadvertently rub the matter in his face.

Virginia rejoined her friends, and Edwin returned a few minutes later. The end of the rodeo was showcased by a dazzling demonstration of Mathis Root's riding and roping skills. For a man in his seventies, he was in incredibly good shape, and his timing and reflexes were impeccable.

While the announcer finished making his closing comments, Edwin hurried them both down to the barn dance area that had been set up as a reception hall. They claimed good seats on the bales of straw near the front that had been set up for Mathis Root's fans.

The only drawback to sitting so close was that they couldn't politely get up and leave if the program ran long.

Fortunately, they were thoroughly entertained by his stories. The sun-leathered cowboy spoke, his voice captivating the listeners. In the cadence of his carefully chosen words, Sadie could hear the *clip-clop* rhythm of a horse ambling along a quiet dirt road. The pacing of the adventure stories, on the other hand, galloped up and down hillsides, leaving the listener feeling the breeze in her hair.

The melodic, husky-voiced flow was intended to send the listeners to a simpler era, when people judged time by the shadow of the sun and enjoyed the tactile experience of mending a fence, chewing a stalk of timothy grass, or easing oneself onto a creaky leather saddle.

Sadie was no exception. She closed her eyes and imagined cowboys gathered around the campfire after a long day of riding the range. She could almost smell the baked beans, grilled steak, and corn roasted in its own husk.

Edwin's stomach growled. He cut his gaze toward her and quietly mentioned that he was ready for the buffet dinner that was to follow.

Of course! That was what she'd smelled. She grinned to think that she'd been fooled into believing that Mathis's reading had summoned up the delicious aromas in her mind.

By now, Mathis was wrapping up with a reading of a familiar poem...the same one that had been included in the tin with the ring. A few words were different, but it was essentially the same.

Edwin fidgeted beside her.

She reluctantly opened her eyes. "Do you want to go?" she whispered.

He shook his head and continued looking straight ahead, his gaze fixed on the speaker whose melodic voice had captivated everyone in the room.

When it was over, the crowd surged toward Mathis, who stationed himself at a table stacked full of his books for signing. With devotees like his, it quickly became clear that she would have a long wait if she wanted to speak to him tonight.

She and Edwin made their way to the buffet table, and when they were through eating, she asked if he'd mind sticking around a few more minutes while she looked at the souvenir table.

"Sure. We can stay as long as you'd like."

He made his way through the crowd to a side table filled with books of poetry and witticisms, as well as DVDs of Root's TV shows. But something had caught her eye at the other end of the long table.

"I'll be right back," she said and maneuvered her way through clusters of people looking over the photos, figurines of the cowboy poet, lariats for young buckaroos, and other souvenirs that featured Mathis Root's face or endorsement.

The kitschy horseshoe earrings, boot-shaped kitchen towels, and oversized belt buckles commanded no more than a glance. The items she was most interested in sat in a neat row at the back of the table.

Various commemorative tins that had been issued over the years, dating all the way back to...yes, 1973.

She picked up the one from that year.

The woman stationed behind the table, perhaps sensing a potential sale, moved closer. "That was a popular design from Loveland around the time his TV show debuted. Are you a collector?" The gingham-clad woman gestured toward the other tins. "This is the perfect opportunity to fill in any holes in your collection."

"Um, no," she said, still holding the tin that looked much fresher than the one that had come out of the tree. "It just reminds me of one that was"—Edwin, having purchased a book or two, as evidenced by the flat brown sack he carried, joined her—"given to me."

He glanced down at the commemorative tin in her hand. "I'm ready to go," he said.

She returned the tin to its place on the table.

Despite the good time they'd had during the rodeo and reading, the silence echoed around them on the drive home.

———

The previous night's awkwardness all but forgotten, Sadie and Edwin teamed up to assist Edith in any way they could. Even so, the most they could do was answer questions presented by the hired help, who already seemed to have everything under control.

After Sadie's planning meeting with her last week, Pauline's "Silver Peak royalty" friend had spared no expense to put on the party of a lifetime. The woman had hired a party stager to decorate the house, a caterer to provide the food and cake, and servers who dressed in Edwardian garb to commemorate the period in which Pauline had been born. And, for the occasion, Edith had bought herself a new dress to go with her sparkly gold shoes.

Pauline's friends, of whom there were many, gathered in the grand room that Edith, in a moment of extreme understatement, called the parlor. In attendance were fellow church members of all ages, many of whom Pauline had taught in Sunday school or at Bible camp. Joanie and other members of Edwin's family had turned out, as well as Bodie—who didn't want it known he'd been "babysat" by her—and his family.

A little unnerved by being around so many people, the teen had taken to reciting lists—whether to others or to himself, Sadie wasn't sure—as an apparent self-calming tactic. Right now, he was going through the US presidents and their occupations prior to being elected. In chronological order, no less.

So far, they had played a few games, and Sadie had won a small Lenox goblet, engraved with today's happy event and filled with exotic chocolate truffles. She set the elegant party favor in her open purse on the floor beside her to protect it from being accidentally knocked over and broken.

From the wingback chair on the other side of Pauline, Edith suddenly rose, rubbed her right wrist, and started searching among the porcelain knickknacks on the marble-topped side table.

"Is something the matter?" Pauline asked from the wingback chair that had been designated—and decorated—as the birthday gal's throne.

"My bracelet." Edith continued looking, pushing aside piles of wrapping paper from Pauline's gifts. "I must have taken it off, and now I can't find it."

The latticework-cuff bracelet had apparently been causing her arm to itch and, like the eyeglasses she'd lost when Sadie was last here, been absentmindedly removed.

Conversation among the guests came to a halt while they searched around the chair and through the large pile of gifts

Pauline had been given. Edwin's aunt had specifically asked that any gifts be in the form of donations to her church, but the people who cared so much for this delightfully quirky and outspoken lady had brought tokens of their affection anyway.

Pauline, of course, had been ever so gracious and grateful, but Sadie and Edwin had exchanged surreptitious glances upon each item opened. His aunt already had a problem with too many things in too small a space. Where would she put all of these lovely things?

"Here it is!" Pauline's pastor bent to retrieve the wayward item of jewelry that lay at the centenarian's orange sneaker–clad feet.

Edith thanked him profusely, and talk turned to stories of the bridge games held at her house over the years. Edwin remembered having come along on occasion, and Joanie talked about how she had enjoyed crawling under massive pieces of furniture and pretending she was hiding from bears or mountain lions. Bodie recited his favorite foods that Edith had served him during the times he'd accompanied Pauline here.

Edwin glanced toward the dining room—perhaps better known as a banquet room—and Sadie followed his gaze to one of the knickers-wearing caterers who apparently had a question for him. He rose and went to see what the need might be.

Sadie offered to help, but he urged her to remain where she was in case Pauline needed her assistance.

His aunt leaned toward her and stage-whispered, "I always thought you and Edwin would end up together."

At the time, she had too. But God had His own plans for their lives, and He had ultimately brought them back together.

Pauline chattered on a bit about a family heirloom she had given her nephew for his then-future bride. "A pretty little engagement bauble," she said, "for his pretty little wife."

Sadie nodded. Shortly after they'd gone their separate ways, Edwin had started dating Rose, a woman he met in law school. They had married and gone on to have a daughter, Noelle, who now worked as a nurse and lived in Atlanta with her husband and young son. Rose had passed on about five years ago, and after that Edwin had returned to Silver Peak, to the old Victorian house in which he'd grown up. Needless to say, Edwin's and Sadie's paths had crossed again, and now they were rekindling the relationship that had begun so many years ago.

"Edwin was home for a short visit from college and shoveled the snow from my driveway for me," Pauline said as if remembering an event that had happened only yesterday. "He told me he was serious about a sweet girl, and I gave it to him so it would stay in the family. It was a Virgil Kamen. It was named after one of the states. Utah or Nevada, I can't remember which. Lovely craftsmanship, though."

Sadie was familiar with that line of jewelry. The designer was known for his delicate artistry and gently swirling patterns, as well as for giving the pieces distinctive names.

"I love old things that have a long family history," Sadie said. "Which side of your family did it come from?"

"The Marshalls, I suppose." Pauline wore a vague, faraway look, as if she couldn't quite recall who exactly had worn the item before it had come into her possession. "They were quite a large family, and I'm sure it went down the line from eldest to eldest."

Then Pauline went on to lament that she'd never received an engagement ring from her husband.

Sadie tilted her head, attempting to follow the older woman's logic. Perhaps the piece she spoke of had come to her from her husband's older brother, who had never had children and therefore no one to pass on the heirloom to. She chalked Pauline's vagueness up to the shaky recollections of a hundred-year-old woman.

Edwin returned with a personal-size cake topped with a solitary lit candle for Pauline to blow out. When she had puffed out the flickering flame, the partygoers dug into slices of Pauline's favorite: chocolate fudge cake with vanilla buttercream frosting.

He set the personal cake aside for his aunt to take home later and served her a slice from the larger sheet cake. Then he took his seat beside Sadie, who resumed the topic he had interrupted a moment ago.

"We were just talking about the heirloom jewelry Pauline gave you. I'd love to take a look at your family tree sometime and trace it back."

Most likely, the piece had been bequeathed to their daughter, Noelle, after Rose had passed away, or it would be eventually. Sadie decided it would be a nice gift to Edwin to research the ring's family history as well as information about the artist who had designed it. It might not be a big deal to Edwin, who wasn't much of a jewelry kind of guy, but she was confident Noelle would like to have the information.

"More punch?" Edwin asked and drained his cup.

She declined the offer, and he rose to get more of the pale pink drink.

Sadie turned to Edith, who was now rubbing her left wrist. "Did you lose your bracelet again?"

"No," their host said. "This time it's my watch."

Sadie recalled the diamond-encrusted timepiece. Quite impressive. Why Edith had insisted on wearing such an expensive item when she knew she would be taking it off, Sadie had no idea.

"Did you tuck it in your pocket?" she asked. The silk and lace pocket on the older woman's dress had been used to stash an embroidered handkerchief earlier. Perhaps she'd absentmindedly put the watch in there by mistake.

Edith patted her pocket. "No, it should be right here on the end table."

Repeating her earlier actions from when the bracelet had gone missing, Edith checked among the figurines and scouted the floor in case it had fallen as the other had.

After the last fiasco, the wrapping paper had been gathered and disposed of and Pauline's gifts moved into a collection of Burberry and Nieman Marcus shopping bags on the other side of the room for her to carry home later. Once again, the guests fanned out and searched, this time for the expensive watch.

"I know for certain it was here on the table a minute ago," Edith insisted.

Pauline stayed seated, but she patted the cushions beside her. She leaned over and scoured the floor between her armchair and Edith's.

Having no luck there, the birthday gal proceeded to tell anyone who would listen about the time Edith had taken off her reading glasses—"on a silver chain around her neck, mind you"—and placed them in a flowerpot.

Pauline turned to Sadie and tapped her own temple, then mouthed the word *forgetful.*

If it had been anyone else, Sadie might have thought she was mocking her friend's momentary lapses, but it was clear that Edwin's aunt truly cared about her friend. She suspected Pauline was just proud of her own sharp mind and perhaps even liked to lord it over her absentminded friend.

While the group continued looking, Bodie recited in detail the items he'd seen in Pauline's apron pocket when he had stayed with her in the past.

"Mirror in the gospel pocket. Little-bitty Bible in the gospel pocket. A screwdriver. A pocketknife. A tiddledywink. Earrings in the gospel pocket." And on and on.

Recalling how heavy the apron had been when she'd picked it up at Pauline's apartment, she now understood why it had felt like a lead weight. At the time, she hadn't had a chance to ask Pauline what a gospel pocket was, so she turned her inquiry to Bodie. Perhaps it would interrupt the current litany and direct him to a normal conversation.

"What's a gospel pocket?"

The boy kept on reciting.

Pauline was saying good-bye to several people who were preparing to leave, so Edwin paused in his search and addressed her question.

"Aunt Pauley used the items from her gospel pocket to teach object lessons to the kids at church," he said. "The stories always tied in to a Bible verse, and even the adults enjoyed them."

"How quaint." Sadie rubbed her chin. It occurred to her that a short lesson would be a nice touch to open the church's upcoming chocolate festival. She touched Pauline's arm to gain her attention. "Would you consider presenting a gospel pocket lesson at my church? Your payment would be all the chocolate you can eat."

Pauline's face nearly glowed with delight. "My dear, I would be absolutely thrilled! Just tell me the date, and I'll be ready."

By now, it was almost time to go. Most of the guests had left, and Pauline's energy seemed to be flagging. They needed to get her home, but Sadie felt compelled to offer to help clean up, even if only for a short while.

"Perhaps your watch will turn up while we're putting things away," she suggested.

"No need to bother, dear. I have people to help with putting the house back in order," Edith said, gesturing to the staff costumed in butler-style garb or long black dresses topped with white aprons and finished with white caps. They looked like characters from the set of the *Downton Abbey* TV series. "It will turn up eventually."

In contrast to her words, she glanced toward the door where the guests had departed, the action seeming to suggest that one of them might have taken the pricey watch. Edith mumbled something about saving the guest list.

At first Sadie thought the party hostess intended to save it for Pauline's 101-year birthday party next year, but then she realized that Edith might want it as a list of potential suspects.

Disappointed at not being able to help their hostess find her lost watch, Sadie reached down to gather up her purse.

She set the floppy tote on her lap and checked inside for the party favor she had placed on top of it earlier. No sign of the goblet.

Now she turned her attention to the floor around the area where the purse had been sitting, but the plush oriental rug was bare. This was frustrating, because she had planned to give the decorative glass to Edwin so he could always remember this special day in his aunt's life.

How odd.

Despite the quality name brand of the piece, it was reasonably affordable to purchase if someone had wanted one like it. But now it was gone, with no earthly explanation for its disappearance.

Her gaze followed Edith's out the window at the departing guests.

Two items were now missing. Might they merely be lost, or had they been stolen?

18

SADIE INVITED EDWIN TO STAY AND VISIT AFTER HE'D DROPPED Pauline off and brought her home. He had some tasks to take care of at home, however, so he jokingly scratched Sadie's ears and pretended to kiss the dog good-bye before reversing the gestures.

After he'd gone, she searched her purse once again. No goblet, but the journal invited her to pick it back up, and she was pulled once again back to 1973.

Sadie watched out of the front window until Edwin drove off, then drew in a steadying breath and returned to the kitchen, where T.R. was putting away the coffee makings. Sadie turned away, afraid that her face would show the uncertain emotions that still lingered there.

"Cool!" T.R. said and reached into the cabinet.

From across the kitchen, she could tell he was investigating something he'd found in her drink cupboard. "What is it?"

"Uh." He coughed lightly. "You've got raspberry tea."

"Yes, it's delicious even without sugar. Feel free to take some of the tea bags home with you if you want."

He stuffed a few into the pocket of his fleece overshirt and closed the cabinet door.

"Who's Mathis Root?"

Sadie spun away from the sink where she'd drained the now-unwanted coffee. A look that was both puzzled and guilty crossed her friend's face. Had he overheard the conversation between her and Edwin?

Not that it mattered, because even if he had, she was doubtful he would have gleaned anything from her odd conversation with Edwin. She certainly hadn't.

"Mathis Root is a cowboy poet," she said carefully. "He has a locally based TV show where he reads his poetry and tells cowboy stories. Why do you ask?"

T.R. shrugged. "I don't know. He seems to be getting some publicity lately." T.R. seemed at a loss for what to say next, then asked, "Have you read any of his stuff?"

Relieved for the distraction from the confusing time with Edwin, she allowed herself to be lured into a discussion of their favorite authors while T.R. lounged against the counter and sipped what remained of his coffee.

A few minutes later, Roz emerged from her room and started talking about what to have for dinner.

"Would you like to join us?" Sadie asked T.R. He was one of those rare friends whom she could spend the entire day with and still look forward to their next outing.

"Thank you, but I've probably already overstayed my welcome."

"Never!" Sadie and Roz said at once.

He couldn't be persuaded to stay, so Sadie walked him to the door, and this time Roz hung back in the kitchen.

Sadie pulled back the lace curtain covering the glass beside the door and peered out at the quickly darkening day, brightened only by the snow that stubbornly clung to the ground. T.R.'s apartment was only a couple of blocks away, but it was still rather cold out.

"Would you like me to drive you home?"

"Nah, I'll be fine."

Then, in a move so quick and smooth she barely saw it coming, T.R. leaned in and stole a kiss. Well, maybe *stole* was the wrong word. *Planted* would better describe the forthright kiss he'd placed on her forehead, much the way the astronauts had purposefully planted a flag on the moon almost four years ago.

In the next instant, T.R. opened the door and picked his way down the snow-covered sidewalk.

He turned back, lifted a hand, and smiled at her, then headed home.

Sadie touched a hand to her forehead. T.R. had never kissed her before.

Hank sidled close to Sadie and licked her arm.

"Now?" she asked. "Just when it's getting good?"

To be honest, she had to admit that her youthful writing was at times a bit melodramatic and perhaps a little sappy. But she commended her younger self for getting the facts and emotions down on the page despite the difficulty of probing what, at the time, had been so fresh and raw and often confusing.

Hank wagged his tail in answer to her question.

She picked up his leash. "Okay, come on. I've got to go out and pick up the mail anyway."

19

"HAS THE *KISSING SAILOR* ARRIVED YET?" SADIE STRODE TO THE front of the shop in the hope that the mail carrier had already been here and dropped off the packet she'd been waiting for. "The customer is a tourist who'll be leaving town in a few days, and she wants to take it with her when she goes."

When Sadie had found a copy of the 1945 edition of *Life* magazine for a customer, she had offered to have it shipped directly to the World War II memorabilia collector's home. But the woman had insisted on seeing it herself before agreeing to finalize the sale.

"Not yet, but Dell is coming around the corner now." Julie leaned out into the glass-front bay window and watched his progress up the street.

With her employee on the lookout for the mailman, Sadie walked back to her desk at the back of the shop to finish up some bookkeeping.

"Oh no!"

Halfway up the block, Dell stopped and turned to look back at the mailbag he'd dropped, but he made no move to retrieve it, even though by now the bird had abandoned pursuit.

In a moment of overkill, Dell retreated farther and ducked behind a large trash container.

Sadie tried not to laugh at the comical sight. Especially not after remembering his fear of animals when she'd brought Hank to the shop one day last year to keep an eye on him after minor surgery. She and Julie had to lock Hank in the back room before Dell would come into the store to get her signature for a package he was delivering.

"My people don't get along with animals," he'd said as if that was all the explanation needed. The funniest part of his ridiculous statement was that he was a self-proclaimed melting pot of red, yellow, black, and white. "Just like the kids' song at church," he'd told them one day. So it would have been impossible to pin down which line of his "people" had influenced his fear of animals.

Julie had no such compunction about laughing, and her giggles were nearly Sadie's undoing.

She stepped away from the door and grabbed the bicycle helmet she'd worn that morning and her coat from the hook. She didn't bother to put the coat on, but ran outside to where Dell peeked out from behind his barricade.

With the helmet on her head, she sprinted into the street, grabbed the mail sack, and took it to him.

"The coast is clear," she said. "They're not going to hurt you."

Well, not more than a firm pinch with their beaks, but nothing life-threatening.

"Who are you kidding? I saw that Hitchcock movie!"

Instead of thanking her, Dell frantically snatched the bag and insisted that civilians were not authorized to handle the US mail. Then he started sprinting to the safety of the mail truck parked at the end of the block.

"Hey, wait! I need my mail."

Dell shook his head and started the engine. "You'll have to pick it up at the post office tomorrow. I'm not coming anywhere near the Antique Mine until those birds call a ceasefire."

"But it's safe where you are, and I'm coming to you."

"Sorry, it's against the rules," he said. "I'm only authorized to deliver to the address printed on the envelope."

Of all times for Dell to follow the rules "to the letter." He'd always been fussy about following procedure, but this seemed a bit over the top.

The mailman gunned the engine and zoomed off down the street.

She clutched the coat he'd refused and returned to the shop otherwise empty-handed.

Julie met her at the door. "What, no mail today?"

Sadie shook her head and returned the coat and helmet to the rack beside the front door. "No. We'll have to go to the post office for our mail until the babies fledge the nest."

"Oh no! That could be a month or more."

She released a dejected sigh. "Yep, unless we can come up with a solution for overprotective mockingbird parents that doesn't include harming the nest or eggs."

"Good luck with that."

―――――――

Later that afternoon, Sadie was cleaning a Civil War sword that supposedly had once been owned by Lewis Addison Armistead, who had fought at the Battle of the Colorado River. According to reports she'd read, the brigadier general had later waved his hat from the tip of this weapon as he'd led his brigade into the Battle of Gettysburg, where he ultimately died from injuries received in the skirmish.

To her disappointment, she'd later learned that Armistead's original sword and scabbard were housed at the Museum of the Confederacy in Richmond, Virginia, which meant that this one, though antique, held no particular claim to fame other than that it had been made during the same time period. However, she had paid a reasonable price for what it was, and she predicted the beautiful sword would sell quickly.

The back door opened, and Theo came swaggering in, waving a spiral notebook.

"Have I got the touch, or have I got the touch?"

Sadie lifted her head from the task of polishing. "You got a date with Ella?"

Theo's enthusiasm deflated slightly before he rebounded with a cocky grin. "No, but I believe that with this evidence, I've cleared her of manipulating Bodie to do her earth science homework."

He rubbed the backs of his knuckles on his chest as if polishing them.

"I expect the date with Ella will come later," he said.

Sadie stretched the kinks out of her shoulders and made a futile wish that she could have manipulated Dell the postman into bending the rules just this once and handing her the magazine she needed for her customer.

Her grandson had arrived just in time to provide a much-needed break, so she happily accepted the diversion.

"Let's see what you've got."

Theo pulled a chair over to the desk and sat beside her. "These are the history notes that I borrowed from Ella. I watched her write the notes, so I know for certain it's her handwriting." He pulled another paper from his back pocket and unfolded it with a flourish. "But first, to refresh your memory, I present Exhibit E."

Sadie looked up from the letter he'd handed her. "Exhibit E?"

He smiled. "Yeah. *E*, for *Extortion*."

"Sounds like an Alfred Hitchcock movie." She looked it over, and it was the same as she'd seen at Bodie's locker last week. "Yes. Hearts over the i's, tight writing. What about it?"

Theo opened the spiral book to that day's date and handed it to her. "And now, Exhibit A."

She waited for it.

"A, because I'm *Awesome* for thinking of it. Compare that letter to the notes Ella wrote today."

Sadie examined the ways in which the writing was different. The letters in the notebook were larger and more loopy than those in the extortion note, and it was written all in cursive. The note requesting Bodie do the term paper, on the other hand, contained handwriting that was smaller and mostly printed.

"These are nothing alike," she said. "Take a look at the lower-case *a*. In the note, it has a left-facing cap, like an *a* from a type-writer, but Ella's notes don't."

Theo chuckled. "Grandma, the only typewriter I've ever seen is in your antique shop."

Sadie laughed as he carefully tucked the letter and notebook in the front pouch of his backpack.

"I never believed Ella would have done anything like that," he said. "She's too nice."

Perhaps his opinion had been colored by his own infatuation with the girl.

"I have to agree that someone other than Ella must have composed the extortion letter," she said.

Her grandson seemed visibly relieved by her affirmation of his own conclusions. "This means I can take her off my suspect list." He grinned at the cloak-and-dagger term.

Sadie leaned back in her chair and folded her arms. "Then what?"

"If I can't find out who did it, I'll keep looking for who *didn't* do it until there's only one person left."

"I'd say that sounds like the best plan."

———————

After closing the shop, Sadie waited at the Alpine Hair Salon while Sally finished cutting Roz's hair. Her own trim was already done, so she perused the bottles of nail polish and every so often picked one up to hold it against her fingertips. Shades of red and pink were her style. The blue, black, purple, and green seemed downright odd.

Someone entered the salon, and Sadie looked up to see Virginia Radcliffe, the teacher who'd taken her job when she'd retired and ultimately become a good friend. "Hi, Sadie!"

"Virginia! So nice to see you!" She leaned closer, giving her friend a quick hug, and asked quietly, "How's it going with the search for the person who posted the picture of Bodie on Facebook?"

Virginia leaned against the counter as if the very thought of the situation tired her. "The school security officer is working on it, and the principal is interviewing students to find out who knows what."

"Have they made any headway?"

The answer was measured. "Progress is slow."

Another way of saying it wasn't likely they'd ever find the boy's tormenter.

Sally walked with Roz to the front of the shop and then pointed Virginia to the styling chair that was now vacant.

Sadie paid first, while Roz continued an earlier conversation about what color Sadie should dye her hair on the next visit.

"I think I'll just stick with what nature gave me," she said. "If you ask me, salt and pepper can be pretty spicy."

Next, Roz pulled out her wallet. During the whole transaction, her friend tried to get Sally to side with her on the hair dyeing issue, but the stylist remained neutral on the matter.

While the two women chatted, Sadie stepped away and perused the artworks on the walls. Some of them were standard hair fashion photos common to many salons. Others were miscellaneous three-dimensional pieces picked up over the years that reflected Sally's personality. And then there was the family art, which Sadie found the most interesting.

Theo and Sara were beyond the age of creating macaroni pictures for her refrigerator, so it was fun to enjoy the experience all over again in the scribbles of Sally's two-year-old grandson.

Off to one side, on the wall behind where Sally stood at the cash register, hung a faded piece in a simple black frame that Sadie had seen many times but never really noticed. What caught her eye this time was the sketch of a mountain—possibly an area near Silver Peak—on which two riders plodded up a tree-shaded trail.

Sally, having counted back Roz's change, noticed her intense interest. "Philip drew that," she said. "He was quite the Renaissance man."

Roz leaned in. "Is that near the old Clearwater Mine?"

In answer, Sally took the drawing off the wall and laid it on the counter in front of them. "I'm not sure. He drew the picture to go with the poem he wrote for me."

A sweep of her hand directed their gazes to the hand-lettered poem on the right. A poem about two trails converging and lovers climbing together to the mountaintop.

Sadie put a hand to her mouth. "Oh my!"

Both women turned at her exclamation.

"Um, it's a beautiful poem. The way it flows, it makes you feel like you can hear the horses' hooves clopping up that trail."

Roz eyed her curiously.

Sadie hadn't shown her the poem from the tin, but her friend must have figured out by her reaction that it was somehow related to the ring she'd found.

"Did you say Philip wrote this?" Roz asked, dragging her eyes away from Sadie's.

"Oh yes. He was always making up rhymes. But I have to say this was the best thing he'd ever written." Sally sighed. "It's special to me, because it captures what our relationship was really like. It speaks to me on such a personal level."

Apparently, it had spoken to other women as well. Namely, herself, not to mention thousands of fans who had carried a torch for Mathis in his youth.

Virginia was waiting for her turn in the chair, so Sadie needed to make this quick.

"Here's an odd question, but did Philip give you any fancy jewelry with this? Earrings, perhaps?"

Sally tilted her head in response to the strange line of questioning, but didn't challenge it. "My Philip? He gave me earrings a couple of times, but..." She shook her head. "Let's just say he was better at picking the right words for his poems and the right subjects for his drawings, but his taste in jewelry and mine did not match. I told him I preferred gifts from his heart, and that's when he wrote that poem."

The hairstylist's taste leaned toward simple and understated. Nothing like the Chameli Youta statement piece. Could Philip have given his wife the earrings? Were they now sitting in Sally's jewelry box at home, unworn because they didn't suit her taste?

Sadie took another look at the poem, noting the *P.H.* in the bottom corner, followed by a tiny version of the Rocking H brand, then handed it back to Sally to return to the wall.

"It's a beautiful poem," she said. There was no way she'd tell her friend it had been copied from a book. "And the artwork is outstanding. It's nice that you have this to remember Philip by."

She and Roz gathered their things and waved good-bye to Virginia. Once they were outside, Roz grabbed her arm.

"You've been holding out on me, Speers."

Roz peered at her with such intensity that anyone else might have been intimidated by her steely glare.

"I just hadn't got around to telling you." No, that wasn't right. "Actually, the truth is that the exact same poem was in the tin I found with the ring in it. I didn't show it to you because I thought T.R. had written it for me..."

"And it felt too personal to share," Roz finished for her. "What about the earrings?"

Sadie started toward the car they had ridden in together. "I was hoping to learn what happened to them before I told you this part." She sucked in a deep breath. "The ring and earrings from Chameli Youta's Verge collection were stolen from the owner in the late sixties."

"And you thought..."

"No, T.R. would never..." She couldn't even bring herself to say the words. She wanted with all her heart to know for sure that he had nothing to do with the theft. And although she would never wish for Sally to have to deal with the heartache of learning that her deceased husband had been a thief, to be honest, it would feel better to Sadie than finding out that her own T.R. was somehow involved. "I thought if I could find out what happened to the earrings, that might answer the question about the ring."

Until this evening, she had begun to believe that Mathis might have hidden the tin near the fishing hole.

Now her suspicion pointed firmly at Philip Henderson.

Tiddledywinks. Sadie had to admit that it took a creative person to wrap a Bible lesson around a child's toy.

"It looks like just a simple game," Pauline said, "but parables are very simple too, and they pack a powerful punch. If you really think about it and apply the rules, you'll win every time... both at tiddledywinks and in life."

She sat at the tiny dinette table in Pauline's apartment, where they went through the contents of the gospel pocket, one piece at a time. The search for the perfect object lesson for Pauline to present at the upcoming chocolate fest was slowed by the older woman providing an interesting backstory for each item, but Sadie didn't mind, because the stories were both illuminating and entertaining. Edwin's aunt knew her Bible, and Sadie enjoyed hearing her insights.

The Swiss Army knife was next.

Pauline winked. "God is handy to have in your life."

"How about the mirror? What's the message in that?" The verse that came to mind was the one about seeing God and His work only as a blurry reflection in a mirror for now, but that someday believers would see Him clearly, face-to-face.

"When I first gave this gospel pocket lesson in the late eighties, a song about a man in a mirror was popular at the time. The lyrics said that you need to change yourself first if you want to see change in the world."

Sadie imagined that the young people who'd heard Pauline's message must have loved that link to popular culture.

"Do you suppose you could find a bit of Scripture that relates to chocolate?"

Now that she thought of it, she couldn't remember ever reading a verse that mentioned the dark confection. Her curiosity piqued, she made a mental note to look up the history of chocolate to discover when it first became well known. Perhaps attendees at the chocolate fest would enjoy learning about its impact throughout the centuries.

"I know!" Pauline raised a thin finger aloft. "Why not locusts? In Matthew and Mark, it mentions that John ate locusts and honey. And in some parts of Mexico, children like chocolate-covered grasshoppers."

Sadie laughed. "Can you imagine the looks on people's faces? What a hoot that would be."

When it appeared that Pauline was serious, Sadie flipped the Bible open and found a verse that might work.

"Psalm 119:103. What do you think of this?" she suggested.

Pauline angled the book and moved it closer and farther until she hit just the right spot. "How sweet are your words to my taste, sweeter than honey to my mouth." She pursed her lips, and starburst lines of red lipstick appeared around her mouth. "Yes, I suppose I could take my old honey dipper and a bit of honeycomb for the children to try."

"That's a great idea!" Much better than passing around a tray of chocolate-covered insects. But she had to admit it would have been hysterically funny to watch the expressions on the faces of the mortified chocolate lovers. She proceeded to put the other items back in Pauline's apron pocket, but a couple of hard objects in there snagged her curiosity. She upended the pocket to empty it.

Two large gold earrings fell out and hit the table.

Sadie drew a breath.

Too heavy to be worn as pierced earrings, the shoulder dusters featured sturdy clips to fasten them to the ears. In the center of the large dangling piece was a pink stone surrounded by green petal-like stones, with everything edged in diamonds.

The stolen earrings.

"Is something the matter?"

Sadie picked up one of the earrings to take a closer look. She opened her mouth a couple of times before she could get the words out.

"This matches the ring," she finally said, referring to the piece she'd found in the tree.

"Why, of course, dear. Edwin was quite taken with it when I passed it down to him."

"Edwin?"

The pieces of the puzzle were starting to click into place. Since this was part of a one-of-a-kind set, the ring Pauline had passed down to Edwin for his wife had to be the same one Sadie had found on her property. The fact that it had been stolen would also explain why Pauline couldn't remember the supposed heirloom's origin in their family, as well as the fact that the initials in the ring didn't match any of Pauline's relatives.

Pauline's attention had moved back to the gospel pocket lessons they'd been discussing earlier, and she chattered enthusiastically about starting a series of them at the assisted living center's weekly Bible study.

Sadie had so many questions, but she didn't know where to start. Or how to make her queries without raising suspicion about her motives.

Pauline seemed to be waiting for a response, so Sadie allowed herself to be pulled back into the gospel pocket discussion while, at the same time, tiptoeing around the question that burned in her mind.

"I was, uh, wondering what lesson the earrings hold."

"Well!" Pauline declared, winding up for another juicy story. "I wanted to teach from Song of Solomon, chapter one, verse eleven, for Valentine's Day. You know, the one about making earrings of gold, studded with silver. Only, these are studded with diamonds." She rolled her eyes in disbelief. "Would you believe the preacher thought it too scandalous? A verse in the Bible, too scandalous. Imagine that!"

Sadie knew the one. Different people interpreted it in different ways. Some considered the book of Solomon to be a love story about a man and his wife. Or was the woman his concubine? Anyway, others thought it spoke of God's chosen people as a whole.

"So what did you do?"

Pauline sighed. "I talked about the golden calf and gold earrings that the people had made while Moses was on the mountain."

Sadie only barely heard Pauline. Her thoughts were already racing back to the earrings and ring. They'd been stolen, as she'd read in her research, but by whom? How did the items end up in the Marshall family? And how did the ring ultimately come to be placed in a tree near T.R.'s favorite fishing spot?

"...and I'll take some chocolates, so the people can compare the sweetness of honey to chocolate and learn that knowing God's Word and understanding His love is sweeter than both." Pauline touched a pencil to her tongue and began making notes on the back of an envelope.

If Pauline had given the ring to Edwin, had he then put it in the tin and hidden it in the tree? If he was going to give the ring to Rose, why would he hide it in a tree on Sadie's family property? And why hadn't he given the ring to Rose, as Pauline had expected? There were so many unanswered questions…questions that teased and answers that eluded her.

"Just make sure you get real chocolates. There's so much artificial flavor out there these days, and the real stuff tastes so much better."

Sadie pulled the list off the refrigerator behind her and pushed it across the table to Pauline. It would be best, she decided, not to say anything to Edwin or his aunt about her discovery until she learned more. For one, she didn't want to accuse his family— either living or deceased—of theft if there was an innocent explanation. And for the other, if one or more of the Marshalls was guilty of having stolen the jewelry, she didn't want to tip them off before she could ferret out the answers.

Please, God, she silently prayed. *Don't let Edwin be involved in this.*

Pauline was staring at her now. "But I'll go along with whatever you think is best."

Sadie clenched her teeth. She'd been caught woolgathering. To avoid hurting the other lady's feelings, she took a stab at an answer that might be vague enough to answer her question.

"Um, yes, chocolate is a wonderful idea." Then her thoughts careered to the past, and she blurted out, "My husband used to give me chocolates on special occasions."

Pauline squinted at her.

Sadie sighed. It now seemed that the tin and its contents weren't from T.R. after all, and she was grateful her husband most likely had not been involved in the theft of the ring.

But that also meant that the romantic poem hadn't come from him either.

20

———

At home that evening, Sadie wandered into the kitchen in search of a snack. Hank was satisfied with his doggie biscuit, but she wanted...she didn't know what.

Yes, she did. She wanted answers. The ring hadn't come from T.R. Sadie was, at once, both relieved and disappointed by that conclusion.

The answers weren't forthcoming, so here she stood in front of the open freezer with frost forming on her eyelashes. Ice cream held no appeal, so she reached past it for the small heart-shaped box—given to her by T.R. shortly before his passing—which had sat untouched for the past couple of years. She'd had one piece when she'd received the gift, but not again unless T.R. encouraged her. At the time, it seemed cruel to enjoy something that he couldn't share with her due to his illness.

So after he'd passed away, she'd wrapped the box with the remaining two chocolates in several layers of plastic to protect the contents from freezer burn until "a better time." She told herself she hadn't touched them because she didn't want to go to the trouble of unwrapping the confections, but the truth was that some strange inner voice whispered that when those final two chocolates were gone, T.R. would be too.

Of course, she knew that wasn't true. It would only mean that she was moving on with her life. She'd been going through the motions of moving on since the day T.R. had gone home to the Lord.

Sure, there'd been plenty of happy times as the months had passed. But sometimes she'd find herself clinging to certain items that belonged to him, afraid to let go...as if doing so would mean letting go of T.R. and all their memories as well.

She started to undo the wrapping, then stopped herself. She wasn't in the mood. For chocolates or for any other food. Instead, she poured herself a glass of water and took it to the bedroom, where she picked up the journal.

Tonight's bedtime reading brought her to Valentine's Day 1973. A day both bitter and sweet.

Sadie had finished classes and was working on an English Comp paper when the phone rang for the third time that day. The first call had come as she was preparing to leave for her midmorning class. Thinking it might be Edwin calling to say it had all been a mistake, her eagerness had gotten the best of her and she had rushed to answer it before the second ring. But by the time she picked it up, all that greeted her was a dial tone.

Disappointed, she told herself that a snow-laden tree branch must have touched an overhead phone line and caused an accidental ring.

Then, about a hour ago, it rang again. She waited a full two rings that time and answered with a strong-as-she-could-muster "hello." Silence followed for the space of a couple seconds, then the line disconnected. A prank call, maybe? Or perhaps phone trouble? Whatever the case, it was only making her Valentine's Day alone even worse.

So when the third call came shortly before dinnertime, she considered not answering at all. Three, four, five rings. Finally, she picked up.

"Good day, Miss Richards. Are you tired of your lightbulbs burning out? Would you like to spend less time in the dark and more time having fun? Let me tell you about the Endless brand of lightbulbs that are guaranteed to…"

"I'm not Miss Richards, but I'll tell her you called." She quickly disconnected and paced the floor, unable to focus on the writing assignment that was due soon. If only those lightbulbs could brighten her mood on this day that was supposed to be happy. Happy for couples, anyway.

The doorbell rang. It couldn't be Roz. Her roommate would have used a key. A bizarre thought briefly occurred to Sadie that the lightbulb salesman had tracked her down, determined to make the sale.

She combed her fingers through her hair and pushed the lace curtain aside to peek out.

T.R. stood there, clad in pressed slacks and a blazer, holding a small box wrapped in red paper and another without a covering. A single pink rose peeked out from where his blazer lapels joined at the button.

T.R.? What was he doing here? She opened the door and swept her hand toward the handsome image he presented. "Hi. You look groovy."

The thought occurred to her that he was stopping by on his way to pick up a Valentine's date, but she hadn't recalled his saying anything about a girl he was interested in.

"Thanks. You look pretty nice yourself."

She glanced down at her paisley flare-wristed top and the faded bell-bottom jeans with ragged hems. She wanted to joke and say "What? This old thing?" but she didn't contradict his sweet compliment. She opened the door wider, and he joined her in the living room.

T.R. handed her the pink rose. "For you. The florist ran a little short. So I made up for it with these." He handed her the smaller box, which contained an assortment of chocolates. "I know you like raspberry, and this has a few raspberry crèmes inside."

"Oh, that's so sweet! Thank you for remembering me today." She leaned in to hug him, and he twisted to the side.

"Careful. This is still damp." T.R. lifted his arm to show her the reddish-brown mark on his jacket sleeve. "I gave my masterpiece a final touchup before coming over here."

After she pulled away, he cautiously offered her the box that contained a strange wooden item on a hanger. The wooden portion gleamed with a fresh stain.

"Let it dry a day or two," he said, "and I'll come back to finish varnishing it."

"Did you make this?"

T.R. nodded. "I would have finished it sooner, but cutting and smoothing those holes took more time than expected." Apparently noticing her confusion, he added, "It's for your scarves. Kind of like a necktie hanger. I keep my ties folded in a drawer, but ladies might prefer to hang up their stuff."

He seemed nervous. As if to channel that tense energy, he set the open box on top of the bookshelf, where it wasn't likely anyone would accidentally touch it until it had thoroughly dried.

"Thank you. You've really made my day," she said in all sincerity.

"That was the intent. You've been hiding away in your apartment with only your books for company for days." His voice softened. "It's time for you to get out. Start living."

In other words, it was time for her to stop sitting around, waiting for a phone call that might or might not come.

"You're right," she agreed. "Tomorrow, I'm going to…"

"No." He grabbed her hand. "Tonight. We're going to Candela's to order a meal off the top of their menu, followed by dessert, and chow down until we groan and say we can't believe we ate so much."

"Candela's? We'll never get in there. They must be swamped today."

T.R. shook his head. "I have reservations. How about it?"

Reservations? Knowing how quickly the restaurant booked up on special days such as this, she realized he must have planned it days ago…perhaps just after that odd visit from Edwin on Saturday. Had T.R. expected Edwin to disappoint her on this romantic occasion?

She smiled up at her friend. "Wait here. I'll be right back."

She returned a moment later, wearing a skirt that went with the top she already had on. The rust-and-yellow scarf that T.R. had given her on her birthday jazzed up the ensemble.

"Thanks for thinking of me," she said.

He gave her an enigmatic smile and offered her his elbow.

21

SADIE HAD PROMISED THEO THAT SHE WOULD BE THERE FOR HIS track meet that evening, but there was plenty of time for her to make a stop next door at Putnam & Sons first. The hardware store had been in Roz's husband's family for generations. Some parts of the shop looked as though the customer had stepped through a time machine into the past, and others were stocked with modern tools and cool gizmos for even the most dedicated handyman. Or woman.

Putnam's carried the usual hardware-store offerings, as well as a small selection of hunting and fishing accessories.

That was the section Sadie headed for. She didn't really expect there to be a GATT fishing lure still sitting on the shelf after all these years, but in a shop this old, it wasn't totally outside the realm of possibility.

Roz sidled up to her. "Don't tell me. You've got so much time on your hands, you're thinking of taking up fishing now."

Sadie laughed. "No, I came across some fishing memorabilia from the sixties or seventies and was hoping someone here might be able to give me some background on it."

She was hoping for a quick in-and-out today, so she didn't elaborate on where she'd found it.

"Roscoe's your man for all things fishing-related," Roz said.

Roz's friend leaned around the corner and called across the store. "Roscoe, Sadie's got a fishing question for you."

Roscoe came around the corner, grinning when he saw Sadie. "Hey there, old friend. What new caper are you working on now?"

Sadie smiled. "How'd you guess? I'm actually wondering if you could help me out with something. Do you recognize this?" Roscoe looked at the printout she handed him.

"Well, look at this. The Great American Trout Tickler," he said. Then he performed the crazy jig from the commercial she'd seen, mimed a fishing cast, and sang, "Gotta getta GATT!" They all laughed. "Haven't seen one of those things in ages," Roscoe said.

"Do you stock it?" Sadie asked hopefully.

"Naw. Many years ago, the company sent us a sample to see if we wanted to carry it, but it's too complicated for the average fisherman. Would have been a waste of shelf space."

"Gotcha." Slightly disappointed, Sadie pulled the necktie out of her jacket pocket and studied the ugly fish image. If Putnam's hadn't carried the device, she didn't know where else to look. Most likely, the store that the socks and tie had come from was out of business after all these years.

"It actually became a joke around here," Roscoe continued. "Whenever customers overcomplicated fishing, we'd say they were going GATT fishing." He pointed to the tie dangling from her fingers. "The company sent junk like that to try to entice people to give it a try."

Roz leaned closer, and she squinted in amusement. "I remember that. There was something else just as bad as the tie, right?" she said, turning to Roscoe. "A T-shirt, maybe?"

"Socks," he confirmed.

Sadie perked up. "I wonder how many people bought the ties…"

Roscoe shook his head. "Actually, they weren't for sale. They were marketing promo items that came with the GATT demo. The socks and tie were so ugly that no one who worked in the store wanted them, so I took them home."

Sadie's eyebrows nearly hit her hairline. "Really? What did you do with them?"

Roz spoke up now. "Well, you can be sure he didn't wear them. I told him I wouldn't be seen in public with him again if he did. So he did the next best thing." She grinned. "He gave them to T.R. and dared him to wear 'em."

Sadie reflected on this latest discovery. That would explain how they came to be on her property. But why had T.R. stuck them in the tree?

"T.R. never wore them," she said.

Roscoe and Roz said in unison, "I don't blame him."

They laughed. Sadie didn't blame him either. But if T.R. hadn't wanted them, why hadn't he just given them away?

She might not have the answer to that question, but at least she felt confident that T.R. had been the person to put the fish tie and socks in the tree.

That meant he was the most likely person to have placed the tin and its contents in there as well…unless someone else had come along later and put the items there on top of the GATT items.

Not likely, but she needed to keep an open mind to all possibilities.

Sadie pushed open the Tahoe's passenger door for Theo.

"You're early," he said and threw his backpack onto the floorboard before folding his lanky body into the seat.

"I didn't want to miss a single minute of your track meet."

She liked watching him work out at the sport he enjoyed so much. But today she had hoped that her early arrival would afford some one-on-one time with her grandson. If it hadn't, she'd been prepared with some reading to keep her busy until the races began.

"Mom and Sara are going to get here right at starting time." Theo rubbed his hands in front of the dashboard heating vent. "The chill is great when you're running, but not when you're waiting for the coach and the other runners to show up."

Curiosity nudged her to ask what he'd learned about the bullying situation over the past three days, but she didn't want to appear to be prying. So, instead, she brought up the topic in a roundabout way.

"I heard from Mrs. Radcliffe that the principal is working to find out who posted that picture of Bodie, but they still don't have much to go on."

Just as it often happened in bullying cases, it appeared as though this one was going to end up unresolved.

"Aren't you going to ask me what I've found out about the bullying?" Theo asked.

She grinned. "Well, spill it," she said and nudged his arm.

"First, I have to say I feel sorry for the kids you used to teach. You have eyes everywhere." For effect, he put his index fingers and thumbs together in two circles and moved them around his head like floating eyes. "Okay, remember Bodie's and Dougie's calculus homework you saw that was in the same handwriting?"

She nodded.

"It seems Bodie *did* do it for him after all."

Sadie turned in her seat to face her grandson. "Really? How did you find that out?"

"I have my ways." Theo cracked his knuckles as if to demonstrate the brute force he had supposedly used to extract the information. "Naw, I went easy on him. I used logic."

"This ought to be a doozy."

"First, I confronted Bodie with the evidence. Showed him the matching handwriting. Then told him I had seen Dougie give him money in the cafeteria. Dougie needed high math grades to get into the School of Mines, and he had paid Bodie to make sure he got them."

Sadie felt her eyebrows rise. "You *saw* Dougie pay him?"

Now her grandson had her hooked, and he was relishing the act of reeling her in ever so slowly.

"Not 'pay.' I said I saw Dougie 'give' him money. Turns out, Bodie needed to make change for the drink machine, so Dougie helped him out." He stretched his legs as far as the seat would allow. "But Bodie thought I saw another exchange of money, when Dougie *did* pay him."

"Oh no." She hated that the poor kid was being used.

"Oh yes. But it's not what you think. Bodie admitted that Dougie had paid him for tutoring."

"But the handwriting was the same. How do you explain that?"

"I asked him about that. He said that he went through each problem with Dougie, and as Bodie stepped him through the process, he wrote down the answers that Dougie gave him."

Sadie pressed her lips together. "That sounds a little too... convenient."

"There are a couple of reasons I know Bodie was telling the truth. First of all, he has this thing about needing to be in control of things that are in his wheelhouse, like calculus. So I can imagine him not wanting Dougie to hold the pencil."

For anyone else, that explanation would seem far-fetched. But Asperger's could make some people very rigid about what they could or could not accept.

"And what was the other thing?"

Theo shrugged. "I don't think he understands the concept of lying. He might refuse to answer a question, but he wouldn't lie."

"So I take it he refused to answer questions about the letter that was supposedly from Ella."

"That's right."

"What about Colin?" She reminded him that if the boy was already taking Bodie's desserts, he might also be demanding other favors as well.

"Funny you should mention him. That slacker suddenly made a B in earth science. Totally unlike him." Theo pulled a tablet out of his backpack. "Even the teacher was surprised."

She watched while he fired up the tablet and loaded the picture that had been on Facebook. "I thought that had been deleted."

"It was, but I saved a copy before the principal made everybody take it down."

Now he enlarged it, but instead of zooming in on Bodie holding his pants under the hand dryer, Theo centered the device's focus on the mirror over the sink.

She leaned in. "What are we looking at?"

"I wish this picture was higher resolution." He kept zooming in on the reflection in the mirror until a small, heretofore unnoticed, image came into view. "Check out the stall door."

The larger it got, the more of a watercolor effect the picture took on. But even so, she could detect a cell phone camera aimed at Bodie from the partially open door. Whoever was holding the phone had hidden himself behind the door. All that showed of the person was his hand and part of his wrist and shirtsleeve.

"Could that be . . . ?" She reached for the device, and he handed it over.

"A bruise on his thumb?" Theo pointed to the shadow that had caught her attention. "I thought so too, but it could just be a blip on the picture. The quality is terrible."

"*Hmm.*"

"*Hmm*, what?"

"The sleeve." She pointed to the white cuff trimmed with a gray band at the edge. "This is a long shot, but I don't suppose you remember who was wearing a shirt like this?"

Theo shook his head. "Girls pay attention to that kind of stuff. It was all I could do to get myself dressed, without looking at other guys' clothes."

"Point taken. But that sleeve might be a start."

"I'll try to ask around without raising any eyebrows. And I'll check social media sites like Facebook for pictures. But something tells me it's going to be slow going."

Sadie couldn't be prouder of her grandson for wanting to help a friend, especially since it was someone he wasn't that particularly close to, and for honing the mystery-solving skills he would need if he followed his current career choice to be a detective.

By now, some of the runners had started to arrive, so Theo collected his things.

"Now that you reminded me of the bruised thumb," he said, "I'm thinking that the homework assignment that showed the guy's thumb might have been copied in the school library. I'll go take a look at the logbook to see who made copies between the time the earth science homework was given and when the paper dropped out of Bodie's backpack."

She handed him the snack she'd brought for him. "Here's a little brain food to keep your deductive powers nice and sharp."

Theo started to extricate his long limbs from her Tahoe. A silver car pulled into the school's parking lot and dropped Bodie off. The coach and a few other runners were on the field by now, doing warmup exercises. A small cluster of early-arriving spectators were taking their seats in the stands, but Bodie didn't go toward any of them.

Instead, the boy looked furtively around him, then headed toward a spot under the bleachers that had been designated as the homework drop-off point.

Sadie reached out and grabbed a fistful of Theo's track jacket. "Come here. You've got to see this."

He climbed back in and watched with her as Bodie pulled a paper from his pocket and left it under the bleachers. Then he headed to join the rest of his team.

"Whoa," Theo said.

He was about to leave again, when the sandy-haired girl who'd been waiting by the closed concession stand stepped away and did a fast hustle-step to the paper Bodie had left behind.

Sadie let out a breath. "Double whoa."

The girl quickly surveyed her surroundings before taking a moment to read what was written on the paper.

"Well, what do you know?" Sadie said. "It appears the over-looked wallflower may be involved."

Now to figure out the best way to approach the girl without spooking her.

Theo gave Sadie a thumbs-up. "I do believe you're right, Grandma. Not bad, considering you hadn't even planned to do any surveillance when you decided to park here."

Pleased that they had solved the puzzle, she was debating out loud whether to confront the innocent-faced bully or just go directly to the principal, when Theo interrupted her.

"Don't count your chickens yet."

Her gaze followed his to the girl, who now refolded the paper and hastily put it back where she'd found it. Then Hayley headed to the stands to join her friends, who seemed unaware of what she'd just done.

Sadie leaned back in her seat and squeezed the steering wheel. "I don't know whether to be disappointed that we haven't found the bully or glad that Hayley is probably not the one. She seems sweet."

Theo touched her shoulder, then turned to push open his door. "As much as I enjoy sitting in here staying warm with you, I've got to go do some stretches."

22

Unwilling to get out of the warm car until closer to
the time of the first track event, or at least until Alice and Sara
arrived, Sadie pulled out the journal she'd brought with her in
case there was some downtime. The next entry brought her to the
Sunday after her Valentine's Day outing with T.R.

"Is this skirt too short?"

Sadie turned from the ballerina jewelry box, where she'd
been searching for an untangled silver necklace, and looked
at her roommate, who'd just barged into the bedroom where
she was getting ready for church.

Roz twirled, and the A-line skirt fanned away from her
slim legs.

"Put your hands down by your sides."

Roz did as asked, and the skirt barely extended beyond
her fingertips. As tall as she was, it was a wonder she'd
found something that didn't fit her like the microminis
that had been the fashion rage for a while.

"It's close, but you're within the level of respectability."

"Good enough," Roz said and invited herself into the room to peer over her shoulder at the necklaces she was trying to pick apart.

"I need a necklace sorter similar to T.R.'s scarf organizer," she said. She smiled to think of his thoughtfulness. Then, changing the subject, she said, "Roz, you should date that guy you met. He's the cat's pajamas."

Roz rolled her eyes. "You mean Roscoe Putnam? He's cute, but we need to have more in common than just similar-sounding first names."

Sadie snorted, and Roz cut her hard-to-get act.

"I've been flirting with him for exactly a month today. I guess that would make this our *monthiversary*. If he doesn't get the hint soon, I'll have to ask him out myself."

"*Ooh*, you liberated woman, you!" Sadie gave up and dropped the tangled necklaces back into the jewelry box. The small sweetheart ring that Edwin had given her sat in the divider next to a coral cloisonné butterfly ring.

Ignoring the butterfly piece, she picked up the interlocking hearts ring that contained a tiny diamond inside each heart. Edwin had bought it with money from his part-time job and given it to her a few days after Valentine's Day when they were high school juniors. She'd worn it until the end of the summer after graduation.

Edwin had taken her to a movie and dinner to say good-bye before they headed off to their separate colleges. And at the end of their date, she had taken the ring off to give back to him in accordance with their agreement to split up temporarily. But he had insisted she keep it, saying he would put it back on her finger someday.

Sadie looked out the window to see if Alice had arrived. She scanned the parking lot. Not yet, but it wouldn't be long.

She thought of the sweetheart ring she'd just been reading about. It had been nowhere near as fancy as the one she'd recently found in the tree, but at the time, those two entwined hearts had been much more valuable to her than any expensive designer piece.

Sadie stared down at the ring in her hand. "Yesterday would have been our three-year going-steady anniversary," she told her friend.

Roz was instantly apologetic. "I'm so sorry. Listen to me, babbling on about Roscoe and our monthiversary. I forgot all about your crummy Valentine's Day." Roz put a hand on Sadie's arm. "And now your anniversary."

Thanks to T.R., her Valentine's Day hadn't been totally crummy, but the look of sympathy her friend gave her now was nearly her undoing. Sadie was determined not to succumb to self-pity.

She put the ring back in the box and lifted out the brightest colored beaded necklaces, feather earrings, macramé bracelets, and stretchy headbands that she could find, then spread them out on the bed.

"Enough with the sad faces," she said. "Let's dress like we're going to a party."

Knuckles tapped on the window of her Tahoe, breaking her attention away from the journal.

"What are you waiting for?" Sara called to her. "Let's get ready to celebrate for Theo when he leaves everybody else in the dust!"

23

SADIE CRUISED ALONG THE FOOD TABLE IN THE CHURCH FELLOWSHIP hall and filled her snack plate with a minipizza bite, a deviled egg, and a homemade lady finger that its whimsical creator had tipped with half an almond dyed red to look like a fingernail.

Sally Henderson and her sons, Milo and Wyatt, had provided most of the food for her in-laws' sixtieth anniversary party, but Campfire Chapel church members loved a good potluck dinner, and many had brought along their own contributions to share. Other than the creative diversions that Sadie sampled now, most of it was down-home food. The catered delicacies provided at Pauline's birthday party last weekend had been attractive and tasty, but Sadie actually preferred the sometimes imperfectly presented dishes made with love by people she knew.

Sally moved in next to her and plucked a couple of pizza bites off the platter on the table, then followed Sadie over to the piano, where they could survey the room with ease.

"Thanks for staying for the party," Sally said, her gaze drifting to her in-laws on the other side of the large room. "Nana and Pop have always cared a lot for you and T.R. I'm sure they're very happy you came."

"We did have some good times together. I've tried to get over there to wish them a happy anniversary, but they've been steadily swarmed by others doing the same."

Since she had Sally's attention and they were discussing the past anyway, Sadie subtly steered the conversation to the question that had been nagging at her. She'd made progress in discovering that the earrings from the Chameli Youta set were in Pauline's possession, but she was still puzzled by the tin with Mathis Root's face, albeit rusted, on the back of the container. And what connection, if any, did his unannounced appearances at the fishing hole have to do with the stolen ring, and perhaps the earrings too? Just as importantly, what connection—other than a copied poem and some fishing outings—did Philip and Mathis have to each other?

"I was wondering about Mathis Root," she began, pondering how to introduce a subject that was decades old, without making it seem random.

Edwin chose that moment to return from making his rounds of the room.

Rather than have him overhear the question she wanted to ask, she smoothly switched to a topic that the hairstylist was more interested in, anyway.

"I love your lowlights," she told Sally. "Looks very sophisticated."

Sure enough, Edwin wanted out. "Where'd you get those little pizzas?"

She pointed to the table where she'd found them, and he was gone again.

"Caleb! No, no, no!" Sally set her plate down on the piano and rushed after her two-year-old grandson, who'd obviously found something interesting to investigate.

The side door opened, and Edith Ryker entered wearing a coat that was much too warm for the spring weather. Sadie hoped the elderly woman would remember to keep her glasses and jewelry on for the duration of the event.

Sadie moseyed over to Buck and Mil Henderson—Nana and Pop to their grandsons and daughter-in-law—and congratulated them on their many years together. She remembered that Mathis had been closer to the pair than to Philip or T.R. because of their similar ages and interests.

"Edwin and I saw a friend of yours last night," she prompted and mentioned the cowboy's impressive riding skills.

Buck rubbed the white whiskers that he'd been growing into a close-trimmed goatee. "Yes, Mathis has been making quite a few appearances lately. He would have come today, but he was already committed for a dude ranch opening in Salida."

Mildred nodded. "He keeps saying he's going to retire, but he never does. I think he just likes being in the spotlight."

"You should come back to our place and go fishing sometime," Sadie suggested.

Buck practically lit up at the idea, but then seemed to think better of it. "Those were great times we had, but my knees aren't what they used to be. Besides," he said, his gray eyes darkening with remembrance, "it wouldn't be the same without the old gang."

The perfect opening. Sadie would not miss the opportunity to grab it. "I remember Mathis sometimes showing up unexpectedly and hanging around the fishing spot back in his heyday."

Buck and Mil glanced at each other.

That look again. The same guilty expression that Mathis wore when she'd caught him prowling her property years ago.

Buck softened first. "I suppose it's okay to tell her now."

Sadie took a seat beside the pair and listened while Mil told about the woman who'd served as the cowboy's muse for all the unrequited love poems that he wrote.

"I remember," she said, glad that she had recently had the opportunity to read Edwin's copy of Mathis's book. "They were very romantic. All that yearning."

"He eventually won her over, and she became his girlfriend. That's when his publicist said his lonesome cowboy image would suffer if his fans knew he was head over heels in love. And that the woman he wrote about returned his feelings."

"He was quite the heartthrob," Sadie agreed. Didn't hold a candle to T.R., but she could see how young women had found him attractive.

"Right," said Buck, "so they had to meet someplace secluded where they could spend time together without being seen."

Mil nodded. "The most private and romantic place Mathis could think of was T.R.'s fishing spot."

Sadie frowned. There had been no need for the man to lurk around her property as if he was up to no good...which she still wasn't a hundred percent sure he hadn't been.

"He could have asked. T.R. and I certainly would have given him permission."

"You did." At her surprised reaction to that announcement, Buck added, "Well, T.R. did. Mathis swore him to secrecy, but we assumed he would have told you."

He hadn't. What other secrets had T.R. been keeping? She wanted to learn more. Maybe ask whether they knew if Mathis had left something behind on her property, but she decided against it.

"Secrecy? I love a good secret." Edith strolled up wearing a new pair of gold shoes she'd bought since Pauline's birthday party last week. Her stylish coat was accented by a Burberry scarf that she unwound from her neck.

The woman offered her good wishes to the anniversary couple and, after a few pleasantries, they excused themselves to mingle with the other guests.

Sadie stood and helped Edith remove her coat. "Did you ever find your watch?"

"Yes. It was on the end table, right in plain sight where we all had looked." Edith gripped the scarf that lay draped over her chest in a way that implied she'd like to wrap it around someone's neck. "You know what I think? I think one of the catering staff must have taken it. Then they got scared and put it back where they found it after they heard all the fuss about our trying to find it."

"Well, I'm glad it's back where it belongs." Sadie still hadn't found the engraved Lenox goblet that she'd wanted to give to Edwin, but that was a small matter compared to Edith's expensive watch.

She took the coat from over Edith's arm and hung it on a peg on the wall. Edith took off the scarf and handed that to her as well.

Nearly choking at the sight before her, Sadie felt her eyes widen. She coughed and tried to cover her surprise at the show-stopper gold necklace that upstaged everything else Edith wore, not to mention everyone else in the room.

"That's why I don't eat those little pizzas." Edith patted her on the back, apparently mistaking her surprise for indigestion. "Too much red pepper for my taste."

Sadie wiped her eyes and gathered her composure. "What a lovely necklace. A real attention-grabber."

Her mind boggled at the sight. And even more at the realization that all three pieces of the exclusive set were now accounted for. But it didn't make sense how the necklace had come to be with Edith, the earrings with Pauline, and the ring placed in the knothole of a tree.

"Thank you. I usually wear it to special occasions and would have done so for Pauline's party, but I couldn't find it at the time." Edith fingered the heavy collar of gold and diamonds and let her hand trail down to the flower-inspired pendant of morganite, emeralds, and diamonds. "It belonged to my mother, who passed it on to me as a wedding gift."

Edith sniffed, the action bordering on haughty.

"It's a Chameli Youta," she added. "The Howells always had good taste."

"Howell?" Sadie's thoughts raced to the initials inside the ring. *A.M.H.* "What was her first name?"

"Ada. Did you know her?"

Sadie didn't answer her question, but asked another of her own. "Ada Margaret?" she said, taking a wild guess.

"Ada May."

Ada May Howell. A.M.H. She shook her head and replied honestly, "No, I didn't know her."

Edith's hand went up to the clasp on the back of the necklace, as if her fingers were contemplating their usual mischief of taking it off while its owner was otherwise distracted. Thin gold chains hung in little curtains from her ears, too wispy to offset the heavy necklace, but pretty nevertheless.

By now, Edwin had made his rounds of the room and was circling back to her. She would have to wrap this up quickly if she wanted to avoid having to explain to him why she was enthralled by a piece of jewelry that was so far outside of her own personal style preference.

"Those drop earrings look very pretty with that necklace," she said, hoping Edith would volunteer more information.

"I used to have the whole set," Edith said. "But the earrings and ring were stolen from my house many years ago. I don't know who cried harder…my mother or me."

Wanting to think the best, Sadie considered the possibility that, since the bridge games of the past had rotated among the friends' houses—which meant the friends had sometimes played at Pauline's house—Edith could have taken off the ring and earrings while there and forgotten them. And Pauline, who could be a bit scattered on occasion, might have assumed the pieces had come from her husband's side of the family.

Sadie preferred that explanation for how Pauline may have come into possession of the items in a law-abiding, if not very observant, way. But what had happened to the ring after Pauline had given it to Edwin? And what path had it taken to get from Edwin's hands to a knothole in a tree?

Edwin returned then with a plate with some dessert on it. "You should try a piece of the cheesecake. It was delicious." He handed the plate to Sadie, then turned to Edith. The older woman held out her hand as if she expected him to kiss it.

"So good to see you again, Mayor. Now, if you'll excuse me, I must go make my appearances to Sally."

As the woman flitted off, Edwin did a double take, his gaze going to the excessive adornment around her neck.

He turned back to Sadie to escort her around the room and chat with the guests they hadn't conversed with yet, but if he had recognized the piece, he never said a word about it.

Sadie would keep mum too. At least for now.

At least until she'd uncovered the truth behind the nomadic jewels.

———

After the party, Roz had followed her home to go through the belongings that Pauline had passed along to Sadie to sell in her shop. With display space limited in the shop, she had offered first dibs on the surplus clothes to Roz, whom she knew would appreciate Pauline's quirky sense of fashion.

Just as she'd expected, Roz loved the clothes. But Roz pushed the bag of clothes away and leaned back on the couch, her palms held out.

"I don't know about this," her friend said. "Edwin might feel funny about seeing me wear his aunt's things."

"Don't be silly. He has already set aside all of the mementos that have sentimental value for him. And he had suggested selling or donating the rest, so he certainly expects the clothes to be worn."

She opened the plastic bag and pulled out a purple and yellow crocheted top from which dozens of strands of yarn fringe hung at various intervals throughout the work.

"Here, try this on. It looks just like you."

Although Roz bumped six feet in height, her build was slender, and she easily fit into the garment. However, it looked like a regular shirt rather than a tunic on her tall frame.

"I love it!" Roz sashayed past the coffee table and struck a pose.

Hank looked up at her. Apparently unimpressed, he moved to his dog bed on the other side of the room and lay down with his back to the fashion show.

"You look like a model," Sadie said in all honesty. Her straight, shoulder-length gray hair looked quite chic, and her glasses added a sophisticated quality to her otherwise Bohemian style.

Roz reached into the bag and pulled out more of the clothes to go through. She set aside some papers that had been included by mistake and pulled out a pair of black leggings that looked like they would go with the tunic.

Her friend wrinkled her gray eyebrows. "Edwin's hundred-year-old aunt wears leggings?"

Sadie giggled. "You'd have to see it to believe it. But she looks great in them."

She didn't bother to mention the bizarre butterfly sunglasses that had captured Pauline's fancy.

Roz's attention was now diverted to a hat whose bow was larger than the portion that rested on the head. She put it on so that the bow sat slightly to the right and mimed a microphone in her hand.

"I'm Aretha Franklin, and I'd like to thank you for coming to this auspicious presidential inauguration."

Sadie snorted and egged her on. "Do Camilla Bowles."

Roz moved the enormous bow to her forehead so that it overwhelmed her slim face and partially obstructed her view. With an affected British accent, she stretched out her arms as if searching for something.

"Do tell, my good man. Have you seen my husband, the prince?"

After the giggle fest was over, Sadie's gaze fell to the papers that Roz had set on the table.

"What's this?" She picked them up and noted the wide-ruled lines that indicated it was elementary-grade paper. The childish pencil scrawls confirmed her impression.

Curious to see if perhaps this was something from Edwin's early years, she unfolded the paper and read the words at the top.

Make Jesus Smile. Beside that, in smaller letters, the name of the student: *Joanie Marshall.*

Next to the title, a drawing that appeared to be that of a bearded Jesus smiled back at her.

Roz pushed the bow up on her head and sat beside her to look over her shoulder.

Instinctively, Sadie started to move the paper away...to keep from having to explain things about Edwin and his family that she didn't even want to consider herself.

Her friend leaned in and pierced her with a knowing gaze. "What are you hiding?"

She started to protest, but Roz cut her off.

"Don't think you can pretend with me. After fifty-however-many years, I can read you like a large-print book in a well-lit room."

So true. She handed her friend the paper. "I wasn't going to say anything, because I didn't want you to think ill of Edwin or anyone in his family. And I've been afraid to tell anyone outside of my family for fear that word might get back to the *Chatterbox* blog. Then everyone in Silver Peak would be asking questions."

Concern showing in her brown eyes, Roz removed the silly hat from her head and set it on the sofa beside her. "Edwin and his folks are good people. And even if they did something wrong, it's not my place to judge."

"That's the problem. I don't know if they've done anything wrong or not."

She gave Roz the scoop, starting with finding the ring in the tree, briefly mentioning the fact that it and the matching earrings had been stolen, and ending with her finding the ornate pair of ear danglers in Pauline's apron pocket.

"Edwin had mentioned that his cousin went through a phase when she was very young of taking things that didn't belong to her," she continued. "Joanie had access to Edith's bedroom, playing dress-up while the ladies carried on with their bridge game in another room. It would have been very easy for her to help herself to the jewelry box."

Edith had only mentioned Joanie dressing in her clothes, hats, scarves, and shoes, and Sadie doubted the woman would have willingly let the child play with her expensive jewelry. Considering the older woman's penchant for extravagant things, Edith most likely did not even own any costume jewelry.

Roz put a finger to her upper lip while she considered what she'd been told. "It seems Edwin's aunt would know the jewelry wasn't hers, even if Joanie brought it to her house and left it there."

"If it were anyone else but Pauline, I would agree with you. But the drummer she marches to plays a beat that no one else has heard before." She examined the paper in her hand. "This looks like a checklist of some sort."

Stuffed bear.

Comb.

Lamp chain.

The items seemed random and inconsequential. Names accompanied each item. The owners that Joanie had swiped them from, perhaps?

"Looks like an inventory of stolen loot," Roz said, confirming her own suspicion.

A smiling, hand-drawn bearded face with long hair accompanied each entry.

Roz flipped the page to the other side. "I wonder if this is all of it, or if there was another page."

"Or we could be completely wrong, and it's a schoolwork assignment." Sadie sighed, the breath long and disheartened. "This isn't much help."

Her friend pushed the paper back into her lap. "Look, you can't just tell me about this bodacious ring and not show it to me. It's not often that I get up close and personal with high-falutin' jewelry, and I want to eyeball that thing up close."

Sadie rose and returned a minute later with the tin and its contents.

Roz, suitably impressed by the exquisite ring, could only shake her head at how the hidden treasure came to be on her property.

"What else is in that box?"

Sadie closed her hand around the tin and hesitated. Even though she no longer believed the poem came from T.R., she felt funny about sharing the intimate message with Roz. For a while, it had seemed like a personal recollection of T.R.'s and her romance, and she had a hard time letting go of the warm feelings the poem had evoked, even if only temporarily.

Finally, after a moment of indecision, she reminded herself that she'd promised to show her friend the poem and handed it over. She and Roz had shared everything since the first day of kindergarten, so it wouldn't make sense to start holding out now.

Just as she herself had done, her friend studied the poem's content for hints as to who might have left it in the tin. But, unlike herself, Roz remained impassive as she read the tenderly wrought words out loud.

Then Roz moved on to the paper itself, first checking for a watermark, then squinting at the carefully inked letters and curlicues.

"Well, bless my soul." Roz tapped her finger against the bottom of the page. "This sure looks familiar."

Sadie took the sheet and held it under the lamp. The calligraphic swirl looped and banked so that it crossed over itself several times.

"I'm not seeing it."

"Can't you see the initials? *F* and *B*."

Something tickled at the back of her memory, but she couldn't quite access it.

"Frida Bullard!" Roz seemed inordinately pleased with herself for figuring it out. Apparently noticing Sadie's uncertainty, she said, "You know. The art student. You took an art history class with her."

Sadie had no difficulty remembering Frida; however, she wasn't so sure her former classmate had been responsible for copying this poem.

"She did calligraphy?"

"For sure. All kinds of letter art in addition to the fine art that she aspired to." Roz stood and gestured toward the hand-drawn and lettered family tree on the wall that Frida had created for Sadie's now-deceased mother. "See? Same signature."

It made sense. Calligraphy was a type of art, and Frida had dabbled in many forms of visual expression.

Sadie flashed back to 1973, the date on the tin, and remembered the fund-raiser carnival that had heralded both an ending and a new beginning in her life.

"You know, I ran into Frida a few years ago," Roz said. "She's living just outside of Silver Peak and works not too far from here."

"Really? What's she doing now?"

Roz shook her head. "She's an apartment manager."

"Wow. I would have thought that even if she didn't make a splash in the art world, she'd probably become a teacher. She was really good at explaining art techniques."

Roz crossed to the bookcase by the hearth where she'd left her purse, fished out a cell phone, and handed it to Sadie.

"Frida's number is in the address app."

Sadie held the phone, wanting to call. Wanting to reconnect with her old friend, but uncomfortable about what she might learn from her.

"I'd go with you," Roz said, "but Roscoe plans to keep me busy at the hardware store most of this week. The spring surge of home improvement projects is upon us."

After a brief moment of indecision, she called her old friend and chatted a bit as if no reason at all existed for her to call out of the blue after all these years and ask to meet her for lunch the following day.

Roz placed a hand to her chest and gestured toward Sadie as if to offer her heart. "My heart will be there with you," she said, "but just in case it forgets to take notes, I'll want to hear all about your meeting afterward."

Maybe it was better that it would be just the two of them. Perhaps, without an intermediary, she could dig deeper and find out what light Frida could shed on the poem that, for a short time, had seemed like a personal message from T.R.

She also wanted to know what connection her old college buddy had to the tin and its contents.

And why Frida had kept the secret all these years.

24

——

After Roz left with many of the clothes from Pauline's stash, Sadie put her feet up on the ottoman and opened the journal.

Sadie slid into the seat beside Frida in their shared art history class. The instructor, who usually moseyed into the classroom just as the clock touched the top of the hour, hadn't arrived yet, so she asked Frida about the final accounting of the fund-raiser for indigent women. Focusing on others sure beat fretting over the phone call Edwin hadn't made.

"We hit our goal, plus some! And, not to brag or anything, but my art booth brought in more than most of the other booths." Frida fished a large folder out of her portfolio and handed it to her. "Here's the family tree you ordered for your mother's birthday."

Sadie pulled the hand-drawn ancestry record out of the folder and examined the elaborate watercolor piece that incorporated her mother's family names and dates in carefully scripted letters.

"Wow. This is just beautiful. My mother is going to love it." Sadie's love of history had begun with the family stories her mother had told her, and it seemed appropriate to thank her on her birthday with a visual rendition of the family's names and links.

She started to put it back, and that's when she discovered a second piece behind the first, separated by a thin layer of tissue paper.

"What's this?"

Frida grinned. "It's for you. I didn't find the history part of Art History very exciting until we started studying together. But it was a requirement for my degree, so this is a thank-you for your help."

"But I struggled with the art part of Art History until you coached me on the techniques, so we should be even."

This class hadn't been required for her degree, but she'd taken it so she would be a well-rounded teacher once she started instructing high school history students.

She carefully separated the two pieces while Frida looked on with an excited smile. And what she found elicited a smile of her own.

"Frida, this is adorable!"

All the name art she'd seen before had been primary-color bright and kindergarten-cutesy, clearly intended for younger recipients, but Frida's version incorporated not only Sadie's first name and the things that represented her interests, but the tasteful colors and sophisticated lines that were exactly what she would have chosen herself.

The border around her name included various bits of Colorado scenery and history: Pikes Peak, ancient barns, miners with pickaxes searching for gold and silver, various battles that had taken place over the centuries, a steam-engine train, the mighty Rio Grande, and the State Capitol building in Denver, among others.

Drawn into her name were her other interests, represented by various antiques—an old crank telephone, rustic furniture, and a horse-drawn wagon—as well as illustrations that depicted the four *F*s that meant so much in her life: Faith, Family, Friends, and Fun. At the bottom right, Frida had signed the piece with an intricate series of loops and swirls.

Sadie gingerly clutched the piece to her chest. "I will always treasure this," she promised.

Sadie got up from the sofa and walked across the room to where the pieces still hung. Even after all these years—and a few years for the name art in the classrooms where she taught—they still looked crisp and almost new. As for the family tree, it had come back to her after her mother passed away. It had remained hanging in her living room ever since.

Just as promised, she had treasured the pieces over the years.

It would be good to see Frida tomorrow. Sadie expected that neither she nor Frida looked as crisp and almost new as the artwork did, but she was sure that their friendship—even after so long—would be just as beautiful.

25

SADIE SHOULD HAVE DRIVEN HER CAR TO THE POST OFFICE, BUT the temperatures, bolstered by the heat of the sun in the cloudless blue sky, had risen to sixty-four degrees, balmy by Silver Peak standards for May. The beautiful weather had beckoned her to walk the four blocks to pick up her mail. So now she looked like a high-wire walker trying to balance an assortment of letters and packages as she made her way toward the town hall building, one of the next two stops she needed to make on the way back to the Antique Mine.

She stopped in the middle of the sidewalk and lifted one knee to help push the pile of bills, advertisements, and antiquers' trade journals higher in her overcrowded arms. To make matters worse, the bicycle helmet she'd brought with her for protection against the overprotective mockingbirds hung by its chin strap from her arm and banged against her hip with every step.

She could have sent her assistant to retrieve the mail from the post office, but Julie had been in the middle of describing for a customer a bizarre decorating suggestion that Sadie would have never thought of, but which actually sounded pretty cool.

An envelope slipped, and she paused outside the broad front door of the town hall building to set her burden down on a bench and reposition the load. A moment of inspiration struck, and she moved the smaller envelopes and loose coupons and flyers into the helmet. The rest of the larger pieces fit tidily in the crook of her arm.

As for wearing the helmet when she returned to the shop, she would cross that feathery bridge when she came to it.

Inside, Kaitlyn McCarthy sat at the front reception desk and nodded to let her know she'd be with her after she finished the phone call she'd just taken.

While she waited, Sadie realized she wasn't sure which office she needed for the request she was here to make. So she signed in on the guest sheet and left the department blank.

Kaitlyn hung up the receiver and turned her bright smile on her. They had come to know each other during Sadie's occasional visits here to take care of business issues or to just stop in and see Edwin in the mayor's office.

"Hi, Kaitlyn. I'd like an application for a temporary permit to display sidewalk signs in front of my shop. Can you direct me to the right office?"

"Advertising signs?"

"No," she said and shifted the mail-filled bike helmet to her other arm. "I'm going to fix a mockingbird problem once and for all."

———

While she was there, Sadie popped in on Edwin to offer a quick hello, but he was out of the office, performing his mayorly duties.

Next she went to the Silver Peak treasurer's office. The sign on the inner door read *Joan M. Tilman, Treasurer.* The assistant's desk sat empty, and Sadie assumed he or she must have stepped away for a moment.

With the list she'd found yesterday tucked into her purse, she started to have second thoughts. Feeling a little silly for considering disturbing Joanie at work with such a trivial matter, she turned to leave.

Her hand had barely touched the outer doorknob when the treasurer's inner office door opened, and Joanie stepped out into the reception area.

"May I help you?"

"Um, I, well…"

"Sadie! I didn't recognize you from the back." Joanie stepped around her assistant's desk and extended her hand in greeting. "It's good to see you again. Thank you for your help with Aunt Pauley's birthday party last week. I heard that Edith Ryker had been stressing over the preparations until you came and helped her make some decisions."

Sadie shifted her burden and shook her hand. "I was happy to help, though I must say that it was nice to turn most of it over to the staff that Edith hired for the occasion."

"It turned out very well, and Aunt Pauley is still talking about what a good time she had." Joanie glanced at the mail in her arms and in the helmet. "Are those for me?"

She returned with a sheepish grin. "No, I'm not here on official business. Just personal." She set her bundles down in the empty guest chair and retrieved Joanie's elementary-grade paper from her purse. "Edwin and I were helping Pauline clear a closet, and I happened to come across this paper of yours."

She handed the sheet to her and hoped the offering would not be perceived as strange.

"I thought it might bring you a chuckle to see something from your elementary school years."

Obviously curious now, Joanie opened the ruled paper and looked it over. She smiled at first, and then she laughed.

Sadie waited expectantly, hoping the other woman would fill in with an explanation that might steer her toward answers about the Chameli Youta ring.

"Oh yes, this definitely brings back memories."

"You were, what, in first grade?" she prompted.

Joanie nodded. "That would be about right. It was around the time my aunt took me with her to see a Pink Panther movie. I was so young that I didn't follow the plot, but I was enthralled by the cartoon character at the beginning of the film."

The treasurer smiled, indicating it had been a fond memory.

"For some reason, I thought Inspector Clouseau was the thief, and I wanted to be just like him," she continued. "So for about a two-week period, I started pilfering random stuff from unsuspecting friends and family members."

Maybe she and Roz were right in their guess yesterday. "So this was your heist list?"

Joanie shook her head and looked down at the items listed there. "Actually, it was my give-back list. When Aunt Pauley found out what I'd been doing, she made me write down everything I had taken and arrange to give them back." She laughed again.

"You should have seen the look of surprise on my neighbor's face when I returned his partial denture."

"Oh, how cute."

Sadie recalled that Joanie had been a sweet kid with large, expressive eyes that seemed filled with innocence. No wonder the neighbor had been surprised by her unexpected thievery. She pointed to the bearded drawings beside each item.

"I don't suppose these were pictures of the people you took from?"

"No, that's a picture of Jesus. Aunt Pauley told me that for every filched item I returned to its rightful owner, Jesus would smile down on me in forgiveness. So I wanted to illustrate it by drawing a picture of Him each time I made things right."

"How insightful of your aunt."

"Yes, it was. Even though it was embarrassing to admit what I'd done, it felt so good to make it right for Jesus."

Joanie let the paper drop to her side and stared off with a far-away expression.

"That was a huge turning point for me, and it wouldn't be an understatement to say it shaped me for the rest of my life."

"Pauline must have been a wonderful teacher," Sadie said and thought of the gospel pocket lessons that the elderly woman loved to share.

"She was. Aunt Pauley said that in everything you do, you should do it with a greater good in mind." Joanie took another look at the paper, then met Sadie's gaze with a sincerity that seemed to soften her somewhat angular features. "Since that time, I've always remembered what she taught me. Honesty and integrity have directed my choices, and I like to think that's why the people of Silver Peak trust me with the town's money."

No lie detector was needed to convince Sadie that Edwin's cousin was telling the truth.

"Edwin and all of the Marshalls that I've met are known for their solid Christian values," she said.

With a silent prayer of hope, she wished that no information would present itself to change her mind on that matter.

Joanie laughed. "Oh, don't let Edwin fool you. He wouldn't have been a normal kid if he hadn't had at least one memorable episode."

Her curiosity piqued by the suggestion that there had indeed been a very memorable episode, Sadie retrieved her mail from the guest chair. She'd already taken enough of Joanie's time, but a comment like that couldn't be ignored. If it had something to do with the stolen jewelry, she needed to know.

"Really?" She tried to take a lighthearted approach, as if it didn't really matter, and that she only considered it a funny tidbit. "I've known Edwin a long time and never saw him doing anything very bad."

Unfortunately, Joanie squinched her nose and grinned as if she'd already said too much. Then the backpedaling began.

"I suppose that's his story to tell."

Sadie considered what she'd learned so far. A stolen ring he'd been given by Pauline had wound up in the same tin as a poem lettered by an old college friend. And now Joanie seemed to be covering up something Edwin had done in the past.

But it didn't make sense. If Edwin had been involved in the theft of the jewelry, why would Pauline hand it down to him as a so-called family heirloom later on? Had that been the story the Marshalls had invented to hide a family secret?

And could that have been why Edwin had abruptly changed the subject when he'd heard Pauline telling her about the ring?

Devastated to even imagine the possibility that Edwin would ever have been involved in anything shady, she pushed the unwelcome thought from her mind.

Now, more than ever, she needed to uncover the truth.

26

While she waited for Frida to join her at Los Pollitos, Sadie turned to the journal to pass the next five or ten minutes. As it happened, the next pages in the journal continued with her long-ago conversation with Frida.

Frida's smile faded as Sadie put the pieces back into the folder for safekeeping. "Have you heard from Edwin lately?"

Sadie straightened and tried not to show the tension that had suddenly formed in the pit of her stomach. She pushed her hair over her shoulder.

"No, but I'm sure he..."

Frida clutched her arm. "What? Not even a call on Valentine's Day?"

Sadie winced. She had expected she and Edwin would get busy and occasionally experience fallow periods of contact, but she hadn't thought they'd drift this far apart.

"We aren't exactly exclusive anymore," she reminded her friend. Even so, it hurt that he hadn't contacted her, especially after she'd called twice and left messages with his roommate. Three strikes and she would be out, so she had refrained from trying again, hoping that he would call and sound like the cheerful Edwin she used to know rather than the serious, non-forthcoming man who'd visited her a week and a half ago.

The only call she'd received on the fourteenth had been a salesperson trying to interest her in buying lightbulbs. Fortunately, T.R. had cheered her considerably. And, to her surprise, he had kissed her again, this time on the cheek, making it clear he'd like to take their friendship further. Although she was technically available to date—as was Edwin—she hadn't given T.R. any encouragement. Sweet friend that he was, he hadn't been offended and, instead, had taken her to a movie after dinner at her favorite café.

Frida's gentle voice broke into her thoughts.

"It's time to move on, Sadie."

"Hey, lady, move your stuff over and make room for your old college buddy!"

Frida dropped her purse in the chair on top of Sadie's and bent to give her a hug.

Sadie pushed the journal aside and rose from her chair to return the embrace. Her friend wore a floral maxiskirt that looked, not surprisingly, like an impressionist painting. Frida's formerly brown hair was now decidedly blonde, and she'd added some weight to her frame and a few lines to her face. If they'd met on the street, Sadie doubted she would have recognized Frida. Her friend looked good and she told her so, but Sadie couldn't help noticing that time had moved on since they were last together.

"Sadie, it's great to see you," Frida said, taking a seat in the empty chair. "I am just bubbling over with questions to ask you."

Sadie smiled. "You're not the only one."

27

THE FIRST HALF OF SADIE AND FRIDA'S LUNCH AT LOS POLLITOS was spent on small talk and catching up on all that had happened in their lives since graduation. It seemed as though the years had melted away and it was only last week that they had sat together in Art History class.

Sadie wished they'd reconnected much sooner and told her friend so.

"Then let's not let any more water flow under the bridge," Frida said.

They set a date for a future lunch outing, and Sadie listened while her college friend regaled her with stories about her job and expressed her amazement at the kinds of things tenants sometimes left behind when they moved out.

"If you ever come across any antiques, give me a call," Sadie said and slid her card across the table.

Frida promised to do so. "I'm so glad you called out of the blue yesterday. I'd been thinking about you over the years, wondering how you were doing."

Earlier, Sadie had told her about T.R.'s passing, and Frida had been sincerely saddened to hear of it.

"I liked T.R. a lot," her friend said and began reminiscing about their college days. "He knew you had a boyfriend-on-hold that first year or two at UC, and I could see that T.R. was taking his time making his move for you."

Sadie laughed at the remembrance. "He later told me he didn't want to be my rebound man."

"While you two were spending so much time together as best friends, he was falling harder and harder in love with you. Everybody could see it."

"Everyone but me." Sadie scooped up some of the contents that had escaped from her burrito and fallen onto her plate. The Garcias, who owned Los Pollitos, made the best Mexican food anywhere. "I may have been blind to how he felt about me, but I knew that he held a special place in my heart."

"It sounds like you two had a lot of good years together."

Sadie nodded, her voice softening as she thought of the man who'd turned out to be the best husband she could have imagined. "We did. Wonderful years."

She and Frida had caught up on so many aspects of their lives, but there was one thing she hadn't told her yet.

"I'm seeing Edwin now." At her age, it still have felt odd to call it "going steady," thought that's really what it was.

A mixture of expressions crossed Frida's pretty face.

Sadie sat up a little straighter, trying to read what had just happened.

"I'm...I'm happy for you," Frida said.

Sadie pushed her plate away and decided against flan for dessert. Their time together was coming to a close for today, and she needed to get to the point of what had sparked their visit.

"I recently came across a piece of your calligraphy."

"Really?" Frida seemed thrilled. "I love doing calligraphy. The vellum and nibs. And even the smudgy ink, if you aren't careful. Every now and then, I address friends' invitations for baby showers or other special events."

"We could have used you recently," Sadie said. "There have been both a centennial birthday and a sixtieth anniversary in the past couple of weeks."

She reached into her purse and withdrew the stiff envelope that held the poem. There was no way she would risk bringing the tin with the expensive ring in it, but the thick envelope kept the paper inside from getting bent or torn.

"This is it."

"How did you get this?" Frida took a moment to examine the work and an even longer time to say anything about it. Finally, "I remember copying this poem for a customer at the fund-raiser carnival in our junior year in college. We raised a lot of money for disadvantaged women."

Rather than answer her friend's question, Sadie steered the subject back to the artwork. "It's a nice poem," she said. "And the calligraphy is beautiful."

"It wasn't my best work. He was in a bit of a hurry for it, so it shows that I rushed."

Now they were getting somewhere. If she could learn something about the customer, perhaps that person could lead her to the answers she sought. But the question was, would Frida remember that person after all these years?

"Can you remember anything about the person who commissioned the work?"

"It was just some guy who showed up at the carnival…"

Ah, so she did remember. But why so vague?

"You remember having to finish the piece quickly," she prompted. "What else do you remember? I take it the customer was a male, but was he a student or a member of the faculty?"

Frida looked away and studied something outside the large pane windows. "Those mockingbirds can be vicious."

"You know," Sadie gently pressed. "Who was it?"

Reluctantly, Frida dragged her gaze back to the table. "It was Edwin. He said he needed it for someone special."

Frida looked away again.

Stunned, Sadie felt as though she'd just had the air kicked out of her lungs. She tried to speak, but a giant invisible band of elastic squeezed her ribs.

"And?" she finally squeaked.

More quietly this time, Frida answered, "And I wasn't supposed to say anything about it to anyone."

Pause.

"Especially you."

Sadie took it all in, trying to process how this sequence of events could have unfolded. She understood why Frida had been reluctant to mention Edwin in relation to the poem, but she had no issue with the fact that he had commissioned the work for Rose, the woman who eventually became his wife. What she couldn't figure out was how the poem and ring, which had apparently been intended for Rose, had ended up on her land.

Apologetic, Frida reached across the table and patted her hand. "I had originally assumed it was for you. But when Edwin hadn't given it to you after a reasonable amount of time, not even for Valentine's Day, it was only fair to conclude that the poem had been intended for someone else. I'm so sorry."

"There's no need to apologize," she assured her. "We had an agreement. He was within his rights to date others, and we each knew it was a possibility that we might find someone else while we were attending different schools."

Like a stealth waitress, Gloria fluttered in and set the check on the table before whisking herself off to another party that had just been seated.

Frida reached for it, but Sadie stopped her and picked it up herself.

"Thank you for this reunion lunch, especially on such short notice," she said. "I hope we won't be waiting so long before getting together again."

These recent developments confirmed what Sadie had already concluded about Edwin's unexpected visit all those years ago and the silence that followed it.

More recently, an awkward tension had developed between Edwin and her, first when she'd mentioned a gift that had been left for her, presumably by T.R. Had Edwin gotten wind of what she'd found? Could that have been why he hadn't seemed interested in hearing about it?

And then there was his peculiar reaction upon hearing his aunt discuss the ring she'd given him for his wife.

With a knowing that settled with certainty in her heart, Sadie resolved that she would put an end to this.

She tucked the poem back in her purse and pulled out her wallet to pay for lunch.

A few minutes later, on the way back to the shop, she debated how she should broach the subject with Edwin.

———————

Still thinking about her conversation with Frida, Sadie braved the patrolling mockingbirds to return to the shop. The feathered parents were as pretty as could be, and she could understand their wanting to protect their eggs from passersby who came too close to the nest, but something had to be done to protect the pedestrians as well.

She pushed the door open and dashed inside, mail spilling from her arms onto the floor.

"Ugh!" Julie stepped out from behind the counter and helped her gather up the dropped envelopes. "This is bad, Sadie. Customers are avoiding the shop because the birds are attacking everyone within a half-block radius. We've only had a few people come in all morning, and one just zipped in here to escape the air raids."

If the attacks had been limited to the immediate vicinity of the tree in front of the Antique Mine, customers could have entered through Arbuckle's and the shared interior door. Unfortunately, customers of all the businesses bordering the nesting tree—even those on the other side of Main Street—had taken pecks from the overprotective parents.

Sadie set the mail on the counter and took off her jacket. If something wasn't done, it was going to hurt the bottom line of the Antique Mine as well as other nearby shops.

"Gloria said it's the same over at Los Pollitos. But don't worry. I'll have it fixed soon."

Without customers at the moment, there was nothing pressing for either of them to do, so Sadie retreated to her desk at the back of the store.

Right now, she wanted more than anything to ask Edwin a few probing questions. She wanted to call him and hear him reassure her that all her concern about the stolen jewelry could be easily explained. But more than that, she wanted to sit with him, face-to-face, and see the blue eyes that, to her knowledge, had always been honest with her.

She pulled out her cell phone. Not to place the call, but to take a look at recent photos of him.

In some ways, the new phones took better pictures than her old film camera did. And it was a lot more convenient to carry around than the bigger camera had been.

First, she pulled up the photos of Pauline's birthday party. Not surprisingly, many of them featured Edwin. And for those in which he wasn't the main subject, his image was frequently captured on the periphery.

She zoomed in on his handsome face and studied the smile lines around his eyes. She touched a finger to the image of his cheek. Unfortunately, the photos raised both questions and mixed feelings for her.

"What secrets are you hiding from me, Edwin?"

28

Her thoughts now on Edwin, Sadie turned back to the essay she'd been reading in bits and pieces over the past couple of weeks. Two weekends after Frida's revelation, she'd gone home to Silver Peak to be with her parents and give her mother the beautifully lettered family tree. Or, as Roz had so rightly put it, to lick her wounds.

"Sadie, this is lovely," her mother said and held the framed document out to admire it. "I'm going to hang it in the living room where everyone can see it."

Barbara Wright's pleasure was evident, but the smile didn't fully reach her eyes. In addition, Sadie's father, who sat in the other room watching a football game, had been quieter than usual when he'd greeted her.

"What's going on?" Sadie asked. "You and Dad seem so... different today."

Barbara folded the wrapping paper around the family tree and carefully set it on the kitchen table. She seemed to be weighing her response.

Finally, "We heard you and Edwin broke up."

Sadie sighed. She had intended to tell her parents herself, but of course the grapevine had been faster. "Technically, we broke up a couple of years ago."

Her mother self-consciously lifted a hand to her newly permed hair. "I always liked him."

"Yeah. Me too." She wondered how she could explain what had happened between them when she didn't quite understand it herself. So she just left it at that. She reached into the fridge and pulled out an apple. "Want one?"

Her mother shook her head. "You're dating that other fellow now?"

Even without his name being mentioned, she knew who her mother meant. "We've gone out a few times, but I haven't decided whether I'm ready to date again."

"Well." Her mother nodded. "I like him too."

Trying to lighten the mood, Sadie joked, "I hope you didn't read about Edwin and me in the local newspaper."

A shake of the head told her the town's grapevine wasn't quite that strong.

"I saw Mrs. Marshall at the hair salon the other day. She didn't notice me waiting for my appointment. She had the drying bonnet on and was talking pretty loudly."

Sadie anticipated what was coming next.

"Edwin met a girl."

She'd suspected as much, especially after her conversation with Frida. But now it was confirmed.

"Sacked!" her father hollered from the other room. "That guy didn't know what hit him."

Sadie put a hand to her head. Neither did she.

That ended the essay for which Sadie had earned an A in English Composition. She put the journal away and went back to scrolling through the pictures on her phone... this time to the prom shots that she'd meant to go through. She wanted to pull out the best ones to share with Edwin and Theo.

Pausing to reflect on a picture of Edwin placing a crown on the head of the newly elected prom queen, she noticed something in addition to his congratulatory smile that caught her attention.

Sadie adjusted her reading glasses and held the phone at just the right distance. It was the person standing off to the side watching the proceedings who interested her.

It was too small to see the detail that had captured her attention, so she spread her fingers over the screen and enlarged the section showing the prom-goer's shirt cuff.

The gray band on the edge of the cuff was just like that in the Facebook shot that Theo had shown her. Just like the shirt worn by the person who had hidden in the bathroom stall to snap the embarrassing picture of Bodie.

She checked her watch. School would be letting out soon.

Quickly, she gathered up her things and scurried to the front of the shop where Julie had pulled out a dustrag and polish to keep busy.

"Would you mind closing up today? I have to go to the high school to take care of an important matter."

29

"THEO, DON'T DO ANYTHING UNTIL I GET THERE." SADIE STARTED the car and waited to finish the conversation before putting the Tahoe into gear. "We're going to take this to the principal and let him handle it."

She arrived at the meeting spot Theo had designated near the student parking lot and scoped the area for one of the tallest guys to locate him. No surprise to her, but he had already figured it out by the time she had called him.

Teens spilled out of the school building. Some zoomed to their cars and others headed toward buses. Still others, such as Ella and her friends, clustered in small groups for a few minutes of socializing before heading off in their separate directions. Hayley stood on the outer perimeter of their group, tucking a limp strand of sandy hair behind her ear, so Sadie assumed Bodie must be nearby.

Sure enough, Theo stood on the sidewalk in deep conversation with Bodie. As Sadie approached, he met her gaze, then turned back to his friend to finish their discussion.

She stayed a respectable distance away, on the other side of a sapling tree to give the impression of disinterest, but she was still close enough to hear large snatches of what they were talking about.

"Bro, I'm telling you, Ella did not write that letter asking you to do her homework." Theo straightened and clawed his fingers through his hair. "She's not the kind of person to use people for what she can get out of them."

Bodie shook his head and mumbled something unintelligible, but it was clear he didn't want to believe what her grandson was telling him.

"And even if she was, you wouldn't want to go out with her."

Another mumble, and Sadie suspected the younger boy wouldn't mind being with the girl, no matter what the cost.

Theo's voice softened, and he laid a compassionate hand on the boy's shoulder. Bodie flinched at the touch, and Theo removed his hand.

"Dude, the letter was a hoax. I'm sorry to say it, but Garrick was playing you."

Stated a little harshly, perhaps, but Theo obviously hadn't made any headway using the softball approach.

Even so, Bodie still clung to the belief that he had a shot at winning the lovely Ella. He muttered something about no harm being done and attempted to end the conversation by walking away.

Theo, determined not to let him off so easily, gently but firmly gripped him by the arm to prevent him from leaving. This time he didn't let go.

True to his nature when under stress, Bodie refused to meet Theo's gaze. Instead he seemed fixated on an electric pole on the other side of the parking lot and spoke to it.

His softer voice was a little harder to hear than Theo's, and Sadie tried not to call attention to herself with her eavesdropping, so she turned to the side and put her better ear toward Bodie.

"Say what?" Theo dropped his hand from the boy's arm and took a step back.

The first part of Bodie's reply was obscured by a brief gust of wind, but she distinctly heard "It all works out in the end."

Theo tried another tack, and the two guys murmured something between themselves. Then the wind shifted again, and Sadie heard Bodie lament, "Somebody should make some rules about this stuff that's easy to understand."

Sadie's heart went out to the boy for his frustration in navigating the challenges of social life. Bodie's comment perfectly captured the struggles that someone with the black-and-white mind-set of Asperger's struggled with every day. Very literal in his thinking, Bodie and many others on the spectrum needed clearly defined interactions that most people picked up naturally, without giving it much thought.

She was about to step out from behind the tiny sapling that did nothing to conceal her from the pair, when Garrick flaunted past the cluster of girls that chattered nearby.

Making sure they were watching, he walked toward Bodie and taunted in a high, girlish voice. "Dear Bodie. Heart-heart, kiss-kiss! Would you do a *biiiiig* favor for me? If you say yes, I'll be your girlfriend and…" He swaggered past Bodie and deliberately bumped him so that the boy was knocked off his feet. "…hold your hand!"

Garrick burst out laughing and glanced triumphantly at the small crowd of onlookers who, by now, had stopped what they were doing to watch the drama unfold.

Sadie had headed toward the boys, but Theo was already making a move. However, it was scrawny little Bodie who beat them to the draw. While Garrick hammed it up, Bodie flung himself at the hulking football player's waist, bringing him down as easily as David had taken down Goliath.

At first she worried for Garrick, who had hit the ground hard, but he quickly bounced to his feet and turned his fury on Bodie.

Sadie's voice got lost in the cheers and jeers of bystanders who swarmed closer for a better view. Garrick's eyes blazed red with rage as he hauled back to deliver a punishing blow to Bodie.

With the crowd's goading and whoops of encouragement ringing in her ears, she pushed past the throng. She had to stop this now, before somebody got seriously hurt.

Before she could insert herself into the fray, Theo intervened. In trying to deflect the blow from the boy, he took a direct hit.

Her tall, strong grandson crumpled like a rag doll and fell to the ground.

———

Her heart pounding and the ringing in her ears intensifying with each hammering pulse, Sadie moved to her grandson's limp form. The sight both terrified her and fueled her to a speed she'd never known before.

But despite her swift maneuver through the cluster of curiosity seekers, Ella beat her to Theo's side. The girl bent over him, worry creasing her pretty face.

Sadie took the other side and knelt beside him to check for breathing. She laid a hand on his chest, and the noticeable rise and fall of air flowing through his lungs filled her with relief.

Theo groaned. His eyelashes, ridiculously long for a boy, flickered briefly, then opened to reveal a hazel-eyed expression of dazed confusion.

"Thank you, God," Sadie said out loud, and the sentiment rippled among some of the others who had leaned in to see if he was all right.

Theo groaned again and tried to push himself up on his elbow, but she put a hand on his shoulder to block him from rising just yet. Ella had knelt down and cradled his head.

Her grandson looked up at the girl who worried over him, and his expression changed from confusion to pure bliss. There was no mistaking the small smile that had found its way to his face.

————

Mere seconds later, the coach whooshed in and collared a stunned Garrick.

"Thanks, Hayley," he said to the girl who had run to alert him to the brewing trouble. Then, to Sadie, with a nod toward Theo, he asked, "Is he all right?"

Theo had sat up during the commotion and rubbed his eyes as if to clear the fog away. He wobbled a bit and still looked woozy. "I'm fine."

By now, the school buses had started up, and the small crowd had thinned of onlookers who had abandoned the excitement of a fight in favor of going home.

Sadie refused to believe her grandson. Addressing the coach, who now had Garrick literally in hand, she said, "When you go to the office, would you send the school nurse out here?"

Turning her attention back to Theo, she noted that Ella still clung to his side.

"You were so brave," the girl said and clutched his arm. "You put yourself in danger to protect someone else. That's heroic."

Hayley, Ella's friend whom she'd been talking to earlier, and two other girls whom Sadie didn't recognize nodded in agreement. Bodie, in his uncertainty, turned one way and then the other, demonstrating that he wasn't sure what to do.

Sadie reached for the boy and gently took his arm. Surprisingly, the gesture seemed to calm him, and she had to admit that it calmed her as well. What she really wanted to do was take Theo in her arms and hug him until she was sure he would suffer no aftereffects from Garrick's blow and then the impact with the pavement. But for now, gaining comfort by comforting Bodie would have to do.

Theo attempted to rise to his feet, but was stopped by Ella's hand to his shoulder.

"You really should lie back until the nurse comes," the girl cooed.

"She's right," Sadie concurred. "You could have a concussion. Please just stay still for now."

She tried not to worry and to trust that God held Theo in His safekeeping. But the very real possibility of a brain injury, no matter how minor, concerned her.

Theo, on the other hand, apparently had no such worries. In fact, he seemed to be enjoying Ella's attentiveness.

He looked up and met Sadie's watchful gaze. Slowly, almost imperceptibly, a tiny smile that could have been mistaken for punch-drunkenness stole its way across his mouth, and he eased his head back onto Ella's lap.

Sadie knew him well enough to understand that he was giving her the all clear.

Not to mention the "steer clear and let me enjoy this moment."

That rascal! Sadie gave a silent prayer of thanks that Theo was at least well enough to flirt.

She looked back toward the school to find the nurse and principal jogging out to meet them.

"I've been thinking about going to that chocolate fest at your church," Ella said. "If you're feeling better by then, maybe we could go together."

Bodie's arm tensed under Sadie's hand, and she turned back to the small group, who waited for Theo's answer.

Hoping to distract the boy from the disappointment that seemed inevitable, she dropped Bodie's arm and called for the nurse to come this way.

But Theo didn't take the hint to drop the subject. Instead, he glanced over at Bodie, who watched the pair with an intense level of attentiveness that anyone else in his shoes might have tried to disguise as disinterest or even boredom.

Clearly, so that Bodie wouldn't misunderstand, Theo closed one eye in a wink of camaraderie and raised himself to his elbows.

"Maybe all three of us could go together," he suggested to Ella, with a nod toward Bodie.

It was times such as this that made Sadie dazzlingly aware that children were one of God's most wonderful blessings. Many people thought of the teenage years as being full of self-absorbed interests and lack of awareness for others, but Theo had just made her heart melt with grandmotherly pride.

And if Ella was all that Theo claimed her to be, she must be aware of the mature gesture he'd just made.

A movement from the corner of Sadie's eye snagged her attention.

Theo must have seen it also.

"You too, Hayley," he said. "There's room in my car for all of us."

30

<hr>

THOUGH THE EMERGENCY ROOM DOCTOR DIDN'T SEEM TOO concerned about the mild concussion he'd diagnosed for Theo, that night Sadie's thoughts kept going back to her grandson. She was certain that Alice, and even Sara, would be checking in on him frequently, but it would make her feel better if she could keep watch over him too.

Barring that, she said a prayer and asked God to watch over her grandson and to grant him a full and speedy recovery.

To distract herself, she picked up one of her later journals. The college essay about her breakup with Edwin was finished, so she skipped ahead to the day she and T.R. had returned to Silver Peak from their honeymoon.

T.R. carried me over the threshold today. Thanks to my athletic tendencies and the muscles that come with them—not to mention a healthy appetite during our honeymoon—I'm not exactly a featherweight. But he made me feel absolutely dainty. And oh, so beloved.

Once inside, he set me down. With his arm draped around my shoulder, he pulled me close and surveyed the place that had been my parents' home until they decided they wanted to move closer to town. Naturally, T.R. and I had jumped at the chance to buy the old homestead and live in this beautiful wooded area that had been the backdrop of so many of my happy childhood memories. My roots were already here. Now T.R. would be adding his roots to mine.

"We need a puppy," he declared.

I looked up at him, expecting to see a glimmer of a smile in the corners of his mouth, but he appeared quite serious. I was more than happy to bring a dog into our little lovenest, but I wondered what had prompted this decision of his.

"A hunting dog?"

T.R. considered it and poked his lower lip out as he thought. "Maybe. A Labrador retriever would be good." He turned back to me and gave me a little squeeze. "Mostly, I was thinking we should practice on a dog before starting a family."

I smiled, and a funny thought occurred to me. "Don't you think people will consider us odd to be putting diapers on a dog?"

We laughed, and that turned into an ongoing joke for the rest of the day. The dog in a baby carriage. Sleeping in a crib. Having its food blended into a puree. It seemed that every conversation went back to our future dog, the practice baby.

His family had brought T.R.'s clothes and other belongings over while we were on our honeymoon…after promising not to prank the house, of course! So after we settled in, T.R. began going through his things to put them away.

Still buzzing with a feeling of honeymoon togetherness, I wanted to help him unpack the boxes and find permanent places for his belongings. The box closest to me appeared to be odds and ends: trophies, an alarm clock, a flashlight, and other miscellaneous possessions, all cushioned among assorted items of underclothing and socks.

Before I could lift the first one out, T.R. shut the cardboard lid and stopped me, saying he would do it himself.

I laughed. "What is it you don't want me to see?" I teased.

He had the oddest look on his face, as if questioning why I would ask such a thing.

Well, that tickled me even more. "You don't want me to see your drawers!"

Honestly, he was so cute! So I teased him a bit more and asked if he was afraid I'd see holes in his socks.

An unreadable frown flickered across his face. Apparently, it wasn't that. He changed the subject, and before we knew it, we were devising even more ridiculous ways to baby our future dog. Putting it in a bonnet. Giving it a pacifier. Burping it. We had never laughed as hard as we did that day...

Sadie closed the journal and set it on her nightstand. What had been in that box that T.R. wouldn't let her unpack?

An uneasy feeling crawled up her spine. Something told her she didn't want to know the answer to that question.

31

"GRANDMA, YOU'RE HOVERING AGAIN."

Theo lay back on the cot that Sadie had set up for him in the back room of the Antique Mine. With his activity and reading restricted, he had complained this morning of being bored. Despite the caution against straining his eyes, he pulled out his smartphone to log on to the Internet.

Sadie swooped past his cot like an owl on the hunt and smoothly lifted the phone from his hands.

"Hey!"

"You heard the doctor," she said and tickled his sock-clad feet. "You're supposed to be resting."

Like herself, Alice had been concerned yesterday when the doctor at the emergency room had diagnosed Theo with a mild concussion. The prescription had called for rest and observation for the next twenty-four hours and to continue to watch for symptoms for the next couple of weeks.

To keep Alice from missing a day of work to be with Theo, Sadie had offered to let him come to work with her, where she would keep an eye on him for the rest of the day. Quite honestly, she was glad to have him here to reassure herself that he would be fine after yesterday's trauma.

The bell over the door rang to signal the presence of a customer.

"I *am* resting. See?" Theo gestured to the camping cot where his feet hung over the bottom end.

"You're supposed to be resting both your body and your eyes. Concussions can be very serious."

Sadie had felt guilty that she had not anticipated the violent turn of events, but both Theo and Alice had insisted there had been nothing else she could have done under the circumstances.

More than anything, she was proud of her grandson for stepping up and trying to do the right thing. Unfortunately, the slim runner had been easily outclassed by the burly football player.

"Not as serious as boredom," Theo complained. "No television, no phone, no reading. What am I supposed to do?" He lifted his arms in an I-give-up shrug. "At this point, I'd be happy to do schoolwork."

The bell up front jangled again, a reminder that Julie might need her. "If you weren't on bedrest," she told him, "you could help with the customers."

"If I wasn't on bedrest, I'd be in school."

"Touché!" She handed the phone back to him. "Find a podcast and listen to it. Those two car repair guys on public radio are really funny, and there's a whole archive of their past shows on the Internet. They should entertain you for a while."

Theo brightened. He put his earbuds in and touched the phone's screen to go to the Web site. With a good-bye wave to her, he settled in to enjoy the radio celebrities' antics.

Sadie smiled. She'd struck gold with that suggestion. Boys plus cars usually equaled a winning combination.

Another jangle of the customer bell, and this time Julie called to her from the front of the shop. "Sadie, I could use your help."

A swarm of tourists milled in the store. Behind the cash register, Julie was busy ringing up an older gentleman who was purchasing an Old World cigar humidor with kiln-dried Spanish cedar. Sadie remembered finding the beautiful piece at an estate sale and had hoped even then that it would find a home with someone who found it as beautiful as she did. This man's eyes made it clear that it had.

Sadie carefully wrapped the box and handed it to him.

The gentleman made a motion as if he were tipping his hat and opened the door to leave. He raised an umbrella to the cloudless sky.

Sadie and Julie peered out the window and watched him cross to the other side of the street to his car. On the way, one of the pair of mockingbirds dipped and circled the umbrella that shielded his shaved head.

Julie turned back to Sadie and lifted both hands for a double high five. "You did it! Your idea was a stroke of genius."

She slapped Julie's palms and returned to the window. Outside along Main Street, cardboard boxes had been stationed in front of Silver Peak Bank, Los Pollitos, the opera house…everything within a quarter-block radius of the tree that the mockingbirds had claimed as their own. A few more boxes sat along the sidewalk for drivers entering and exiting their cars.

Each contained a dozen or more umbrellas with a large printed sign: *Bird-brellas. Borrow here, and drop off at the next convenient receptacle.*

"Congratulations, boss!" Julie moved back to the cash register to help the next person. "I was wondering what you were going to do with all those umbrellas."

Sadie laughed. "Me too."

———

Sadie pulled into Alice's driveway. Her daughter's car was gone, and the house lay dark.

Unconcerned, Theo jumped down out of the Tahoe and carried the cot to the garage. On his way to the house, he paused to shoot invisible basketballs at the hoop on the side of the garage.

Under other circumstances, she would have joined him in a quick game of one-on-one, but today she just reminded him he should be taking it easy.

"My twenty-four hours is up." Theo moved to the house, where he unlocked the front door and held it open for her. He followed her in.

Inside, she turned on the lights and headed to the empty kitchen. "Where is everybody?"

"They escaped because they saw you coming and were afraid you'd make them lie on a cot and stare at the wall all day."

She poked him in the side. Like a six-foot-tall toddler, he jumped and giggled. No matter how old he became, she would never tire of the sound of his laughter.

Sadie held her pointer finger up like a gun aimed toward the ceiling and studiously examined it. "I never realized that one tiny finger could be so powerful that it can make one hundred and fifty pounds jump around the room."

Theo cruised through the pantry and finally settled at the counter with the crumb remnants of a bag of potato chips.

"Hey, what's this?" He picked up a note from the counter and read out loud. "Picking up Sara from Mia's house. Back soon. Love, Mom."

Sadie set her purse down and took off her coat.

"Grandma, you can see that I'm doing great. You don't have to stay and babysit me until Mom comes home."

She poured herself a glass of water. "I don't have to, but I want to. Besides, we never got the chance to talk about how you found out it was Garrick who'd been mistreating Bodie."

Theo pushed the empty potato chip bag aside. "I would love to talk about it, but I think I'm going to pass out."

Sadie set the glass down on the counter and rushed to his side, where she stood close in case he lost his balance on the bar stool.

"Are you dizzy? Feeling sick to your stomach?" The doctor had said to be on the lookout for symptoms such as those. "Look at me so I can see if your pupils are the same size."

Mimicking her earlier action, he aimed his finger at her like a pistol. "That got your attention. I think I'm going to pass out from hunger."

He rubbed his belly.

With a playful swat at his arm, she relaxed her guardian stance and took the stool beside him.

"Mercy, child! Don't ever do that to me again. You almost gave me a cardiac moment." She put a hand to her heart to emphasize the fact, but he just flashed that charming smile of his.

In retrospect, she actually felt somewhat guilty for having underfed him today. She had packed him a lunch that was enormous by her own standards, but he had quickly polished it off as a midmorning snack. At lunch, he'd downed a burrito and the couple of sides she'd bought for him at Los Pollitos. And by midafternoon, he was scavenging for food again, so she had sent him next door to Arbuckle's for a pastry but, of course, that hadn't filled him up either.

"I can't help it," he protested. "My hollow leg is empty."

Judging by the time marked on Alice's note, it would be a while before she and Sara returned, and longer still until dinner was on the table.

"Why don't you make a sandwich to tide you over while I start some lasagna."

"Lasagna!" Theo jumped down from the stool and performed a series of bizarre dance gyrations that he had once called the Carlton after a wacky character on a rerun of an old TV sitcom. Not to be confused with the Charleston, which was mild by comparison.

His twenty-four hours of observation are up, she reminded herself. Trying to contain Theo's youthful energy would be like trying to stuff a mountain lion into a gunnysack.

He settled down to making a sandwich that would be classified as a meal and a half according to anyone over the age of thirty.

While he chowed down, she started making the lasagna. Taking a guess, Sadie asked if Sasha, the girl who had been in charge of handing out drink bottles to thirsty prom-goers, had been responsible for setting Bodie up with the rigged drink bottle.

Theo shook his head and wiped the mayo off his mouth. "No, she was the first one to laugh at him, but she didn't have anything to do with the drink or the picture. She just went around blabbing to everyone to check their Facebook updates."

"Then what was the tipping point for you to find out that Garrick was the guilty party?"

Theo grinned that smile again that seemed like a visit from T.R. every time he did it. "Remember when he was going around on prom night, smacking balloons and popping them?"

She nodded. The showoff had made it look as though the sheer force of impact had exploded the balloons that dangled from ribbons at various points around the gym.

"He had wedged a thumbtack between his fingers," Theo said as if that was all anyone needed to know to solve the puzzle of who had pranked Bodie.

She thought about it a moment, then shook her head. "I don't get the connection."

"I reasoned—correctly I might add," Theo said, holding one finger aloft, "that the thumbtack had been used to poke holes in the plastic drink bottle that soaked Bodie's pants."

"Smooth."

The water for the pasta came to a boil, and Sadie lowered the heat for al dente lasagna noodles that would finish cooking after they were layered in the casserole dish and popped into the oven.

"But why?" she asked, turning the situation over in her mind. "Garrick is a big guy, and you said he was popular because of his position on the football team. Why would he need to pick on a kid who's so much smaller than himself? He wouldn't need to do that to lift himself up. He was already at the top of the social pecking order."

"Simple. It turned out that Garrick had not broken up with Ella after all." He handed her the spinach that would go between the layers of pasta and waited for her reaction.

She lifted an eyebrow, which was enough to urge him on.

"*Ella* had broken up with *Garrick* because all he thought about was sports, and he never focused on his schoolwork like she does. He didn't want anyone to know that he'd been dumped, so he told everybody that he was the one who'd called it off."

"And she let people believe his lie to allow him to save face," she offered.

"Right! But Garrick wanted her back. Understandably so." Theo stirred the onions and mushrooms sautéing on the stove. "He assumed that if he could make better grades in what was *her* worst class, she'd have new respect for him and give him another chance." Still stirring, he added, "But Garrick thought that the only way he could improve his grades was to bully the homework out of the smartest guy in the class."

Sadie opened her mouth to speak, but Theo cut her off.

"I know. Put the work in, and your grades will automatically come up," he said for her.

She and Alice had trained him well.

"Garrick already assumed Bodie was being manipulated to do Dougie's calculus problems for him. And he knew Colin was putting the squeeze on Bodie for desserts, so he must have decided he'd take advantage too."

Sadie filled in the rest. "And in the meantime, he chose to have fun being a jerk to Bodie, the kid who'd had the nerve to ask *his* girl to the prom."

"You got it. Garrick convinced Colin to pass the dribbling drink bottle to Bodie so it could soak his pants."

And provide a moment of mean-spirited humor for the perpetrators.

"It did seem odd that Ella, who could have had her choice of prom dates, would go out with a boy whose social skills are a bit…"

"Remedial?" Theo suggested.

"Yes. Do you like carrots in your sauce?"

"Sure." He snagged a slice and crunched it. "You're right. Ella could have gone with anybody, but she went with Bodie because, one"—he pressed one finger back—"she's a super-nice person who appreciates Bodie's book smarts and friendship. And, two, she really wasn't ready to date so soon after the breakup. Accepting a friendship-only date with Bodie was one way to go to the prom without dealing with other guys who wanted romance instead of just a fun time."

"Like you and your friend-date, Katy."

"Yeah."

She recalled how upset Ella became when people laughed at Bodie with the purple drink on his pants.

"Ella did seem rather protective of Bodie."

Theo nodded. "He's like a little brother to her."

Apparently not to Bodie's way of thinking. Even with the friends-only restriction on their date, the young man had obviously hoped for more.

Theo refreshed the details of how the Facebook photo had gone down. "When Bodie went to the bathroom to take off his pants and hold them under the hand dryer, Garrick grabbed his phone from the sink counter, ducked into the stall to hide what he was doing, and took the picture of Bodie in his underwear. Bodie was so focused on drying his pants that he didn't even notice what was going on."

Theo grinned.

"Even if Garrick knew his sleeve would show up in the mirror, he probably didn't imagine that we'd trace it back to him."

Sadie slathered layers of pasta, spinach, sauce, and cheese into the baking dish. "And with Bodie's phone in hand, it was a simple matter to upload the picture to Bodie's own Facebook page. What about Dougie? He was the first to share the photo, right? Had he been in on the plan with Garrick?"

Theo shook his head. "Even though it looked like Dougie had paid Bodie to do his calculus problems for him, he wouldn't have done anything to risk his chances of getting into the School of Mines. And he didn't need help with his earth science papers because he was already good at it."

"Thus, his interest in a college that specializes in geosciences." Sadie sprinkled mozzarella on the lasagna and set the pan aside. "But Colin was manipulating him. What about the desserts he stole from him? And the better-than-usual grade he made on his homework?"

"The desserts? Because he could. But the earth science grade was legit. His uncle is in the fracking business and helped him with his research."

The practice of hydraulic fracturing—using hydraulic liquid to drill for gas and petroleum—had been making the news in Colorado for the past few years. Politicians didn't want to lose out on the fuel industry's inflow of dollars, but citizens claimed that the method of harvesting the resources created environmental and health dangers.

At least something good had come out of it for Colin.

"It goes without saying that Garrick must have written the letter to Bodie and signed Ella's name to it," she said.

Anyone with eyes could see that the socially awkward boy was sweet on Ella and would do anything to gain her affection.

Theo confirmed her thoughts. "Bodie doesn't understand the ins and outs of the dating scene," he said.

"And the photocopy of the bruised thumb on the homework assignment?"

"Yep. I checked the library's photocopier logbook, and Garrick's name was on there."

The lasagna was ready to pop into the oven. Sadie needed to get home soon to feed Hank. But another thread had yet to be untangled.

"It seems like we're forgetting something," she said. "Or someone."

"Hayley."

"Ah yes." On the day of the track meet, she and Theo had watched Bodie place the completed homework paper in the designated drop-off spot. "When Hayley retrieved the homework from under the bleachers, we thought for sure she must be the one extorting the homework from Bodie. But then she put it back."

Theo chuckled. "She had assumed it was a love letter for someone else. Maybe Ella? I don't know. But Hayley intended to torpedo the letter and get rid of the competition so she could have Bodie to herself."

"It was nice of you to invite Bodie and her to the chocolate fest with you and Ella."

He shrugged. "Everybody but Bodie could see that Hayley has a crush on him. If he would ever notice her, he might see that she's a pretty nice girl."

A car pulled into the driveway just as Sadie covered the lasagna to put it in the oven. It pleased her to know that she had saved her daughter the hassle of fixing a hearty dinner after working all day.

Alice entered the kitchen with an armload of papers to grade, and Sara balanced a large paper sack in her arms.

Theo, having been cooped up all day, proceeded to burn off his excess energy by teasing Sara, moving in front of her every which way she turned.

Alice lightly pinched his arm. "Theo, help your sister."

"Sure." He playfully snatched the sack from the girl's arms. "What's in the bag, Squirt?"

He looked inside to answer his own question.

"Sweet!"

Sadie paused, one hand on the oven door and the other holding the glass pan of Italian deliciousness. A sinking feeling told her that all her cooking efforts had been for naught.

"It was getting late," Alice explained. She surveyed the used sauté pan and drips of tomato sauce on the counter, and her gaze landed on the lasagna pan in Sadie's hand. "So I decided to pick up a ready-made meal from the Market."

"Maybe I should put the lasagna in the fridge, and you can bake it tomorrow night."

"Don't worry about it." Alice hitched a thumb at her son. "If it's here, he'll eat it."

Alice crossed the room to give Sadie a hug. Reveling in the sweet embrace, Sadie returned the show of affection with a tight squeeze.

"It's a good thing my only child was a daughter," she told Alice. "I don't think your dad and I could have afforded to feed a teenage son."

32

SADIE HAD BEEN INVITED TO JOIN HER DAUGHTER AND grandchildren for dinner, but she had declined and come home to feed Hank, who'd already found a dinner of his own.

"Oh, gross. What are you eating?"

The dog pranced into the house, his tail wagging with pleasure. Whether over her attention or whatever he'd just finished smacking his lips over, she wasn't sure. She didn't want to know, but she suspected it might have been a cricket.

"What is it with you dogs?" she asked him. "Eating everything that isn't nailed down."

Hank didn't answer, but he followed her to the food bin, where she portioned out some kibble and topped it with leftover green peas and meat scraps from her own dinner last night.

"Here, I think you'll like this better."

While he ate, she heated up the rest of the leftovers for herself and sat down to the table with the journal she'd been perusing lately. It had been a sad, happy, and intriguing experience to take a peek into her past. After she said grace, she flipped the pages ahead from the last entry she'd read.

My back was hurting today. The baby must have turned and caused pressure. Either that, or the sheer weight that I'm hauling around is straining my muscles. Regardless of the reason, it's miserable, but, of course, still worth it. Alice or Alex, whichever the baby will be, is worth all the discomfort that it takes to bring this precious little one into the world.

T.R. offered to put off his fishing challenge with Roscoe today to stay home and look after me. *The Great American Fish-Off,* they called it. Roscoe was to use some newfangled gadget from the hardware store, and T.R. planned to tackle it (so to speak, ha-ha!) the old-fashioned way: With hook, bait, and "psychology."

Naturally, I laughed at the way he tapped a finger to his forehead when he said that, but he didn't take offense. He just said, "Hey, I caught *you,* didn't I?" And that made me feel great even though, considering the way I've been waddling around lately, he probably hadn't expected to make such a big "catch" as me.

The baby isn't due for another couple of weeks, and if there was any problem while he was out fishing, I could always call my parents. So, of course, I insisted he and Roscoe pursue their challenge. Unfortunately, T.R. lost to Roscoe's gadget, and our friend promised "shame, humiliation, and acts of obsequiousness" would follow as T.R. acknowledged Roscoe as the Great American Fisherman.

Worse than losing the challenge was the mess T.R. came home to. While I had rested on the couch and graded students' papers, our yellow lab puppy, Mosi (an Egyptian name that, in Swahili, means "first child"), had gone adventuring in our bedroom and discovered that T.R.'s "incidentals" drawer, full of underclothes, neckties, belts, and socks, had been left open.

Needless to say, once Mosi finished teething on them, there wasn't much left. The open doors and drawers are something that I've reminded T.R. about in the past. But he still forgets to close them, even after banging his shins on low drawers or knocking his head on protruding cabinet doors.

I expected T.R. to be angry with Mosi, especially when it looked as though there might not be an unchewed or drool-free necktie for him to wear to the Chamber of Commerce's monthly meeting tonight, where he's supposed to address an important matter before the business members. As a young lawyer, he wants people to take him seriously, so it's important for him to look presentable.

Surprisingly, T.R. didn't get upset at all. In fact, he seemed oddly...relieved, if that makes any sense. (It doesn't make sense to me, but it seems worth noting.) Anyway, he managed to salvage a bolo tie and wore that instead. And before he left for the meeting, he laughed and said he expected me to tell Roz about the dog disaster.

I did. I called Roz while T.R. was at the meeting, and she and I laughed until we thought my water would break.

The day's entry ended there, and Sadie flipped forward in the journal to see if any other mention was made of how T.R. had fared wearing what some people called a "shoestring tie" at the important business meeting. But apparently nothing notable had come of it, for there were no other entries until a few days before she went into labor.

33

THE FELLOWSHIP HALL AT CAMPFIRE CHAPEL NEARLY OVERFLOWED
with chocolate lovers of all ages. A disproportionate number of
teens filled the room, thanks to the youth group members paper-
ing their school with flyers. Sadie gave thanks for the outpouring
of ticket purchases and donations that would go toward helping
the Widows' Mite organization for women in need.

Piled on tables crowded into the room were the usual chocolate cakes, cookies, and pies. And to wash them down were
chocolate coffee, tea, and milk. Surprisingly, some of the oddest combinations were also seeing some of the most interest...
chocolate goat-cheese truffles, chocolate-covered sun-dried toma-
toes, and white chocolate and basil mousse.

In accordance with Pastor Don's request, samplings and sales
were not to begin until the food and event had been blessed, and it
was still a few minutes until the official opening time.

Roscoe Putnam cruised by, and Sadie snagged his arm to stop
his trek to the chocolate fountain.

"Got a minute?"

He nodded, so she reached into her purse and pulled out the
ugly fish tie she'd been carrying around lately. She had no idea if

he could tell her any information that she didn't already know, but it couldn't hurt to try.

"I came across this recently. Roz tells me you gave it to T.R. a long time ago." And the journal entry she'd read a few days ago had raised further questions.

Roscoe lifted the tie from her hand, and a smile crossed his face as recognition set in.

"I had forgotten all about this." He handed the tie back to her. "Your husband and I had a fishing challenge to see who could catch the biggest fish in the shortest amount of time. The loser had to wear that eyesore to their next public event."

Roscoe seemed to enjoy reliving the moment with her.

"I won, so T.R. had to wear it to some bigwig event of his that night."

"The Chamber of Commerce meeting?"

He pointed at her. "Yeah, that's it. But T.R. came up with some lame excuse, like he lost it, or the dog ate it. With a stupid story like that, I didn't believe him."

"I wouldn't have either," Sadie admitted. She'd heard plenty of off-the-wall excuses over the years from students who hadn't turned in their homework, but even they had enough common sense not to use the "dog ate it" excuse.

"So I threatened to come look through your trash cans to prove he weaseled out of our deal."

Now it was beginning to make sense. Sadie smiled and urged Roscoe on with his story.

"But you told Roz about the dog tearing up T.R.'s stuff, and that's when I believed it. I knew you wouldn't cover for him, even though he was your husband." He laughed, the sound full of warmth over the long-ago memory. "In fact, you'd be right there with me, egging T.R. on. Daring him to wear that ugly thing."

The thought of her husband wearing the awful tie tickled her to no end. "You're right. I most certainly would have."

T.R. must have known that too. On a couple of different occasions, he had confessed that he had done things he wasn't proud of. Welching on a deal—hiding the fish tie and socks in the tree to keep her or Roscoe from finding them—appeared to be one of them.

But what about the ring? Was that something else he'd hidden away because of something he'd done that he wasn't proud of?

———

Sally Henderson, who'd been going from table to table to see if anyone needed help, paused in front of the area that had been set up for Pauline's opening gospel pocket lesson.

"Just a few more minutes," she said. "Do you and Mrs. Marshall need anything before we begin?"

Pauline slowly rose from the chair she'd been seated in and turned her back to Sally. "If you don't mind, would you retie my apron strings? Sadie's a sweet gal, but she has them all knotted up like a fist in my back."

The wallpaper-pink apron that had probably fit Pauline twenty or more years ago now hung from her slimmed-down frame. A large bulge in the pocket weighed it down on one side so that it gave her a lopsided look.

Sadie might have taken offense at the comment if it had been anyone other than Pauline who'd said what she did about her bow-tying abilities. But she just chalked it up to the woman's unfiltered personality.

Sally did the honors of retying the knot, and Sadie had to admit their friend created a much tidier—and flatter—bow than hers had been.

"Sadie, you were right about chocolate being a better fundraiser than a bake sale. People will have nothing to do with starchy carbs, but show them a table full of chocolate goodies, and they'll fight to be the first in line."

"Thank you, dear." Pauline sat back down in the comfortable chair designated for her.

"You're very welcome." To Sadie, Sally said, "I'll give you the high sign when we're almost ready to open the event. Just let me know if you need anything."

Edwin joined her as Sally left. A smudge of brown at the corner of his mouth indicated he'd already been sampling the fares.

Sadie removed a clean tissue from her purse and wiped away the evidence.

He grinned, whether out of guilt or satisfaction, she wasn't sure. "Orange crème chocolate," he said. "I couldn't resist."

She smiled back at him. "Thanks for being here to help with your aunt's gospel pocket lesson."

Pauline waggled her fingers in greeting to her nephew. "Sadie, it was so nice to have you over to my place the other day. We should do it again sometime, and I'll tell you more stories about our family history and show you the rest of my heirlooms."

"That would be delightful," she said in all honesty.

An uncharacteristic awkwardness had settled between her and Edwin these past couple of weeks, and Sadie thought she detected a slight stiffening in his smile.

Pauline opened her Bible. "I could use a minute to get my thoughts straight."

"Oh, of course." She and Edwin stepped away, and the tension followed them.

As much as she disliked the inevitability, she needed to confront Edwin about some pretty serious issues. One thing she knew was that they couldn't go on the way they had been recently.

She cleared her throat, and her words came out on an ominous note. "We need to talk."

He appeared startled by the serious tone. "Now?"

"How about tomorrow? After church."

"Yes. Of course." Edwin glanced at Pauline and back at her. "Is everything okay?"

Before she could answer, Pauline rose and started moving the small folding table that would be used for her gospel pocket display. Sadie hurried to assist her, and Edwin was called away to help at the chocolate fondue table, thus ending their awkward exchange.

After they had the table just the way Pauline wanted it, Sadie pulled her aside and led her to a chair in a quiet corner.

Without much time before the short Bible lesson was to start, she got straight to the point.

"The earrings in your gospel pocket," she began, and noticed that Pauline's hand went to her apron. "And the family heirloom ring that matches them. I want you to know that they were stolen."

Pauline smiled sweetly. "No they weren't, dear. I gave the ring to Edwin for his wife, and the earrings are right here in my pocket." She patted her lap.

"They weren't stolen from you. They were taken from Edith Ryker."

The older woman laughed, her voice high and airy. "Oh, I wouldn't say they were stolen. Appropriated, perhaps, but not stolen. The eighth commandment says thou shalt not steal, and I certainly wouldn't do that, now, would I?"

Sadie blinked at what seemed like a casual admission to the theft. "*You* took them?"

She had known for a little over a week that Pauline had the earrings in her gospel pocket, but she had supposed that someone else had been responsible for having brought the stolen jewelry into the household and leaving the older woman to assume they were Marshall family heirlooms. But she had never once thought Pauline would have committed the heist herself.

"Took? You make it sound like a crime." Pauline smoothed the apron skirt over her black slacks. "Those items, and all the things in my gospel pocket were *appropriated* for a good cause. To teach God's Word."

Unable to think of a reply to such warped logic, Sadie sat in stunned silence.

"Besides," Pauline offered by way of explanation, "all of my gospel pocket pieces were acquired from people who were too rich—and too forgetful, in Edith's case—to even notice they were missing."

Oh, she was certain they noticed. Especially in the case of the expensive Chameli Youta jewelry. Remembering Pauline's birthday party, when Edith's diamond-encrusted wristwatch had gone missing and reappeared later, she knew they needed to discuss this further. But time was ticking down to the opening of the chocolate fest. She'd have to cut straight to the point.

"What about Edith's watch?" she said. "The one that she was looking for at your birthday party?"

Pauline shook her head. "I don't draft into service anything that anybody wants. When Edith kicked up a fuss, it was clear she wasn't going to be happy until she got it back." The elderly woman grinned, revealing even, white dentures. "So I made it reappear."

Stunned at the woman's audacity, Sadie found it hard to believe what she was hearing. But going by Pauline's skewed logic, she herself hadn't "kicked up a fuss" over the missing Lenox glass that she'd won as a party favor.

"Do you know anything about the Lenox goblet I won? It had been sitting on top of my purse to take home later."

"Oh yes, dear." Pauline reached over and patted Sadie's arm in a sweet, grandmotherly way. "That one lends itself beautifully to a verse in First Corinthians. 'So whether you eat or drink or whatever you do, do it all for the glory of God.'" She nodded in a self-satisfied way. "That's how I try to live my life."

Dumbfounded, Sadie realized there was a disconnect between the teachings of this intelligent, mentally sharp woman and her actions. And it had apparently been going on for a very long time.

This was the same person who had made a young Joanie write those punishment sentences for swiping things, yet Pauline had somehow convinced herself that her own stealing was justified because she was using the pilfered pieces for what she called a higher good...teaching God's Word to others.

Sadie took a moment to laugh inwardly at the irony.

Pauline was watching her with the piercing blue eyes that reminded her so much of Edwin's. "Don't tell me. You're going to say that Lenox goblet was yours and you want it back?"

Pauline had the nerve to look annoyed.

"No, I don't need it," Sadie said in all honesty. "Just save it for Edwin after you're done with it." She paused to let what she was about to say sink in. "But there is something in your gospel pocket that needs to be returned to its original owner."

Pauline pulled some of the items out of her apron pocket and spread them on her lap. A plastic tape dispenser. A sock with a hole in it. The Swiss Army knife that Sadie recalled from Bodie's recitation.

"It's going to be hard to find those people after all these years." Pauline peered up at Sadie. "Does mercy have a statute of limitations?"

"Of course not. But there's something very valuable in there that belongs to your friend Edith and it should be returned."

Pauline looked down and pursed her lips.

"That's my Proverbs piece. One of the proverbs is 'apples of gold in settings of silver.' That's a nice one about minding your mouth. And then there's one about being more precious than rubies." Pauline rubbed the pink morganite stone in the center of the large dangle earring. "But I don't think this is a ruby. It's much too pale. It surprises me that Edith would buy some cheap knockoff."

Although shocked that Pauline would call the stunning piece of artwork "cheap," Sadie was even more amazed that the quirky centenarian remained unrepentant and was still marching to the beat of her own drum.

"...and this stone represents the unnamed woman in the Bible who dropped a rock from a tower on the head of her enemy." Pauline grinned. "That gal had spunk!"

Sadie helped Pauline to her feet to go back to the small table where her gospel pocket talk would soon take place.

If Pauline's Bible lesson was anything like the one about the woman with the rock, she'd better stick around for what was sure to be an amusing, if not informative, lesson.

———

Sadie and Edwin managed to snag two chairs beside Pauline where it would be easy to assist—or intervene—if necessary. On the floor, small children sat cross-legged in the front, while parents and other chocolate aficionados claimed the rows of chairs.

Edwin leaned close. "She's a pretty amazing lady, isn't she? So much spunk."

How fitting that he would use that very word to describe his aunt. Sadie chuckled at the thought that Pauline would drop a rock on the head of her enemy if necessary.

Pauline fumbled in her gospel pocket, her shaking fingers apparently having trouble fishing out the item of her choice.

Sadie leaned in to help but was waved away.

The gospel pocketeer finally retrieved the silly butterfly glasses she'd made and put them on, much to the delight of her audience.

"How do I look?" Pauline asked the children.

Applause and laughter followed, along with a bit of warm-up chatter.

Sadie's mind wandered to the talk that she dreaded having with Edwin tomorrow. It had been hard enough confronting Pauline about Edith's stolen jewelry. It would be harder still confronting Edwin.

Pauline pulled out the brass-framed hand mirror from her pocket and explained how mirrors had been made in biblical times. She passed it around for the children to see.

"Unlike my mirror, the people in the Bible used mirrors made of bronze and polished to a high sheen," she explained. "But even at its best, the reflection in those old mirrors was wiggly and warped. It was like looking at your reflection in the chrome bumper of my 1952 Packard Coupe."

Sadie could identify with what she was saying. She herself had been very unclear on a lot of things lately. But she planned to change that.

"So with this mirror in mind, what do you think we're going to talk about today?"

Children's hands were raised, and the expected answers came. Vanity. Pride. Even one that took everybody by surprise: why God made ugly people.

Sadie glanced down at her hands. Without thinking about what she was doing, she rubbed them like she sometimes did, and her fingers automatically closed around the silver band on her right hand.

She looked up and found Edwin watching her. With her hands now resting in her lap, she turned her attention back to the lesson.

"This mirror is about love!" Pauline declared. Obviously taken with all the attention she was getting, the older woman directed everyone to 1 Corinthians 13:12.

Sadie didn't have to open a Bible. She knew it by heart and mentally recited along while Pauline read to the group.

For now we see only a reflection as a mirror; then we shall see face to face. Now I know in part; then I shall know fully, even as I am fully known.

"Because we can't see it clearly yet, we don't know or understand just how magnificent God's love is," Pauline said. "But one day, when we see Him face-to-face, it will be an amazing experience. We will see what authentic love really looks like."

There were still a lot of things Sadie didn't know or understand. So many things lately that she saw through the wavy reflection of a polished brass surface. For instance, why would a sweet lady who lacked for nothing find it acceptable to steal from others?

And then there was the issue she needed to clear up with Edwin.

"We don't have the answers now," Pauline said, wrapping up her talk. "So we have to read our Bibles to learn about God, then trust in Him and go in faith."

Sadie looked up at Edwin. She needed to go in faith and do the right thing.

Pauline's perky way of explaining her message had captivated the children, and they actually seemed disappointed when the lesson was over.

Sadie joined in the applause as the audience rose to their feet.

"Wait! Don't go yet," Pauline called. "Here's something I made just for all of you." She reached for the grocery sack under the table and withdrew a large plateful of chocolate treats to share.

Sadie and Edwin got up to help distribute the sweet confection. *Fudge.*

34

AFTER THE CHOCOLATE FEST, SADIE TOOK HANK FOR A HIKE TO walk off some of the calories that most certainly had attached themselves to her hips today. Following that, she finished tidying the house, read her Bible lesson in preparation for church the next day, then rewarded herself with some TV time.

When it became apparent that the best she could find on all the channels was a cooking show featuring exotic foods that weren't even sold in her local grocery store, she switched off the television.

She spent the next fifteen minutes jotting an entry in her current journal and laughed to herself at some of the things Pauline had said today, as well as the children's antics. Kids—especially those hopped up on sugar and caffeine from chocolate—were always good for a funny story.

When she was done writing, she found the journal from a few years ago and fell upon one of the later entries featuring her husband.

I'm worried about T.R. He hasn't been feeling well. An understatement, to say the least.

Since the diagnosis, he's been focused on trying to keep things as normal as possible. That's just like T.R. Always thinking of others before himself. The sicker he gets, the more effort he puts into being strong for me and the rest of the family. Not to mention all the friends and church members who are praying for him.

His determination to keep things normal is why he drove to town this afternoon. I wanted to keep him at home, where I could take care of him, but he wouldn't have any of that. He was gone a long time. So Hank and I sat and waited, checking out the window every time we heard a noise. Whether Hank was worried about T.R., or about me worrying about T.R., I'm not sure.

Eventually, T.R.'s car returned, and he slowly made his way up the walk to the house. He held a package in his hand.

I tried not to let him see me peeking out the window. Didn't want him to think I'd been worrying, which I was. But one glance at his handsome face set my worries aside, and relief and joy filled my heart.

After he made it inside—without my help, I might add—he handed me the sack from the pharmacy, containing the item that he had purchased.

Without opening it, I asked, "Where else did you go?" After all the time he'd spent in town, I imagined he must have made several stops and visited with many friends and acquaintances.

"That was it," he said, taking a seat on the couch. "For you. Open it."

His face was pale. I joined him on the couch, knowing without his saying so that he must have gotten tired from the outing and spent much of his time on the chairs set out for people awaiting their prescriptions.

I started to ask if I could get anything for him but stopped myself because he wouldn't want me fretting over him. So I turned my attention to the small bag in my hand.

Inside was a heart-shaped box filled with an assortment of chocolates, including raspberry and dark chocolate, one of my favorites.

T.R. smiled and encouraged me to sample them, but he refused to take one for himself. At this point, his body was unable to handle the sugar. But it seemed to please him to give the sweets to me.

I took a raspberry chocolate and enjoyed it thoroughly. Watching me, he seemed to enjoy it even more.

"You really shouldn't have gone to all the trouble," I told him.

"I want you to be happy," he said. He wiped a chocolate smudge off of my lip and kissed me. "The sweetest sugar."

I took his hand and told him I *am* happy. That being with him brings me pleasure.

But he persisted. "I want you to be happy...always. You're not yet sixty years old," he told me. "God willing, you can still fill your life with joyful experiences"—he looked at me, his gaze significant with meaning—"and with people who are good to you."

I didn't want to talk about it, and I told him so.

But he was insistent. "Fill your life, Sadie. Don't hold back on account of me and what we've had until now." He took my hand and squeezed it with what strength he had left. "You honor me best by filling your life with good. By enjoying the sweetness of life."

35

―――――

HANK RAN AHEAD OF SADIE'S AND EDWIN'S HORSES, CUTTING through the brush and sniffing for rabbits or whatever else he could find. The golden retriever, well familiar with this path, seemed to know where they were going.

Sadie reined Scout around a puddle of mud, and Edwin's horse dutifully followed.

"Thank you for coming up here with me today," she said. They were nearing the area where she and Theo had removed the lightning-struck branch from the dirt trail. "There's something very important that I want to show you."

Edwin was riding one of Milo's horses that preferred to lag behind. When they reached the wide part of the path, he guided the animal alongside Sadie's.

Sitting tall in the saddle, Edwin looked officious despite the jeans, boots, and pearl-button shirt that he wore. He gave her a long, questioning look.

"I always love spending time with you," he said.

His expression told her that he was curious about the reason for this outing. And maybe a little wary of "the talk" that was to come.

They dismounted at an open patch of grass and swapped the horses' headgear from bridles to halters to allow them to graze. Sadie lifted a small canvas tote from the saddlebag and led Edwin off the path a short distance.

"Theo and I found something in this tree over here."

Wordlessly, Edwin stepped closer and took a look, then brushed away some of the bark that had been chipped off.

"When I first saw it, I thought it was a gift for me," she said. "From T.R."

Edwin rubbed his forehead and turned back to her. "I remember your mentioning something about it, but you never said anything else."

She clutched the tote under her arm. He hadn't asked either, but none of that mattered now. What was important was that they get to the heart of the truth.

"I didn't tell you sooner because I was trying to spare your feelings."

He shook his head and draped an arm around her shoulders. "And I was trying to respect yours by not prying. I thought you would tell me as much as you felt comfortable divulging."

She stepped away so she could face him. She had to see his face to know his reaction.

"The gift," she said. "It wasn't from T.R. It was from someone else, and I was hoping you could provide some answers."

"I'll help however I can, but I must say, this is quite mysterious."

She opened the tote and removed the rusted tin that she had put in there for safekeeping.

A flicker of recognition crossed his face, the same look she'd seen the night they went to Mathis Root's poetry reading and she had examined a similar tin.

Slowly, carefully, she pried open the rusted lid and showed him the contents.

"There are a ring and a poem in here. Do you know anything about them, Edwin?"

He gave her an incredulous look. "Of course I do." He stood silent for a moment while he processed what was going on. "Wait a minute. *This* was in the tree? And it was the first you've seen of it?"

No hesitation in his answer. But what did he mean by "of course I do"? As if she should have known he was familiar with it.

"Yes. It was a total shock."

Carefully, she took out the ring and poem and handed them to him to look them over.

"When I read the poem," she said, "I thought it seemed to mirror my romance with T.R. Our trails converging and love blooming in the spring thaw. Promises of climbing to the peak together. So, of course, I latched on to the hope that he had left it here for me to find."

She looked away, toward the view of Silver Peak that rose like a protective guardian over her house and the rest of the town.

"But then I learned about the ring...the designer, the value, the fact that it had been stolen many years ago—and I didn't think so."

Edwin lifted his gaze from the ring. "Stolen? Then that would explain..."

He stopped and seemed to be considering the facts that she'd just given him.

"Explain what?"

"When I came to visit you at UC Boulder in 1973"—he tapped the date printed on the tin as if to confirm the time frame—"it was to apologize to you for letting my schoolwork and part-time job get in the way of keeping in touch as much as I would have liked."

To apologize? "You mean you didn't…"

He stopped, his gaze peering into hers. "Didn't what?"

She shook her hand. "No, go ahead. You were saying?"

With a small nod, Edwin continued. "I had brought with me a gift of a ring—a family heirloom." His fingers traced the ornate ring in his hand. "And a sentimental poem that perfectly expressed my feelings for you."

"For me." She had already decided that the poem hadn't been from T.R. And once she knew that Edwin had hired Frida to copy the poem for him, she had assumed it had been meant for Rose. Not for herself.

"Yes, for you. The ring was my way of asking you to wait for me. And I had the calligrapher at the fund-raiser carnival write the poem because my own handwriting was so atrocious."

He put the items back into the tin that Sadie held.

"And this," he said, placing his hand over hers, "was a souvenir from Loveland. That's where I had asked you to go steady with me in high school."

She looked up at him and smiled. "I remember."

"The tin was intended to commemorate that special time in our lives, and the ring and poem were to move us on to a deeper level of commitment."

She let him lead her to the large branch that she and Theo had pulled aside, and she sat down with him. "So you came to tell me…"

"That I wanted us to be together forever."

This was feeling like an alternate reality. She had lived most of her life believing one thing, and now, with one simple statement from Edwin, she discovered she had been all wrong.

"But your letters and calls. They were…" How could she say it without sounding accusatory? "Dwindling. I thought you had shown up that day to break up with me. And that you couldn't bring yourself to come right out and say it."

"No. No, Sadie, my dear." He hugged her, his arms folding easily around her. "Schoolwork was all-consuming. That's not an excuse. It tore me up, not to be able to keep in touch with you as well as you had with me."

She had spent a lot of time—when schoolwork had been overwhelming for her as well—crafting chatty letters about her days, the people she met, the things she did. And she'd received very little back. She didn't hold his lack of reciprocation against him, but she wanted to understand why he hadn't been as diligent.

"Regular phone calls were out of my budget," he continued, "and I kept putting off writing to you until I had the time to compose a proper letter."

She squeezed his hand, which still clutched her shoulder. "I would have been happy with a postcard."

He had the decency to look abashed. "I should have done that."

Edwin released her and dropped his elbows to his knees. His head drooped as he let his mind drift to the past.

"Then, while I was visiting with you that day, I met T.R. A nice guy. I saw something, though, in the way he looked at you."

"I don't…"

"Devotion, Sadie. That's what I saw."

She shook her head. "We were just friends at that time."

"It wasn't him that kept me from telling you what was on my mind that day." He straightened and drew a long breath. "I didn't want to put you on the spot in a choose-him-or-me showdown."

Unbidden, the thought of Pauline's gospel pocket mirror came to Sadie's mind. She had certainly been looking through ripples in that particular glass.

"I left the gift in your apartment. The family heirloom ring was a sign of my sincerity. After I left it, I went back to my university and waited for your answer."

The thought of him waiting and not knowing was nearly her undoing. "I never saw it."

"It was in the cupboard, with your coffee and cups. Roz didn't drink coffee at that time, and I knew it would stay safe there until the next morning when you went to make your morning java."

She shook her head. "It never turned up."

Unless… She wondered if the possibility had occurred to him as well.

If it had, he didn't say anything. Edwin reached for the tin. He seemed to want to keep his hands busy.

"I bought this container to put the ring and poem in because Loveland was that football date where I'd asked you to go steady with me. If you had said yes after receiving these things, we would have moved our relationship forward."

He opened and closed the lid several times. Then, apparently realizing what he was doing, he handed it back to her.

"And even if we were to part, I would have considered the ring a gift for you to keep."

She remained silent for a beat or two. The pawing of the horses' hooves reminded her that, although Edwin's and her trails had parted ways for a while, they had inevitably crossed again. And the chirping of birds as they flitted through the tree branches overhead reminded her that spring was blooming once more.

"I saw Frida recently and showed her the poem." At his questioning gaze, she added, "Her initials were at the bottom. Anyway, she told me you had commissioned her to write out the poem."

"I had wanted to call you after I left that day. I even tried twice on Valentine's Day, but I hung up without saying anything."

She met his gaze and remembered the brief surge of hope that it might have been him, and the thud of disappointment when she had picked up the receiver and heard only a dial tone.

"I didn't want to pressure you for an answer," Edwin said. "I knew you liked to pray about important decisions, and I wanted to give you the time you needed to listen for the answers."

"When you didn't get in touch with me after some time had passed, Frida told me you'd moved on and found someone else. She thought the poem was meant for another girl."

He gave her a wry smile. "And so you wrote the letter wishing me well. I took that as a no. And inside, I wished you well with the man whom I was convinced would love you and treat you like the gem you are."

She touched Edwin's hand. "He did."

"I'm glad." He stretched his legs and adjusted his weight on the log where they sat.

And, like the gentleman Edwin was, he'd never mentioned the ring again.

"I still don't understand what happened to the tin after you left it at my apartment. If Roz had found it, she wouldn't have taken it without saying something. And T.R. certainly wouldn't have…"

Edwin met her gaze and held it. If his thoughts had taken the turn hers just had, he didn't say so. But he didn't need to.

"T.R. stayed in the kitchen while I walked you to the door to say good-bye. When I returned a few minutes later, I remember him looking in the cupboard and finding something. At the time, I thought it was raspberry tea."

She was having a hard time reconciling this scenario with the T.R. she knew. Or the man she thought she knew.

"He must have found the tin and put it aside where I wouldn't find it. But why?"

Edwin rubbed the afternoon shadow on his jaw, and the action elicited the sound of sandpaper. "Maybe he wanted to wait to show it to you until he knew how you felt about him," he speculated.

"When T.R. and I started dating, he mentioned that he wasn't perfect. And he mentioned that fact again after we were married, when he confessed that he'd done something he wasn't proud of. Now it's beginning to make sense."

T.R. must have circumvented her finding Edwin's gift, and then struggled with his conscience over doing so.

And if he'd had possession of the tin at that time, as she now believed he had, it would also explain why he hadn't wanted her to help him unpack his things when he moved in to the house with her. He hadn't wanted her to find the tin.

"I can see that," Edwin said.

His voice sounded calmer than she felt at the moment. Edwin didn't appear angry, as some other men might have been under similar circumstances.

"Knowing what you know now," he ventured, "do you think T.R. was the one who put the tin in the tree?"

She slowly nodded. "He must have hidden it in the tree after I came close to discovering it while I was cleaning."

On several occasions, he had stopped her from moving his possessions to clean around them. At the time, she had just thought he was fussy about having people mess with his belongings.

The tin had been the first item she'd found in the tree, which indicated it was the last thing he'd placed there. First, into the tree went the fish tie and socks to hide them from Roscoe. And who knew how many years later the tin was placed in there?

"I wonder if T.R. held on to it, hoping to find the right time to tell me about it."

After Alice had come along, he'd loosened up and stopped being so fussy about whether she touched his personal belongings. At the time, Sadie had assumed he'd just gotten used to their toddler investigating everything in the house—the pots and pans in the kitchen, Sadie's makeup when her back was turned, and ultimately T.R.'s personal things. That must have been around the time he had removed the tin from the house and hidden it in the tree.

"The fishing hole was T.R.'s favorite thinking spot," she said. "I don't believe he would have ever gotten rid of your gift, but it would have made sense for him to take it there to decide how best to broach the subject with me."

"Maybe he never could find the right time or circumstances to come clean with you," Edwin suggested.

Edwin rose from the thick branch where they sat. After giving Sadie a hand up, he dusted the bark and grit off of his jeans.

"Judging by how long it took the tree bark to grow around the tin," he said, "T.R. thought for a long time about how to find just the right way to talk to you about what he'd done."

Sadie nodded. "I believe that's what happened. After we had Alice, the stakes would have been so much higher. That's likely when he decided to hide the box permanently. He didn't want what he'd done to put our family at risk over a secret that had begun as an impulse and then grown into an albatross that hovered in the back of his mind."

Edwin walked with her back to where the horses had been patiently waiting. "T.R. must have interpreted my, er, sporadic correspondence and phone calls during our first couple of years of college to mean that I wasn't that interested in you."

He took her by the shoulders and turned her to face him.

"But I was. And I still am."

To prove it, he dropped a brief but gentle kiss on her lips.

"I know." Sadie smiled, pleased that he still wanted to be with her. "I am too."

T.R.'s perception that Edwin had lost interest in her might have been his ultimate justification for claiming her as his own.

And now, talking to Edwin face-to-face about his gift that had been hidden away for so many years, she could more clearly see why he had responded as he had when she'd pointed out the identical tin at the poetry reading.

Edwin hadn't wanted to rehash the fact that her answer to his request had seemingly been a "no."

She couldn't blame him for not wanting to relive what he had perceived as a rejection.

In retrospect, she admired the restraint Edwin had shown when he had learned of T.R.'s and her engagement. He'd seen how happy she was with T.R., and he hadn't wanted to do anything to interfere with her joy.

"There's one more thing," Edwin said as they returned to the horses. "You should know that it wasn't until after the time of my visit to you that I met Rose."

They headed back to Milo's stables, but they were walking now, with the horses following on their leads. Neither was ready to end their time together, and a springtime stroll was one way to prolong the day.

Sadie relished the warmth of her hand in his. Feeling a little like the teenage kids they used to be, she kicked a pebble from the path.

Bringing these issues to light had created yet another new beginning for them.

"It's going to take a while for all of this to sink in," she admitted.

Edwin nodded his agreement. "It does make me curious about what 'might have been,'" he said, curving his fingers into quotation marks, "if circumstances had worked out differently."

"Me too." She considered the many differences they would have encountered if they had ended up together. With all of their compatibilities, she expected they would have gotten along fine and been very content together. But it wasn't up to either of them to second-guess the outcomes of their lives, and she said as much. "I believe things turned out the way they were meant to be."

He lifted her hand and touched it to his lips. "We've both been incredibly blessed with our respective spouses and children."

"With life's usual ups and downs, of course." Nothing and no one was perfect. Especially not her. But despite that, she could honestly say she wouldn't have had it any other way.

Edwin nodded. "Indeed. And now God has blessed us further by bringing us back together during this stage in our lives."

"If you could go back in time…"

"I wouldn't change a thing." Edwin stooped and plucked a slim stalk of grass from beside the path and bent it to form a circle.

Curious, Sadie watched him wind and twist the green blade. She'd made grass whistles before, but not like this.

Edwin smiled and continued his work while they walked.

Finally, he twisted the piece into a complete circle and tied it off into what looked like a makeshift ring. He paused to take her hand and held it in his.

"You'd think with practice this would get easier," Edwin said, a shy grin forming on his handsome mouth.

With shaky fingers, he placed the grass ring on her left ring finger.

"A symbol of second chances." He paused for a moment, then gave her a shy grin. "Sadie, will you go steady with me?"

It was not the first time they'd had a similar conversation, but against the backdrop of Sadie's discovery in the tree and revisiting her essay from 1973 once more, it somehow carried a new layer of significance, as if they had come around in a full circle.

She smiled and wiggled her fingers as she admired Edwin's handiwork.

Impatient now, and ready to go back to his stall, Scout emphatically bobbed his head.

Edwin laughed, his voice deep and throaty and full of pure joy. "Well, I know his vote, but what do *you* say?"

He angled her hand as if the excellence of his workmanship might influence her.

"This time I want to hear it straight from your lips. No more letters and misunderstandings."

She touched the fragile ring and gave a playful pout. "It might fall off."

"It's okay. I know that, whatever your answer, you'll abide by your word, with or without a ring."

He was right about that.

Sadie stepped into his embrace and looked up into his amazing blue eyes. Finally, after all these years, she gave him the answer he'd been waiting for.

"Yes."

36

_____

THAT NIGHT, SADIE TURNED TO A FRESH PAGE IN HER JOURNAL.
Up until a couple of years ago, her thoughts and feelings had been
logged in its pages fairly consistently, never going too many days
in a row without a new entry. But ever since T.R.'s passing, her
writings had been more hit or miss.

She admired the sentimental grass ring on her finger. The
grass fibers strained with every movement of her hand and probably wouldn't remain on her finger until morning. But that was
all right because, as Edwin had said, the ties between them were
stronger than any physical object that represented their bond.

She uncapped a pen and touched the tip to the page. Sometimes she recounted the day's events as if she were telling the story
to herself. Other times, she turned an experience into a prayer of
sorts, preceding the entry with two simple words: "Dear God."

Tonight would be a little different.

My dear T.R.,
    This morning, I had to dash to the Antique Mine
before church to retrieve a beautiful pair of silver collection

plates that I wanted to donate to Campfire Chapel. Just as expected, Pastor Don and the members were thrilled to replace the old ones. Hey, maybe they'll inspire us to be even more generous in our offerings. ☺

While I was at the shop, I happened to see the last two of a clutch of baby mockingbirds flutter out of their nest. It's amazing how life comes in full circles, sometimes quite quickly. It was only a short time ago that the parents—in a courtship that reminded me of yours and mine—met and started their family. It's a new beginning for the little fluff balls, and by next year, they'll find someone to pair up with.

In other matters, there's been another full circle. Edwin Marshall is back in Silver Peak, and back in my life. Has been for some time now. I just wanted you to know, T.R., that I'm doing as you asked.

I'm filling my life with good. I'm enjoying the sweetness that life has to offer.

She capped the pen and put the journal down. Hank followed her to the kitchen, where she opened the freezer and withdrew a plastic-wrapped package.

The last time she'd looked at the box of chocolates, she couldn't bring herself to touch either of the two remaining pieces. But tonight, her heart light, she set the frozen candies on a saucer to thaw.

In a little while, she would savor the raspberry-filled chocolate in a toast to T.R., just as she'd savored the many happy years they'd spent together.

And then, to salute the continuation of the circle she'd started so many years ago with Edwin, she would take delight in the orange crème.

Edwin's favorite flavor.

Sadie's thoughts drifted back to what her granddaughter had said that day when they found the ring hidden in the tree. Sometimes, anyway, lightning did strike twice. It certainly had for her and, because of it, she felt immeasurably blessed.

About the Author

CAROLE JEFFERSON IS THE PEN NAME FOR A TEAM OF WRITERS WHO have come together to create the series Mysteries of Silver Peak. *When Lightning Strikes* was written by Carolyn Greene. In addition to her mystery writing, Greene is a best-selling romance author. She has won two HOLT Medallion Awards, been nominated twice for the RITA award, and was presented with the Romantic Times WISH Award. Her romance writing background came in handy for exploring Sadie's past and present loves in *When Lightning Strikes* and the secret that began more than forty years ago. Greene and her husband have two children and one granddaughter and live in Virginia with their two hyperactive miniature pinschers. She welcomes e-mails from readers: Carolyn@CarolynGreene.com.

God Bless Us, Every One

"Oh, Sadie, this is amazing." Roz Putnam's pink and yellow broomstick skirt flared out as she spun around. "This book is over a hundred and fifty years old."

Roz held a lined acrylic case that contained a clothbound book with gilt lettering. The bottom half of the case was velvet-lined, and the book nestled into the plush fabric, visible through the unlined top of the case.

"I know." Sadie Speers straightened the box she was packing up for the Silver Peak Opera House, where she had been asked to create a Victorian Christmas display in the lobby for the Christmas season that was just beginning this late November morning. She, Sadie's grandson, Theo, and her part-time shop employee, Julie Pearson, were packing a number of antiques for the display. "I wish you could have seen my face when Edwin told me he owned a signed first-edition copy of *A Christmas Carol*. I couldn't believe it."

Edwin Marshall was Sadie's high school sweetheart. They'd parted as friends at the end of those years, but since Edwin's return to Silver Peak after more than four decades, during which each of them had loved and lost a spouse, he had begun courting Sadie again.

"Have you seen Dickens's signature yet?" Roz's brown eyes widened behind the red frames of her glasses, which sported tiny clusters of ceramic holly leaves and berries at the corners where the earpieces met the frames. The glasses were only one of many pairs of unique and amusing eyewear Roz collected. Just yesterday, she'd worn a pair with red-and-green-striped frames. No one could say Roz didn't have the spirit of the Christmas season.

Sadie nodded in response to the question. "Edwin took it out of the case and showed it to me. Before I put it in the display case at the opera house, I'll show it to you."

"I want to see it too." Sadie's grandson, Theo Macomb, had his arms full of silk holly and ivy, which Sadie's employee, Julie, was packing into another box. An inch taller than Roz's six-foot frame, Theo had the same green eyes that his grandfather T.R. had had, along with a mop of thick brown hair. He had come straight from school to lend a hand. The greenery he held contrasted vividly with the light gray sweatshirt he wore that featured the high school's mascot, the Silver Peak Miners.

"Hey, can I borrow it, Grandma? I'm doing an extracredit project about Dickens for my AP English class. My last exam didn't go as well as I'd hoped, so Mrs. Weld told me I could do this project to try to bring up my grade. I really need an A in this class to be considered for some of the colleges I want to apply to."

Sadie winced. "No, Theo, you may not borrow a valuable antique that has been lent to me." She softened her refusal with a smile. "It is worth a lot of money, according to Edwin, and the thought of it leaving my sight until it's locked in a display case is giving me heart palpitations already."

Theo sent her a wry grin that told her he'd known the answer before he'd asked. "Bummer."

"I'm sure it's insured." Julie was dressed much like Sadie today in a fleece jacket and jeans. The difference between them, Sadie thought ruefully, was that Julie's jacket was fitted with slenderizing princess seams, her jeans had fancy little designs on the back pockets, and the small stack-heel on her boots dressed up the outfit, as did the hammered copper Native American cuff on her wrist and sparkly copper scarf that graced her slim neck.

Julie tossed her long blonde hair behind her shoulder as she removed some of the greenery from Theo's arms. "However, I'm with you," she said hastily, as Sadie opened her mouth. "I didn't mean Theo should borrow the book. I don't think the high school is an appropriate place for a one-hundred-and-fifty-year-old book."

Undaunted, Theo said, "Maybe I can take some pictures of it." He pushed a lock of dark hair out of his eyes with an absent gesture.

"Good idea. I'll ask Edwin if he has any objections. Maybe you also could take some pictures of the production," Sadie said. The display she was creating was for an "equity," or a professional production of *A Christmas Carol*, which was slated to run next Friday, Saturday, and Sunday during the final weekend of Holly & Ivy Days, an annual celebration in Silver Peak at the beginning of the holiday season. Sponsored by the town council every year, the celebration was held the first full week of December and featured special shopping bargains, caroling, the annual tree lighting, a window-dressing competition, and much more. It was one of Sadie's favorite weeks of the year in her beloved little town. "It's a one-man show in which the character of Dickens reads the story, using different voices for all the characters. So it would fit in with your report. You'd need to ask the director if that would be okay."

"The starring role is played by Davis Pickering," Roz added in a "he's dreamy" voice. "He's so talented."

"Who's Davis Pickering?" Theo asked.

All three women turned to stare at him.

Theo's green eyes danced. "Uh-oh. Davis Pickering is an older-lady heartthrob?"

Julie, who in her midthirties was nearly three decades younger than Sadie or Roz, swatted Theo's shoulder. "Hey. Watch who you're calling an older lady."

He chuckled and ducked away.

"Yeah," said Roz. "Age is just a number."

"For your information," Sadie said to her grandson, "Davis Pickering is a British actor who works in the United Kingdom and on Broadway. He's on that show *Cosmic Quest*. So he's much more than just a pretty face." *Cosmic Quest* was a television series about futuristic space travel that had spun off into several popular movies as well.

"That's the guy," Roz said.

"That's an awesome show." Theo suddenly looked animated. "My favorite episode was the one where he had to rescue his old mentor who was being held on an alien planet."

"And he starred in a movie version of *A Christmas Carol* a few years ago too." Julie put a hand to her heart. "He's amazing. I can't wait to see him in a stage role."

"So what's a famous guy like him coming to Silver Peak?" Theo said. "I mean, we're not exactly the center of great entertainment here."

Sadie chuckled. "That's putting it mildly. Davis's grandparents used to live here, and I guess he has fond memories of visiting the area as a child. His aunt, who still lives here, is on the opera house committee that books entertainment, and she asked him if he'd do it. He said yes and then asked Quinlan Masters to direct it. He's apparently a highly respected stage director, so we're all in for a real treat."

"It's all about who you know," Julie murmured.

"Seems like a one-man show would get boring," Theo commented. "So he just sits up there and reads the book?"

"Oh, I don't think you'll be bored," Sadie said. "Dickens himself did this reading for a number of years. He assumed all the roles, using different voices and different postures and body language for the characters. It was said to be riveting, and I imagine Davis Pickering will more than do Dickens justice. I got you a ticket for opening night," she said to her grandson, "so you can judge for yourself."

"I hope I can get my picture taken with him," Roz said. "And I'll have to get him to sign a program for my mother-in-law. She loves Dickens."

"*Oooh*, me too." Theo put the back of his hand to his forehead and crumpled to the floor.

"Go ahead and laugh," Julie said, swatting him playfully with the end of her scarf. "But think about this: your chances of getting an A surely won't be hurt if you submit pictures that you took of Davis Pickering in your report. I know Amanda Weld, and I wouldn't be surprised if she's a fan of Davis Pickering like we are."

"Consider it done," Theo said as he snapped back to his full height. "And if I get an A from Mrs. Weld, I'll give each of you copies of the photos. Until then, I'm holding them hostage."

Sadie laughed. Then she gestured to the boxes around them. "Let's close these securely and get them over to the opera house before the snow falls any harder. We're supposed to get a couple of inches again tonight." At the moment, it was snowing lightly, fat flakes drifting lazily down from the overcast Colorado sky, but Sadie knew it would probably get heavier as the evening progressed.

Since the first snow had fallen in late October, they'd had regular accumulations ever since. This week, it appeared, would be no exception, but Sadie was thankful the forecast wasn't calling for any major storms. Really bad weather could affect her Holly & Ivy week sales, which almost always significantly added to her holiday total.

Her three "assistants" quickly followed directions. They all bundled into their outerwear, and everyone picked up a box.

Fifteen minutes later, all the boxes of display goods had been carried across the street from Sadie's antique shop to the lobby of the restored theater.

The Silver Peak Opera House had been built in the last quarter of the nineteenth century, when Silver Peak's mining boom had been well established and an upper class of citizens had begun to emerge in the town. Constructed of solid red brick, the opera house boasted beautiful arched windows and the lavish embellishments that characterized the Victorian era. For the holidays, each window had been trimmed with a wreath of live greens complete with a large red bow. Massive carved stone flowerpots flanked the doors, and in each of them had been set small Christmas trees decorated with white lights and red bows.

The heavy front doors with their large glass upper windows also bore wreaths. Currently, they were locked, and she used the key she had borrowed earlier in the week to open them, then relocked them behind everyone.

The lobby of the opera house had a floor of highly polished wood with a wide burgundy carpet runner stretching from the door back to where it met a second runner placed perpendicular to the first. The second runner led to doors at each corner of the space, through which the audience members entered the theater proper through short passageways. A staircase toward the back left angled up and turned back on itself midway toward the second floor.

On her immediate left were two large glass display cases; to the right, a ticket desk. Behind the ticket desk was a small office, and just beyond it, a coat-check room. Sadie had always imagined it was typical of many opera houses of the era.

While they were shrugging off their coats and stuffing hats, mittens, and gloves into pockets, Julie said, "Oh, Sadie, I almost forgot to tell you. I got a decorating job yesterday."

"That's great." Sadie pulled out the box cutter she'd brought along and sliced the tape with which they'd closed each box. "What is it?"

"It's for a Victorian-themed Christmas party the week before Christmas. The client was planning to use a Breckenridge decorator, but the company flaked out at the last minute." Julie pulled a wry face. She gestured to the boxes they were opening. "I didn't realize you'd be using all this stuff when I accepted."

"Who's the client?"

"Do you know the Eckstrands?"

Sadie shook her head. "Not personally, but I've heard of them. Willis and Deborah-not-Debbie Eckstrand? Very wealthy? They're good friends of Simon Riley and his wife, right? I thought the Eckstrands went south in the winter."

"Not until after Christmas this year." Julie lifted a sterling-silver calling card receiving tray from a box and laid it carefully on a sheet she had spread on the floor. "Aw, rats. I was hoping to rent some of our inventory for the party, if you didn't mind, but I see you're using a lot of the Victorian items here."

"Anything I'm not using would be fine to rent out," Sadie said. "All I ask is that you place a discreet card somewhere in your display mentioning that some of the items are from the Antique Mine."

"No problem," Julie said promptly.

"I can help you brainstorm," Sadie offered. "I do still have some things left, and maybe we can come up with some decorating possibilities from other sources."

"I'll take all the help I can get," Julie admitted. "Thanks."

Theo pointed to an elaborately fluted cranberry epergne with a trifold trumpet-form base that was ruffled and crimped. "Hey, Grandma, what's this?"

"A flower vase, to put it simply," Sadie said. "From the Victorian era when almost anything that could be decorated was heavily ornamented. One could even say the Victorians were ostentatious. Actually, the roots of the interior decorating profession came from this period."

"Well, this vase, or whatever it is, is seriously ugly," Theo said skeptically. "I'm not sure I'd want it in my house."

"Tastes have changed in the past hundred years." Sadie grinned. "The Victorians might have said the same of many of the

things we find attractive today. And then they'd have added orna-
mentation to them to make them lovelier—at least in their eyes."

Julie chuckled. "Totally."

"Oh, hey, Grandma, did Mom tell you about our Christmas
trip yet?" Theo said. Then he clapped a hand over his mouth.
"Forget I said that." Only it sounded more like, *"Fuh-geth uh sedth
thet."*

Christmas trip? Sadie turned to face her grandson fully. "What
Christmas trip?"

A Note from the Editors

WE HOPE YOU ENJOY MYSTERIES OF SILVER PEAK, CREATED BY the Books and Inspirational Media Division of Guideposts, a nonprofit organization that touches millions of lives every day through products and services that inspire, encourage, help you grow in your faith, and celebrate God's love in every aspect of your daily life.

Thank you for making a difference with your purchase of this book, which helps fund our many outreach programs to military personnel, prisons, hospitals, nursing homes, and educational institutions. To learn more, visit GuidepostsFoundation.org.

We also maintain many useful and uplifting online resources. Visit Guideposts.org to read true stories of hope and inspiration, access OurPrayer network, sign up for free newsletters, download free e-books, join our Facebook community, and follow our stimulating blogs.

To learn about other Guideposts publications, including the best-selling devotional *Daily Guideposts*, go to ShopGuideposts .org, call (800) 932-2145, or write to Guideposts, PO Box 5815, Harlan, Iowa 51593.

Sign up for the
Guideposts Fiction Newsletter
and stay up-to-date on
the fiction you love!

You'll get sneak peeks of new releases, recommendations from
other Guideposts readers, and special offers just for you . . .

And it's FREE!

Just go to Guideposts.org/newsletters
today to sign up.

Find more inspiring fiction in these best-loved Guideposts series

Secrets of the Blue Hill Library
Enjoy the tingle of suspense and the joy of coming home when Anne Gibson turns her late aunt's Victorian mansion into a library and uncovers hidden secrets.

Miracles of Marble Cove
Follow four women who are drawn together to face life's challenges, support one another in faith, and experience God's amazing grace as they encounter mysterious events in the small town of Marble Cove.

Secrets of Mary's Bookshop
Delve into a cozy mystery where Mary, the owner of Mary's Mystery Bookshop, finds herself using sleuthing skills that she didn't realize she had. There are quirky characters and lots of unexpected twists and turns.

Patchwork Mysteries
Discover that life's little mysteries often have a common thread in a series where every novel contains an intriguing mystery centered around a quilt located in a beautiful New England town.

Mysteries of Silver Peak
Escape to the historic mining town of Silver Peak, Colorado, and discover how one woman's love of antiques helps her solve mysteries buried deep in the town's checkered past.

To learn more about these books, visit ShopGuideposts.org